Longing of Lonely Ladies

Greg MacBride

Printed by CreateSpace

A CIP catalogue record for this book is available from the British Library.

Paperback ISBN-13: 978-1539752110
eBook ISBN: 978-1-63535-302-0

Typeset in Garamond 12.5pt.

A WORD FROM THE AUTHOR

We were in Tim Hortons.

On one side of the table, their hands around hot coffees, sat my daughter-in-law between two friends, all nurses. I sat opposite, a mug of tea with a double double.

We discussed books. I had published a book on World War II. Polite, but I knew they were not all that interested.

"So what grabs your reading attention?" I queried.

"I like a romantic book," replied one.

"Yeah a romance which makes me laugh," said another.

I looked at the third.

"What I like is an erotic romance".

Her companions nodded heads, grinning.

"So, to write to please you ladies, I need to come up with a funny, romantic, sexy book?"

"Yep!" they chorused.

"It will never happen," said my daughter-in-law.

I sipped my tea, and questioned, "Why not?"

"Because it's a long way from the stuff you write," she replied.

Already a story was forming in my head.

"Maybe I will surprise you," I said.

"Bet you don't," she laughed.

"What do you bet?" I said.

They all looked at each other, giggled, then told me.

This is for the three cheeky nurses.

I will collect later!!

ACKNOWLEDGEMENTS

My thanks go to Petrina for deciphering, typing and retyping my atrocious handwriting into understandable prose.

My thanks also go to Mark for his important editing.

Finally my sincere appreciation to Stephen for his formatting and the books final production.

CONTENTS

This one is for
Petrina.

CHAPTER ONE

Ricci

IT HURT! At the bottom of the scrum, somebody's backside in my face I dazedly feared for my manhood. The bang on the head put me out for a few seconds. The shrill whistle of the ref seemingly far away. A size twelve boot had ripped into my tender parts.

With Vernon looking anxiously and Tom standing bemused by me, the tangle of bodies was pulled off me. The stretcher guys knew their stuff and I was manhandled off the field.

"A medic took a look. Wow!" he said. Then, "Hospital."

* * *

Lying in clean sheets with the smell of antiseptic clearing my head I looked up at the young doc as he pulled back the covering. "Wow!" he said, looking at my personal parts!"

A white coated female with a stethoscope around her neck heard his exclamation and came to take a look. "Wow!" she said

1

and made a comment below her breath, something like "Lucky man!" as she continued her journey.

They had asked my name. "Riccardo Macdonald, interesting name", said the medic. "My mother was Italian," I said.

The young doc made a detailed examination. Straightening up he said, "That rugby boot must have had metal studs. It has torn into the side of your crotch and bruised some blood vessels. It needs a couple of stitches. Luckily that boot missed your whatsit by a few centimetres otherwise you would have a pattern of stud marks as decoration." This guy had his own sense of humour! He went on about the medical aspect, about damage to the varicocele or some such thing, and lost me in the detail. He regained my attention, "This means although you will be able to continue sexual intercourse you will be unable to produce or pass any sperm.

"What does that mean?"

"It means you will be unable to be a Daddy." He looked at my perplexed face. "This will continue until everything is back in order." He grinned, "Fortunately a small operation can then reverse the situation and if so required you could start building up your own rugby team. It will be as if you had had the 'snip' and wanted it to be reversed."

He pulled the cover back over. "In short you will be firing blanks from that big gun of yours until the situation is amended." He went to move away, turned and said, "oh yes! No more rugby for a while!"

*   *   *

Walking was painful. I recalled old cowboy films where the cowboy, after a horseback journey, ambles off to a nearby saloon on bowed legs, my similar walk caused by a mud laden rugby boot.

I hadn't bothered to explain my name to the nursing staff other than mention my mother was Italian. I have something of a mixed pedigree. My grandfather, Hamish Macdonald, a dour Scot from the Highlands had been a government official of the Foreign Office or whatever it was called at the time in India. Here he had met and married an Indian lady, my grandmother. They had one son, my father Robin, who became a talented pianist who, while giving recitals in Italy met and married a beautiful Italian singer. These nuptials resulted in a daughter, Anne-Marie and three years later a son i.e. me. We were living in Italy, I was fourteen at the time, when they were both killed in a four car accident when in a taxi. My grandparents had retired and purchased a property in South London possibly on the assumption it was too cold for an elderly Indian lady to reside in the Scottish Highlands. On the death of our parents they became the legal guardians.

Grandfather Hamish subsequently past away a couple of years ago. Anne-Marie is in a volatile relationship with a boyfriend. And now, edging towards twenty, I live in the home owned and occupied by my grandmother. The only other person in the household, another, younger Indian lady who is the companion of my grandmother during the day lives nearby. That is the family history. Scots, Indian, Italian blood will have something to do with the lovely good looks of Anne-Marie, my broad shouldered build and thick black hair, brown eyes and long slender fingers with which I play piano but not to my father's standard.

* * *

I walked into the room cowboy fashion. Grandma was seated in her usual high rise chair, her walking stick beside her. She had an audience of two young ladies. Anne-Marie and her best friend Leona Pinkerton, known to one and all as "Pinky." The young women swivelled round on my arrival.

"What on earth have you been up to?" asked Grandma.

"Where's your horse?" said Anne-Marie as sympathetic as ever.

I settled carefully in a nearby chair. "Rugby incident", I explained.

"So what exactly happened?" From Anne-Marie.

I was in no mood to give my sparky sister details. "A kick in the leg. Had a couple of stitches. That's all."

"Show us. Sounds bad." Said Anne-Marie.

"I'm showing you nothing." I replied, shortly.

"I think you have taken a kick in the whatsit!"

I glared at her. "That would be painful", said Pinky.

"Especially in his case," said my sister.

"Why in his case?"

"Shut up, the pair of you," I muttered.

"I know things others don't," smirked Anne-Marie.

"You know nothing," I said, angrily.

"I used to look after you when you were younger."

Grandmother interrupted. With a smile. "That's enough. Change the subject."

Anne-Marie ignored her. "I broke up his first romance," she declared. Pinky looked interestedly at her. "We were in the playground and he had a pimple on his face. I think he was seven at the time. He liked this little girl with blonde hair," "You got a spot on your face," she said. "No I haven't," he said. "You have," said the girl. I interrupted, "he has got lots of pimples." "Where?" asked the girl searching his face. "On his bottom," I fibbed. "No I haven't," he said. "Let me see," said the girl. "No way!" he yelled. "Lots of them", I insisted. "If you don't let me see, I won't talk to you!" the girl said. He then said "I'm not pulling my pants down and I haven't any pimples on my bum!" "I'm not speaking to you anymore." She turned and flounced off!"

Pinky laughed. "All lies. All lies." I muttered.

"Time we were off," announced Anne-Marie rising. Giving Grandmother air kisses. Promising another visit, they grinned, a pair of Cheshire cats. Offered any medical care or assistance, should I require it.

They giggled at my muttered response, blew kisses towards me and finally departed.

* * *

I looked around. "Haven't seen Rupinda about." Grandmother said, "She phoned me earlier to say she is unwell. Bad cold. Might be Flu. I told her to take a hot bath, a couple of aspirins, a tot of whisky and go to bed."

"I'll fix us something to eat." I walked uncomfortably towards the kitchen. "Something simple Ricci. A salad will do fine. Oh, yes. There is some apple pie and ice cream."

"Steady with your order. I am not a cordon bleu chef, I'll have you know," I joked.

"I'm well aware, Darling. That's why I suggested a simple salad."

We ate, drank tea and later a "wee nip" as Gran called it. Always sounded a bit strange coming from a cheerful dark faced Indian lady. Must have heard it often from her Scottish husband. No longer young she still retained a smiling face and no extra weight, so enabling her to move slowly around comfortably despite arthritic legs. At bedtime she refused all assistance and subsequently fell into a gentle sleep. Probably occasioned by another "nip".

I sat for a while reading. The pain slowly diminishing. I called it a day. Switched off most of the lights, went to my own room and so to bed.

I spent most of the following day in the local library. Interested in Modern History I was drafting the outline of a World War II book. With the advantage of having individual means following the death of my parents, I was seeking to become a writer.

I returned home. Grandmother Kumari who approved, doted on and loved her only grandson, and knew I felt pretty well the same way about her, was seated in her favourite upholstered chair, a welcoming smile on her dark exotic features. I place a light kiss on her cheek.

"Hi! Grandma," I greeted.

"Hello Darling," she replied patting my hand. "Is it still painful?"

"Just a little ache now, that's all. How have you been today?"

"Oh, I'm the same as usual. But Rupinda is still unwell. I've told her to take thing easy and not to return until she feels better."

Grandma looked around the room. Her dark eyes passing over the comfortable furnishings, the mini grand piano I played for her pleasure, the comfortable chair Rupinda occupied as they cheerfully chatted and constructed fine needlework on cushions and covers.

"I will miss her," she murmured half to herself. She collected her thoughts. Addressing me, "I will make her some soup. Later this evening would you be kind enough to take it round to her, Darling?"

"Of course, it will be a pleasure." I then surprised myself, "But you will have to give me her address."

Knowing I wasn't aware of Rupinda's address made me realize I actually knew little of the woman who arrived daily, usually after

I had left the house and who returned to her own little world each evening.

What I did know was Rupinda, a quiet spoken widow had answered an advertisement for a companion and had quickly become a good friend and welcome company. Not surprising really. For Grandmother Kumari, widowed now for over two years with the passing of her husband the elderly Hamish leaving her – the love of his life – an Indian lady from Kashmir. Delighted to find a pleasant and helpful younger presence also widowed and also from the Indian continent. Then the pleasure of finding they had a mutual interest in fine needlework made each enjoy and spend many happy hours in each other's company.

The evening meal over I placed the flask of hot soup and the wrapped various sweetmeats in a duffel bag having removed muddy rugby boots and miscellaneous items.

"Tell Rupinda I hope she is feeling better and to take as much time as she wants," instructed Grandmother. "Oh, and here is her address. It is only a couple of roads away, a ten-minute walk I would imagine."

I knew the road. Had often used it on my way to rugby practice. So I was not surprised to find the address was one of a neat row of detached bungalows. Opening the gate of the small front garden, I knocked on the front door.

A short delay and then the door was opened slightly and a woebegone dusky face appeared. Sleepy eyes widened on realizing who was standing smiling on the doorstep.

"Rupinda! I am sorry to disturb you. I am the messenger from Grandma Kumari. The deliverer of hot soup and other things."

CHAPTER TWO
Rupinda

Rupinda responded in a hoarse voice, "that is so kind of Kumari. Give me a moment to get back into bed and then close the door behind you." As she turned I saw she was bundled into a blanket around her shoulders.

Counting to twenty then closing the front door I stood in the hallway, heard her call my name and so entered her bedroom. Glancing around I saw the influences of the land of her birth.

Bright coloured pictures vied with richly embroidered tapestry over backs of chairs. A faint attractive perfume competed with that of medication. She was sitting up. A double bed with satin sheets and propped by large pillows. Tousled hair enclosed a heart shaped dark eyed face.

Rupinda indicated a chair near the foot of the bed. Seated I undid the tie of my shoulder bag and brought into view the flask and package of sweetmeats. Under instruction from the patient I placed them on a tray in the kitchen.

I returned to the bedroom. Rupinda was obviously unwell and after a few moments I rose to depart. She waved me back into my seat.

'Please don't go yet. You are the first person I've seen all day." She stopped, considered. "In fact you are probably the first visitor to enter this house since my husband passed away. That was four years ago."

"Your Grandma Kumari has been a lifeline to me." She lapsed into silence. Her mind on the past. Then her eyes re-focused on her visitor. "Oh Ricci, I'm so sorry, you must be off somewhere and I am keeping you."

Hastily I replied, "Not at all." Then continued, "Forgive me mentioning it but I know so little about you. I know you to be widowed but don't know much more than that. Do you have children for example?"

"No. I married Brijesh when I was twenty. He was a few years older than me. A chemist – a very good one. He was offered a senior position with a well-known parfumeries company with headquarters in London, England. It was an offer he just could not refuse. We came here and were very happy. It was then he became unwell and passed away. They found it was his heart. As he hadn't been with the company very long the pension was not over generous, but we had this place paid for and I manage quite well. He was a good man."

She stopped talking. Then looking at me, smiled mischievously.

"But I know quite a lot about you. Your Gran is so proud of you. She is always talking about her only grandson." She sat up, "Would you bring me more soup tomorrow? I am feeling better for your visit and I would like to talk some more." She indicated towards a key on a side table. "Take the key so you don't need to stand on the doorstep like a salesman."

I rose to go. She was obviously tiring. "I'll be back tomorrow evening with more soup," smiled and stepping forward I picked up her hand resting on the sheet and kissed it.

"You are a gentleman and I thank you again for this visit."

Walking home my mind was a jumble of thoughts. I had a feeling of undertones between us but couldn't put it into words. Despite the watery eyes and sniffling into a handkerchief I realized there was far more to Rupinda than just a companion to Gran. The pain in my groin seemed to have eased, or had it shifted slightly?

*   *   *

I spend most of the following day in the local library, researching the outline of a War II book.

"Hi, Grandma," I said, on returning home.

"Hello darling," she replied patting my head.

After enquiring how Rupinda was, Grandma announced she would make a special soup to help combat her cold. Later that evening, I, who for some reason hadn't mentioned I now had a key to Rupinda's home stood again on her doorstep. Fumbling with the key I let myself in and called out to let her know.

"Come in please," her voice from the bedroom sounded closer and stronger. I entered and stood in the doorway for a moment. She, in a dressing gown, was seated in one of a pair of armchairs alongside a small table. She smiled and indicated the empty chair. "Your visit and the soup must have perked me up. I'm feeling much better." I sat facing her. I brought out the flask of soup. "Grandma informs me this is a special anti-cold soup." I passed the flask to her. Leaning forward she exclaimed "Pepper Rasam! A lovely clear soup well known for combating colds. As I'm feeling much improved today, please take it into the kitchen. I will enjoy it later."

I did as I was told and returned sat facing Rupinda who said, "I believe you are off to university later in the year?"

"Well I thought of taking a gap year. Truth is I think I need a break before I have several years of study."

"What are you thinking of studying?"

"I'm interested in Modern History and hoping to become a writer. Fortunately, I have no one depending on me and I'm financially secure."

She fixed her dark eyes on me. "what, no girlfriend?"

"Nope!"

She smiled and said, "Now I am going to be personal and ask you if you have had girlfriends."

"Oh, yes. I've had several, but they amounted to nothing

special. After all I'm nearly twenty." I grinned.

Rupinda said, "Did you ever sleep with any of them?"

I was taken aback by the question. "No. It wasn't that kind of relationships."

"So you are celibate, a virgin?" she said with surprise.

Eyes wide at the question, I felt my face burning, "I guess I am."

I felt I should ask something personal to see her reaction. After all it was only fair. "how long have you been living on your own?"

She thought for a moment. "Four – nearly five years."

"That is quite a while. You must miss your husband?"

"I will always miss him. He was a good kindly lovely man. I miss him in many ways. But I know I must get on with my life."

"You were married for some three years, yet you had no children?"

"Brijesh and I had made plans. We wanted four or five years together enjoying each other in a personal way before we became parents. Perhaps unusual, but that is what we wanted." She smiled. "After all we came from a part of the world that produced the Kama Sutra."

"But that was written many years ago!"

She nodded. "In about the third century, actually. By Vatsayana Mallanaga. Kama is the Hindu God of Love and it is the Treaty of Pleasure. The sexual positions described are but part of the Kama Sutra which is viewed by many as of scholarly importance in the way life should be conducted to bring goodness and kindness to each other and promote happiness."

"And do you know the positions?" I asked cheekily.

She smiled gently. "My husband and I both had university backgrounds and so were regarded to have some intelligence. Brijesh was also a research chemist who, in addition to exotic perfumes was also researching medical sexual related issues to act as stimulates for those who suffer low unhappy sex drives." Rupinda's eyes twinkled. "Yes I know and have experienced and enjoyed many of the sexual positions described." Again her eyes sparkling held mine.

Mischievously she continued. "In fact I could be a very good teacher to a young man who could become a very good and thoughtful lover for the rest of his life."

I sat stunned, speechless. I looked into her eyes. I knew I was seeing a beautiful and open minded modern woman, knowing this could be a subject for discussion. "Would you teach me?"

She sat silent for a moment studying my face. "It could be a secret between the two of us. You would have to become a willing student. Don't decide now. Come back tomorrow evening. Tell your Grandma I am much better but will like a few more days to recover. We will then talk about it and you will decide."

* * *

I arrived at Grandmas house to be met with a perplexed Grandma. "Anne-Marie phoned and she is not at all happy," Grandma said.

"What's the problem this time?" I queried. "Anne-Marie and her city boyfriend are always annoying each other."

"She thinks he has another girlfriend and he is two timing Anne-Marie," said Kumari. "He is protesting it is not so and that his absences are due to meeting clients – although he admits some may be female. She is so wilful and has a lot of her excitable mother in her."

"Not like a nice sensible person like me." I grinned.

"Oh. There are plenty of things about you that always remind me of your mother, God bless her. But you have many traits of your father. Your beautiful piano playing, your build and many other things." Grandma Kumari recalled where I have been. "How is Rupinda?"

"She has almost recovered from her cold but asks if she could remain home a few days longer."

"It looks as if your visits have been helpful." She looked at her grandson shrewdly.

I said, "we've had long conversations. She is an interesting woman. I am thinking of taking some flowers to her."

"That is a wonderful idea, darling. I'm sure she will be delighted, and tell her to take all the time she wants."

"Will do," I replied.

I left the room. Kumari looked at the closed door. "Well, Well, Well," she murmured. Her mind was still sharp as ever.

*   *   *

The following day I took a walk into town heading for the florists. Passing a pharmacy I considered my possible immediate future and purchased a pack of contraceptives. Not without some embarrassment. The ache in my groin was now barely noticeable. That evening, putting the key in the lock I felt unknown anticipation prickling my skin.

Rupinda was in the kitchen when I proffered the bouquet. Smiling her pleasure she said, "Roses! This must be the nicest gift I have had in ages. I can't remember – it must be years since…" Her eyes crinkled. She said coquetry, "Do you know the presentation of flowers has long been considered to having a secret meaning?"

"I have heard something along those lines," I admitted.

"In India and many other places red roses can mean 'I love you, I respect you, you are beautiful!'" I tried not to look embarrassed. Then grinned and said, "Well, two out of three can't be bad!"

Rupinda stepped forward, kissed me lightly on the cheek. "Thank you for these, they are so beautiful!" I knew the smiling woman facing me had a sense of humour, when she continued. "Perhaps one day you may give me a bunch of sweet pea."

Puzzled, "and why would I do that?"

"The presentation of sweet peas can mean 'thank you for a

lovely time!"

* * *

Whether it was my visits or the soup that aided her quick recovery Rupinda's cold had fast disappeared. Something, seemed to have revitalized her or was it anticipation? Soft drinks were on the nearby table. Rupinda and I sat facing each other. Quietly she said, "if you are comfortable we will begin. I am going to outline the attitude, the conduct, the goodness of a gentleman described by the author of this treatise on the path to obtaining and providing happiness. You may know much of what is written for we have had over two thousand years to ponder on his meanings many of which are still being interpreted by scholars."

I nodded. Feeling as if I were back in school.

"At all times a gentleman will be good mannered. He may be angry or insulted on occasions but he must never succumb to retaliation or insulting behaviour no matter how he is pressed. This is of particular importance in the presence of ladies, ladies of all walks of life. A gentleman must always possess a gentle smiling visage. This doesn't mean he goes about with a silly expression on his face. I mean having a friendly, unthreatening honest look about him that others are instinctively drawn to him. He may be a man who lives a life alone, who prefers his own company or be a gregarious person who likes to be the life and soul of the party. He remains kind and always seeks to provide assistance to others when it is required and withdraw quietly when it is no longer necessary.

One should always be truthful. Even a little lie can develop into large ones and far as possible he should not lie. If one is dealing with an unpleasant person there will always be something about them a comment on which will give them a small pleasure. Even an uncouth woman may have attractive hands or beautiful eyes.

"A gentleman is or should be a people watcher. A simple exercise is watching passers-by, crowds or single people. Such as those that stand silently outside underground stations. Sit in park seats. Who are disabled. Who seem lost or unhappy." Rupinda stopped talking, studied me, her attentive companion.

"What I am trying to say, is this. Human beings are immensely interesting. One can learn simply by being aware of their existence. Each person is different. They may wear the same uniform or live the same type of life but each beneath the skin is a fascinating entity. Each was given birth into this world and throughout their life desires and requires certain things and cannot be happy without them. Food, shelter, companionship, warmth and at times in their lives the urge to cohabit and finally to find happiness or at least contentment."

She was quiet. Taking a sip of fruit juice, she looked at me. Taking in my physical features, dark eyes, considering. Appearing satisfied, seemingly I would be a good subject. Or perhaps she was considering my background. A strong Scottish grandfather, a beautiful graceful Indian grandmother. An artistic expressive father and a comely enchanting Italian mother had produced a person, who despite the difference in age she knew she would always be attracted to.

I was almost on the same wavelength. For she was spell bindingly exquisite. Fine utterly smooth caramel coloured skin, long black shining hair, graceful figure and – I couldn't get away from - black twinkling humorous enticing eyes.

"There is one word I want to explain," Rupinda said. "That is pride."

I shifted in my seat trying to ignore the tightening of body parts. "Pride?" I queried.

"Yes. The feeling of self-worth. A confidence of one's personal importance. Just polishing one's shoes can be a moment of pride and satisfaction. Being clean and nicely dressed can give pride to oneself. It has to be a quiet, private feeling. Not pretentious ostentatious of vanity or arrogance. She fell silent. Then "All the things I have described are part of the whole."

"Finally, 'shyness'. Shyness in dealing with other persons. Shyness exhibited by other persons, where, when necessary it should be confronted." She stopped again. Eyes sparkled. She tried to suppress a grin.

"If I said to you go into the bathroom, take off all your clothes and come back into this room and stand before me, what would you say or do?"

I didn't think I had heard her correctly. "Say that again."

She repeated the question. I had heard it right. I looked at her. The steady gaze and slight smile remained. I took a deep breath. "I would strip to my skin and stand before you," I replied. Then my grin matching her smile, continued, "providing you are also standing unclothed."

There was a silence.

"We will begin in the art of instruction tomorrow.

CHAPTER THREE

She was standing in the centre of the room. Her hands clasped in front of her facing the door. Her hair was tied off her face. Her body outlined the crisp white blouse and black skirt.

She said nothing as I entered the room. For a moment I slowed. Then, inevitably drawn, moved towards her, stood close, placed my hands on her waist drew her towards me. My lips found hers. For a moment she stood rigid. Then her back relaxed. Her hands moved up my shirt, clasped around my neck as she responded.

I felt the warmth of her body and desire stirred. She was aware. Unclasping her hands, she took hold of mine and moved slightly back.

"We have things to discuss. I have something for you." She released herself and holding my hand moved to the armchair, ordering me to sit. Moving to a side cupboard her hands closed around a small object.

Seated opposite she placed it on the table between us. A small square shaped phial containing a golden yellow liquid.

"You may recall my mentioning my husband Brijesh researching exotic perfumes and sexually related essences." She said quietly. "Well, he was successful. After many tests he found certain extracts when combined in particular quantities resulted in improving physical attraction. When animals note a particular odour about another of the species it prompts a sexual interest. Although not precisely the same Brijesh was able to produce small quantities of an extremely subtle perfume. He found if a man just transferred the slightest touch of this essence to certain body areas it combines with his body heat and a subtle awakening of interest if submerged or blocked sexual desires are there in the first place, from a woman." I looked again at the small square phial. It was a beautiful container. Four golden shoulders continued down the four corners. The cap, also of gold had the facet design of a diamond ring.

"How do you know it works?"

A small smile played around Rupinda's lips. "I know it acts like it was designed to do. Although it was somewhat superfluous. For at that time my desires were not submerged or blocked in any way." She looked at the tiny bottle. "You probably won't realize it but the smallest amount gives out an extremely fine aroma yet even women would not be aware of its presence. I remember Brijesh saying during a test several women had made comments that it gave out some kind of an aura but couldn't account or explain it. Before you go today I will show you where to place it on your body and how incredibly small the amount to use."

"So what would happen if I used more than I should?"

"Firstly it would be extremely wasteful of this small amount. Secondly you must know of perfumes and the like which if used in excess revolts you and you move away from it. And finally overdoing it could make your skin itch and becomes an irritant.

"Take off your shirt," she commanded.

I stripped to the waist.

Carefully opening the glass phial, using the tiny enclosed brush she touched the surface of the golden liquid, brushed it against the inner surface as she withdrew, it glistening in the light. She placed a finger in the slight hollow of my shoulder. "You just make a brush stroke here on each shoulder and the same action here," she said touching just above my navel.

"How often?"

"Not often, Perhaps once a month."

"But won't it wash off when I shower?"

"No. Wait a few seconds. It will be absorbed through your skin. You can forget all about it." She completed her task. Carefully returned the brush to the phial.

"You are unlikely to be aware of its action. It is extremely subtle. Should others become aware of it they would probably think of it as an expensive body wash. The only way I can describe it is rather like an invisible aura. And remember, just a tiny touch. This is like gold dust. Rajesh was only able to manufacture a small amount before he died."

Replacing my shirt, I said, "Is it working on you?"

Rupinda smiled, "I'm not telling. I won't be seeing you for a couple of days. Tomorrow I am visiting my doctor. To arrange an oral contraceptive. What they call it, - going on the pill- I think it will be better to do so. You can tell Grandmother Kumari I will return to her in two days for I am feeling much better."

CHAPTER FOUR

Her words surprised me.

"Tonight is your night. No instruction," she whispered. "I just want you to hold me. To feel your body against mine." Lights were low. Faint Hindu music murmured in the background. A perfumed Rupinda stood at the side of the bed. A silk sheet held, following the soft outlining curves of her body.

So we stood for a moment.

"You first." She spoke softly.

I sighed. From the bathroom with just a towel about my waist I had stepped into her bedroom. I let slip the towel. Slowly it dropped to the floor. She gasped, staring. I could feel it hardening. She muttered something in her own language. Then, "Wow!" Her imagination taking hold. "That is really something!"

"Now it's your turn."

Rupinda moved her hands. The satin sheet crumpled to the floor. Her long black hair falling thickly about her neck.

Shoulders held well back, firm neat breasts, nipples rising. My gaze moved down her elegant slim body, skin shining faintly.

She held out her hands. I stepped towards her, her breasts pressed against me as I sought her soft partly opened mouth. Slowly she fell backwards on to the bed, my body following down.

Rupinda's breath quickened as she looked up into my eyes. Half leaning, I lowered my head, my lips brushing softly against her ear, teeth tugging gently. She responded cupping my face as my lips and tongue moved slowly gently to meet the rise of her breast. Her fingers ruffled my hair. I took the swollen nipple between my lips, teasing gently with tugging teeth, then sucking the distended hot hardened tip as she pressed it invitingly towards me. Her fingers slid from my head to the sides of my face. I felt her hands pressing. She pulled my head down, my lips to meet hers. Her tongue slipped wetly to mine for a moment. Her hands, still each side of my face, she moved her other breast with its heated nipple and positioned my lips above it pulling my mouth down towards it. Perhaps it was soreness of the other or jealous desire. A swollen hot nipple felt my lips enclose and a sigh of pleasure escaped her.

The tips of my fingers brushed across her body. Halting against her hips for a slight moment before traversing across her navel to brush the dark olive drawn tight skin of her other hip. She shuddered. My hand moved lower. For a moment I covered the bush of black wiry hair then gently sought warm inner thighs.

Her legs parted. A finger slipped into wetness, gently pressing, massaging her clitoris to be joined by a second finger and finally a third. Rupinda's body crumbled. Her arms about me tightened. I rolled my body to kneel between parted legs. She uttered a low cry as her distended vulva parted as I pressed, sliding rigidly into her. Her knees lifted, limbs widening to encompass me. Sensationally she cried out at the fullness, the tightness. For a moment I was still. She relaxed   Slowly I pressed into her. She responded. Perspiration filmed our heated bodies as we gripped each other and movements became more insistent, desiring. Then Rupinda, violently shuddering, called out, arched her body as the hot tide of repeated orgasm flooded her whole being.

*   *   *

"That had little to do with the Kama Sutra," I observed. We were lying comfortably, both naked, resting. Rupinda smiled at me. "I had waited a long time. Your arrival started a new rather erotic train of thoughts. I desired you so much. Thank you."

She pondered, "perhaps we can begin again, tomorrow. Eagerness on my part and desire gave me no time to think. The missionary position is the known, accepted basic and the most urgent position and is mentioned of course in the Kama Sutra." She smiled. "And no advice was required or needed." She looked at me under her eye lashes, "even for a celibate."

"Well, animals receive no initial instruction and they manage quite well," I commented.

"All these alternative positions, despite being given names or numbers, descriptive or otherwise are essentially when desiring, seeking exotic romantic alternatives. Abandoning all shyness, all inhibitions. Must have willingness and desire from both parties."

"I believe my future is to be more enlightening than my past," I said, putting my arm around her warm glistening shoulders.

"Not only enlightening. Think pleasurable, entrancing, risqué sensational, beguiling, sexual - even funny!"

Rupinda sat up. "Always remember. It is the happiness, the fulfilment of desire by the woman you are endeavouring to provide. The lonely, the unhappy. Those to whom you are providing succour. Think not of your own pleasure which may be an incidental result. Foremost must be your intention to provide happiness, contentment to those who may require it."

"So in actual fact I am providing a service."

"Exactly. Remember. In the heat of the moment not to forget that fact."

*   *   *

The following days, the weeks so quickly passed. During daylight I sat at my desk writing, researching and on occasions visiting ex-servicemen to hear long remembered recollection of their wartime youth.

On a number of occasions, I made use of the key Rupinda had provided. She was an excellent instructor. My knowledge of the various positions grew. My celibate way of life had long disappeared. Enjoyment, and that is the appropriate word for undergoing such personal instruction increased as my friendship with Rupinda strengthened. I found a particular delight in the old Hindu naming of the positions. Secretly and without commenting very much upon it I was quite happy to settle most times for the missionary position – at least initially. Varying came later!

But Rupinda insisted that although our intimacy may be delightful, the object of all instruction was the fundamental happiness of sad, lonely women through courtesy, kindness and where required, companionship.

With the cessation of instruction but the forming of a long and enduring friendship, and with my move to Uni to study Modern History, a period of happy youth closed.

With farewells to Anne Marie, Grandma Kumari and a passionate evening with Rupinda I took up my role once again as a student. Somehow it won't be quite as enjoyable!

CHAPTER FIVE
Beth

I glanced at my watch and realized I would have to step out for I was running late. Not that it was all that important. A couple of pints with a bunch of rugby guys in their usual pub. But it was good enough way to keep in touch with my personal friends, Vernon and Tom.

Turning into Panton Road I was the only pedestrian other than a woman some twenty yard ahead. She was pulling a wheeled holiday case which seemed to have a cracked left wheel, a bulky backpack and a heavy carry bag. It was as she dropped the bag I saw her right arm was held across her chest in a black sling. The lady was certainly having difficulties and as I came up to her I saw she looked on the verge of tears.

"Excuse me Miss, but can I be of help? You seem to be a trifle overloaded." I said.

She wearily raised her head. "Oh, I think I can manage, thank you. I just need to get my breath back."

Through misted eyes she saw only a stranger offering assistance. "I really think you need a helping hand to sort of replace the one you have out of action," I insisted. "Have you far to go?"

She rubbed the back of her good hand across her face wiping her eyes and looked again at the figure in front of her. She was aware of a friendly voice and took in I was really concerned. She smiled at my reference to her arm and looking down at the sling aid, "It was a bad time to strain my wrist and it's about the worst day I can remember. For it is not only my wrist, I've had my bag stolen with all the things I own and need. Then on collecting my case from the airport carousel I find that somehow it's inherited a broken wheel." She remembered my question. "Another couple of hundred yards to go and I will be home."

I stepped forward and collected the large bag and the disabled trolley. Despite her refusal she looked relieved. "it's very kind of you."

I walked alongside the weary traveller. The clickety click of the broken wheel keeping time with our steps.

You have obviously been on holiday," I said.

"Spain." She looked down at the pavement then blurted, "I just had to get away, even if it was only for two weeks."

"And did you enjoy yourself, out there?" I guessed she was in her early twenties and by the tone of her voice not particularly happy.

"It was alright," she replied quietly. "It made a change, but being on my own..." she stopped and looked down again. "It could have been better."

We were approaching the end of a line of houses. Beyond I knew and could see a group of shops, mini food store, butchers, chemist, pizza house and book makers in a small square.

She indicated her house with her head. "This is where I live. I've got to break a window or something, for my keys were in my bag that was stolen." She looked mournfully at the front of the house.

"Perhaps I can find a window ajar," I said, "and get access that way."

"I'm a bit security conscious, living on my own," she muttered. "Unlikely, I'd say."

I dropped the bag on the step inside the gate and slipped the back pack from her shoulders. I took the bag from the woman, and said "I'll see what I can do," and moved to the ground floor windows. Without smashing the double glazing, no chance of entry. I walked around the side of the house to the rear garden and the kitchen door. Inspecting the door lock I considered it may have possibilities. There was a slight gap between the door and the frame edge. I slipped a credit card from my wallet and inserted it in the gap. Putting pressure on the card I tried to slide the ward of the lock. No luck. The card wasn't sufficiently rigid. It was then I remembered the pocket knife I used to scrape mud off rugby boots. I again inserted the card and at the same time pressed the sharp point of the knife against the metal tongue of the lock. Carefully and successfully I managed to retract the tongue and pull the kitchen door open.

Entering the tiny kitchen, I moved to the front door, unlocked it and pulled it open to confront a wide eyed tenant of the property.

"Wow!" she cried, delighted. Then, "You are not a professional burglar by chance?"

I smiled. Pleased to see she had cheered up, now she had access to her home. She was about to pick up her bag. I said "leave that to me," and I stood aside as she entered. I followed placing the articles in the sitting room.

She turned to me and the thought suddenly struck her. "Oh! I'm sorry I must have made you late for wherever you were going."

"No, nothing important. I'm more concerned with your difficulties." I reassured her.

I think I may have a spare key to the front door." She went to a cupboard. On the inside hung a bunch of keys. "Yes, success. I have found one. Tomorrow I must get another key cut after I have been to the bank and sorted out my stolen cards." She sat down and looked around. "Would you like a drink? I'm dying for a cup of tea. You have been so kind. I can't thank you enough." Then she remembered "Oh Lord. No milk!"

I checked my watch. The mini-market would still be open. Rising, I said, "be back in five minutes. Put the kettle on. I'll get milk." Her mouth still open in surprise I dashed to the shopping precinct, bought milk from the store and checked out the Pizza parlour. Returning, it actually took ten minutes, I handed her the milk and the cardboard box of pizza.

"Thought you might be hungry. Didn't know which was your favourite but the guy had a pineapple and ham on the go so I opted for that." Then, "By the way I'm Ricci," and stuck out my hand. I felt her soft grasp.

"Elizabeth," she replied with a smile, "but known as Beth."

During the next hour drinking hot tea and munching pizza I found Beth was a nurse, had volunteered to work six months with an overseas charity, shared the house with a friend, also a nurse and was awaiting details of her soon to be posting to Africa. I heard how her holiday alone had been occasioned by a row with a boyfriend which hadn't worked out and indeed had frightened her with threatened violence. I also found that Jenny, the nurse she shared the house with was in Surrey looking after a sick mother. Beth had cheered up considerably. Following enquiries about myself I had trotted out the usual story of Indian, Italian and Scottish bloodline.

"So I'm a sort of mongrel," I joked.

Beth was intrigued, "You are certainly no mongrel," she flushed, and without thought continued. "So that's where you get your dark good looks…" She stopped. Her face flushed pink. She didn't want to show her feeling of interest in this young stranger.

"Since my parents died and my grandfather passed away, my grandmother with whom I live with has looked after me." I continued "She has taught me a great deal about good manners and respect for others." I stopped. "I sound a bit of a twit," I smiled and stood up. "I've taken up too much of your time. I had better get going."

Beth rose saying, "Not at all. You've kept me interested, and I thank you for helping me."

*   *   *

It was the following day, surprisingly our paths again crossed. I was seated in Pinatos in the high street with a café latte in front of me when she walked in carrying shopping bags. Few people were in at that time and she saw me immediately. I waved an acknowledgement and she veered over in my direction.

"Hi," she said smiling a greeting.

"Hi, yourself," I said. "Let me get you a coffee or whatever. I see you are overloaded again."

She grinned at the memory. "I'll have what you are having, no sugar," she said.

Placing a tall latte before her, I asked, "Have you now sorted your problems?"

"Yes, thank you," she smiled. "I'm back to work tomorrow so

I need to sort things out rather quickly," she continued.

"May be our paths will cross yet again," I said.

"I hope so," she smiled without thinking. "That would be nice."

"How about dinner tonight?" I asked.

Laughing, she looked at me, "seriously?"

"Of course I'm serious. I'll put it another way...I would be honoured if you would care to dine with me this evening"

"I would love to." She smiled.

"I'll book a table for eight-thirty." I looked at her now bandaged wrist.

"It's a lot better," she said. "At first I thought I had fractured it, but it was a bad strain. Should be okay in a day or two."

*   *   *

I had chosen a popular restaurant and the evening went well. I picked up a smartly dressed young lady with made up sparkling eyes, dark hair down to her shoulders wearing a green dress. I had appreciated she was a nice looking young lady when I first laid eyes on her downcast face. This evening I realized how stunningly good looking she actually was. "You are quite a lovely lady and I am delighted I have met you." I made these comments when I held the door of my car open for her. She was pleased at my remarks and throughout the evening, during a pleasant meal, through to coffee we found pleasure in each other's company. As I was driving I drank mostly water providing Beth with her choice of wine, which resolved any reserve of shyness.

Beth spoke at length of Uganda where she understood the chosen charity was operating. "Friends spoke of the hardships, the illnesses and way of life of the poorest, particularly of the children," she paused, "And so I am going, for six months as part of my nursing career."

"What happens with your housing situation over here?" I asked.

"I have an arrangement with Jenny. We are buying it between us, she will continue with payments and I will arrange my share to continue. Perhaps the situation will be reversed when I come back, for Jenny is interested in the charity and may, on my return decide to do the same thing."

We spoke some more particularly of travelling until it was time to move out. On the drive back to her place I noticed Beth was quiet, seemingly run out of words.

I pulled up before her house. We sat for a moment in silence. Then, "So back to work is it tomorrow?" I checked.

Beth nodded, "And Jenny will be back from visiting her mother." Another silence. Beth turned to me, "Come in for a coffee?" that broke the silence and I followed her into the house.

"Coffee or wine?" she asked me. I hesitated. "A glass of wine won't do me any harm," I decided.

"I'll have the same," said Beth.

We sat opposite each other. After a few comments about the

wine we lapsed into silence, Beth looking into the distance. "A penny for your thoughts," I said.

Beth looked up and said, "What?......Oh, I am sorry. I was miles away," she laughed, yet seemingly nervous.

"So what was taking up your thoughts?" I asked.

For a moment she was silent. Then, quietly, "I was thinking it would have been nice if you could have stayed tonight."

Just as quietly I replied. "There is nothing stopping me from doing so." I continued, "I would never have mentioned it, but I'm pleased you have done so for you are a lovely lady." I glanced at the couch and said, "It might be rather uncomfortable but my feet can always hang over the end..." For a moment she looked confused. Then laughed as she realized I was joking.

I stood and moving to her I bent and kissed her. "Been wanting to do that for quite a while." She put her arms up around my neck and with my hands on her waist I lifted her. She was warm, I could smell her perfumed body. Her lips parted and she pressed against me as we kissed again and again. Deep open mouthed kisses.

"What are we waiting for?" she asked in a whisper.

Lifting her into my arms I moved to her bed.

CHAPTER SIX

The room half-lit, the moon shining onto our bodies one moment bathed in silver then a movement enclosing us in shade.

We clung together, my hands on her warm glowing body. I lowered my head as the sheet slid away. She sighed as my lips closed on a swelling nipple.

Her hand slipped between us, moving down seeking me. I was hard. Big and hard. Her hand went around me. Tightened. She gasped. In the half-light I saw her questioning look. "Wow" she said. She squeezed. "Wow!" again. "This is big!" she whispered.

"Are you complaining?" I whispered back.

"My Goodness, No," she giggled

"Well stop squeezing it like it's a banana," I commanded.

"A banana?" she breathed. "More like a cucumber!"

The imagination of such a vegetable seemed to tickle her and she burst into laughter. She released the item, sliding her arms up around my neck, her breasts hard against me.

"I hope you are going to put it to good use, soon, very soon," she breathed. She pressed harder into my chest. My hands slid down her back. Fingers curved in line with the two swellings at the bottom of her spine. I squeezed and she made her anal muscles respond.

As she again relaxed my fingers gently slid between the mounds and curved once again as they found her distended vulva. She pressed hard against my fingers, relaxed, her legs parting slightly. Fingers entered her soft wetness seeking her clitoris, gently massaging. Her grip tightened on me as she shuddered, seemingly unaware she was whispering my name over and over.

She was pulling at me. Hot, wet, perspiring. She smelled delightful. I moved down towards her opening, inviting thighs, wetting her hardened breasts as I did so.

Beth was panting, her breath irregular. Now pulling her wide I pressed stiffly into her. I placed my lips on her as I relaxed for a moment. Desperately she pulled her face to one side, needing air as I moved further into her. Now hardness replaced gentle action as I massaged anew her clitoris. Now she was lying perfectly still, her nails gripping into my back as I lay between her extended legs massaging internally. I stopped for a moment. Motionless we remained. Gentle movements. She drew up her legs and her eyes widened as I began again. Tight, hot against each other. Now she came into action coming up to meet me each time as I went down into her. Her actions became faster. Arching she gave a tiny scream as shaking, shudderingly she came, her orgasm wetly, hotly, flooding me.

*   *   *

Now relaxed head pressing into my chest. "Oh, my goodness," she said. Then raising her head smiled and kissed me.

"I could do with a drink," I said, dry mouthed.

She turned on to her back. "The kitchen is that way," she said pointing in the direction if the kitchen. I took the hint, found my boxers, slipped them on and moved from the bed.

Returning with glasses of wine I found the other occupant missing. I watched her as she returned from the bathroom wearing a white t-shirt that barely covered her thighs. Demurely she slipped under a sheet sitting up as I handed her a glass.

"Are you okay?" I asked not sure.

"I'm feeling great! In fact, I'm feeling wonderful, like a liberated woman. Thank God I take the pill. The way I feel, just about anything could happen."

I laughed. "Perhaps I should have mentioned it. You were in no danger of conceiving. A small accident some time ago saw to that."

She was puzzled and said so. As briefly as I could I explained the rugby incident and its outcome. Finally, I used the descriptive phrase summing it up. "So at this time I'm shooting blanks." She had been listening intently.

"But this – er- accident hasn't interfered with -er-action, er- otherwise?" she then realized and giggled.

"I will leave you to decide on that." I said.

She clung to me. "Can we do it again," she whispered.

"In due course, if you are up for it." I answered.

"I'm up for anything with you," she whispered again squeezing my arm.

"Should you wish we could always take another route," I said.

Surprised, she questioned, "Another route?"

"With the same eventual result, I hasten to add!"

She giggled. "I like you talking like this. Tell me more."

"Well," I said. "Imagine you are going on a rail journey. Say there are three alternative routes. The first train takes a straightforward route, but stopped at the small stations. The second train takes a country route which takes somewhat longer but gives time to enjoy the country side. The third is more of an express going direct to your destination." I stopped. "Are you still with me?" I asked.

"You bet," she answered.

"The Kama Sutra describes a number of alternative method of arriving at the eventual destination, if you follow me!"

"All the way. She breathed. "The Kama Sutra? You have a surprising way of describing your reading material, but then you are an author. Carry on!"

"For example I could give you the names describing sexual positions which do not necessarily follow the – er- method used - er – recently. Although I have to say such positions are in use somewhat enthusiastically by thousands of -er – couples."

She wriggled. "You are making me feel – er- warm. So describe the positions."

"I'll just name three. Samdamsha Position. This gives all decisions to the woman.

Then there is the Kaurma Position, where we are seated face to face. Finally, there is the Uthranta Position. The woman is completely exposed- er – I think that is all I need to mention."

"Don't stop now! Tell me more." Beth pulled on my arm, still wriggling.

"Remember you are back at work in a few hours," I said. "You need your sleep."

She used a swear word to give her opinion on that, and so I explained more details of each position. "So tell me which you would prefer and I will endeavour to fulfil your wish," I joked.

Beth pulled herself up. Her hot body deliciously against mine. She was breathing warm air in my ear. "I want them all, in turn," she whispered.

"It's not possible!" I exclaimed.

"Maybe not. But we can try!" she said, slipping her hand down towards me.

*   *   *

It was still dark when, dressed, I left the house. Delicious exhaustion I reflected what Beth was probably sensing. A quick hug, a kiss and a promise to keep contact had left her with a smile.

Few people were about at this time of the morning. The air was fresh and dawn breaking. I was feeling in a good mood as I let myself into my home. For I had met up with an unhappy unfortunate ex-holiday maker and left a happy contented young nurse.

*   *   *

Beth returned home, tired after a busy first day back at work. Entering, she found a note on the carpet. Package outside kitchen door it read. Mystified she entered the house and walked through to the kitchen and unlocked the kitchen door to find a large package.

Taking off her coat, she unravelled the thick brown paper. Displayed was a large pink and grey holiday wheeled case with a note attached. Keys inside. Unzipping the case Beth gazed at a beautiful bouquet of red roses. Keys to the case were nearby. Lifting the flowers Beth read the attached note.

I thought you might be needing a replacement with non clickety click wheels! Have a good and safe six months in Africa.   LOL Ricci XXX

CHAPTER SEVEN
Vanessa

I was seated opposite a man in the bar of a London pub. It was evening. Offices were closing for the day, in fact for the weekend for it was a Friday evening. The bar was filling quickly with workers eager to relax before heading off to destinations. A trio of females grabbed one of the few unoccupied tables close to the one where we were seated. Spare seats at our table were whisked away to provide seating for larger groups. What had been an almost empty bar became a crowd of laughing, noisy drinkers.

My companion was talking. He pushed a file of papers towards me, his fingers hovering above as if reluctant to part with them. "As I was saying, my father put down his memories of the war a number of years ago with the intention of turning them into a book. Instead they languished in a drawer for years, forgotten. He passed away last year some six years after the death of my mother. It was when I was clearing out their home I found this old file." The man stopped talking, slightly irritated by the crowd noise. He swallowed beer and continued. "I sat down and read what my father had written all those years ago. You will understand he was not a writer in fact most of his life he was a builder, a bricklayer. But some of the things he wrote, incidents, death of friends, he had been an infantry man, brought tears to my eyes. Now I'm no writer and know I couldn't do justice to these memories of my father. It was then I saw your ad in that army magazine asking for war time memories for incorporation in a forthcoming book. I've decided to offer them to you, to see if you can use the contents. There is just one proviso. You take a copy and return this file to me. Oh, yes, and I would appreciate if my father is mentioned."

I had thumbed quickly through the file and scanning paragraphs here and there knew there was much of interest I could use.

"I would appreciate use of your father's writings. Real 'I was there' description of incidents are extremely useful and are becoming rare. I can undertake use of this file and can promise a copy will be made. I will return this original file to you. I will of course give credit where due to your father in what will be my third book on World War Two. You may know ten percent of book profits go to Armed Forces Charities." This seemed to satisfy the young man.

"Can I get you another beer?" I asked.

He set down his empty glass. "Thanks, but I'm driving. I'll be off now, and thanks for what you are doing."

"No," I said. "Thank you for taking the time to contact me. I will send you a copy of the book when it is published. That, I'm afraid may be in a year or so."

He rose, shook hands and with one last glance at his father's file, left the pub. I sat glancing through the sheets of paper. The crowd began thinning out, the sound level dropping. There was movement at the nearby table. The two young girls had risen, still laughing at something the older person had said, flapped hands in her direction and left the pub. The smile on the face of the person now seated alone faded, her gaze dropping to the half-filled glass before her.

Something about her had caught my attention. Now that the girls had departed she sat gazing at the glass her mind obviously elsewhere. I sensed her sadness. She seemed a lonely person as chattering workers passed her heading for the door.

I placed the file in my briefcase rose and moved away to stop immediately in front of the woman at the next table. She had glanced in my direction several times whilst the girls had been chattering away.

She looked up in surprise as I halted. "Forgive me bothering you, I've been sitting alone at the next table just looking into my drink and couldn't help noticing you were doing exactly the same. Being alone in a pub doesn't seem to be the best thing in the world. I know I am possibly being intrusive but I did wonder whether I could be cheeky and ask if I may join you in a glass of wine, or what else you may prefer."

She looked at me. Not flustered. Possible suspicious. She studied my features, seemed to be satisfied with what she saw. She looked at my briefcase. "You are not selling me something?"

"Good Lord No. Actually I am a writer. I was talking books with the man you may have seen me with earlier."

Suddenly she smiled. "I'm drinking white wine."

"White wine it is then," I said somewhat relieved. May I leave my briefcase whilst I get the drinks?"

She nodded her eyes still studying me. I returned, placed a glass before her. She was still looking at me intently.

"Look," I said, opening my wallet. "I'm Ricci. Here is my card indicating the books I have had published. Honestly I am quite genuine. Not a con man or anything."

She glanced at the card. I noticed her thick black hair and pleasant brown eyes. One could not help noticing she was full bodied, in short, slightly overweight. Her skin pleasant, lightly brown, a slight colouring indication perhaps parents from overseas.

She was now relaxed. More accepting. "I'm Vanessa." She said.

I smiled, "It's a lovely name."

She was again studying me. "Where are you from?" she asked.

"South London." I answered

"No. I have a feeling…"

"Oh, I see," I said understanding. "I am the result of Scottish, Indian and Italian ancestors. Although born in England."

Now she seemed satisfied. "I thought you had some foreign blood. Just like me, but from Jamaica."

"So what do you do to earn a crust?" I asked.

She smiled. "To earn a crust is about right. I work in the bowels of a tall business building where the workers rarely go unless they are seeking an old document or information. My job is to keep the files in order. Tend to be boring with little contact with the other workers. Those two girls who sat with me were on a trainee course and happened to be with me when the bell rang and work ended. I was asked if I would like a drink, said yes for it was the first time in ages I had company." She looked at me. It must be my lucky day." She smiled. Then, "So what do you write about?"

I gave a light hearted answer and moved into an easy conversation, with her providing humorous comments on fellow workers, or bosses. She seemed to have fully accepted me, chatting away easily. Time passed. I glanced at my watch.

"Vanessa, would you care to join me in a meal, unless of course you have some other commitment."

"Some other commitment, I like that," she laughed. "I was about to return to my little flat, have cheese on toast or something similar and spend the evening watching boring TV programmes. I will be delighted to have a meal with you."

We found a small Italian restaurant tucked away in a side street which provide excellent pasta. Over coffee as she thanked me for the meal I brought up what had been puzzling me;

"How is it a woman like you, with a great sense of humour is not being escorted by a regular boyfriend or indeed is still unmarried." I noticed she had no ring on her finger.

She looked at me, unblinking. I thought I might be stepping over a boundary line and was about to say so.

"It may seem strange. But not to me. I have no sisters or brothers. Both parents have passed on. I have little contact with eligible people with my job. I was out of work for a while and was pleased to get this job, despite it not being very exciting. I live in a small flat in a block of flats, where people seem to keep to themselves. Some are unpleasant. Abusive. Once I am home I don't go out, especially at night. The idea of internet contact doesn't appeal to me. You can look in newspapers or magazines and see lines and lines of people trying to make contact. But can you trust them? I am nearly thirty-five. Overweight, eat and drink too much and you may not think so but I am rather shy." She said curiously, "You are much younger. What are you, twenty-four?"

"Twenty-five." I answered.

"I still can't understand why a person like yourself is bothered with me? You are, I am sure, a very nice man in fact I was just wishing I was younger. And slimmer. I could go for you."

"You shouldn't put yourself down like that. I have a friend of Indian birth who, when I was a few years younger explained the subject of happiness. In brief she taught me that happiness is not what I should want for myself but to help others to seek it or give them happiness in what they might want or need." I said, "I've put that rather badly, but since then I've conducted myself as far as possible along those lines."

We spoke late into the evening. The time came when I said we can take a walk and can probably pick up a taxi in a few minutes. Indeed, we did just that. She gave the driver an address and in five minutes or so we were outside a tall building lights flickering in the darkness. I was about to wish her a good evening when she said "You must come in for a coffee," I settled the taxi and joined her. "I'm not all that keen on being on my own in the darkness," she whispered putting her arm through mine. "I'm feeling a lot safer with you."

CHAPTER EIGHT

The lift wasn't the cleanest in the world and Vanessa's wrinkled nose indicated she thought the same. "Housing problems get worse and worse in London," she muttered.

Her flat was, compared with my grandmother's house, tiny. A sitting room, no dining room, a kitchen, bathroom and a largish bedroom seemed to be it. Yet it was clean and tidy, things put neatly away in cupboards and the air was fresh and pleasant.

"Take a seat, Ricci," she said, making for the kitchen and coffee cups. I sat in a comfortable armchair thinking despite whether a sitting room is large or small there is always a sofa facing a television set. In the kitchen Vanessa switched on a radio and turned down the music until it only provided background. I then realized I was quite comfortable in this little flat and could understand how Vanessa felt safe. She returned with the coffees.

"Help yourself to sugar and cream, and here are some biscuits." She settled comfortably on the sofa.

"So how do you spend your evenings?" I asked.

"I like music, watch certain TV programmes and I find some interesting talk on the radio. I cook for myself of course. So you can see I eat too much. Eat in between meals often because I am bored. I read quite a lot – don't broadcast it, but I've taken to reading – er- rather exotic – er – to be honest – more erotic books. They tend to be more interesting."

"Boyfriends?" I asked.

"You have to be joking! The last boyfriend was before I started putting on weight. He found he preferred a younger woman. But that was quite a while back."

"But you are obviously a sensual woman, don't you miss the – er – company of men?"

She looked down at her hands. Almost dreamily she said. "Of course I miss it sometimes I yearn for it. Sometimes I just have to do something about it. I just have to."

"How do you mean?" I asked

She looked at me, then rose, entered her bedroom and returned with something in her hand. It was a vibrator.

"This!" she said. Held it up, unsmiling. She returned to her bedroom. I heard the drawer close. She returned to the sofa. "It's an open secret. Many women use them or something similar even married women. But of course the arms of a gentleman are infinitely better." She smiled.

"Are you a gentleman? Or are you rough with women?"

I laughed. "Oh! I think I'm quite gentle. I was telling you

about this Indian lady giving me advice. I like to think that apart from the advice from Rupinda my background invites me to be- er – kind to animals and the human race. My grandfather was someone of importance in India with a reputation for kindness, my father was a well-known pianist in Italy where he married an Italian singer both known for their generosity."

She looked at me steadily. I kept her gaze. "I want you to know one night stands do not appeal to me. It is a thing I have never done. I don't really know why I'm telling you this. But I have to say I like you tremendously despite the fact we hardly know each other. There is something – I don't know what – that draws me to you. if I was younger, I would be flirting with you and- er- sort of hoping."

"I don't understand the younger bit. You are an attractive woman with lovely features. In fact, quite sexy. About the hoping – you don't have to be shy. Just ask!"

There was a long pause. Then, "You understand it has been a long time. I've been lonely. I am lonely. Just looking at you gives me warm feelings. You came into my life from nowhere and I don't want you to go!" Then, she whispered, "Could you stay the night?"

I stood up, walked the few steps held her hands and kissed her. "Whatever you want. In fact, if you wanted I could stay over for the weekend. That might overcome your aversion to a one-night stand.

Her face was one big smile. "Oh boy!" she said. "I'll drink to that! Let's open a bottle of something stronger than coffee!" she jumped up animatedly.

"There is just one problem," I said. "All I have brought with me is a briefcase, no change of clothing. Not even a tooth brush. I can survive the night but I must buy some shirts and things tomorrow. Maybe we go out, shop around and have lunch someplace." She clapped her hands together.

"That's a lovely idea. My! Just think, shopping with a man!"

She poured two fingers of golden liquid in to two squat glasses. "I've had this since Christmas. Must be matured by now," she joked, handing me a glass of rum. A drink I was unused to. It hit me creating a warm glow. If this doesn't relax us, I thought, nothing will!

After a second large glass Vanessa jumped up. "I must have a shower, I'm sweating."

I trotted out the old cliché Ladies don't sweat, they perspire. Only men and horses sweat.

It was certainly warm in the small flat. I undid a couple of shirt buttons. As Vanessa returned from the shower wrapped in a dressing gown, rubbing hard at her thick black hair, she saw what I was doing and said. "It is warm. I'll open a window." With her back to me she continued. "Have a shower. It will cool you down. I'll get towels out for you. There are plenty of lotions and shampoos, to make you smell nice."

I took up her offer. I stripped off, leaving my clothes in a dry spot and entered the shower. Soaped all over I was definitely feeling cleaner and cooler. A voice called out, "Do you want your back washed?" She had cheekily stuck her head around the door. I turned to reply, then saw her eyes widen. She pointed, as though lost for words.

I stated, "Some ladies say 'WOW.' I've also heard others say, 'Oh My God'!"

Vanessa stood as though transfixed, staring. "Wow!" She said. "Oh My God!"

I came out of the shower still wet. "You can dry my back if you like," I said. She grabbed a towel, rubbing. Partially dried I turned, slipped my hands under her robe. It came apart. We stood pressed against each other. I kissed her and felt her lips part.

"I think we should find my bed," she whispered.

*   *   *

We were lying on our sides pressed against each other. My hand slipped over to her stomach. It moved down to her thick black bush. I gently scratched amongst her hair.

"That's nice," she said.

I continued scratching. "I'm looking for lost golf balls," the stupidity of the remark made us both burst out laughing. I turned towards her, hand on her breast as she turned on her side towards me. I kissed her. Her lips were soft and as they parted our tongues searched, meeting.

I bent towards her large breast and drew her teat into my mouth. It had the pleasant roughness of a strawberry. She was enjoying me. I felt her hand slip down past my stomach and grasp the subject of her surprise. It began to enlarge.

"I like this," she whispered. I went to move onto her. She said still holding me, "Whatever you do, do not roll off," followed by giggling laughter. Disregarding her warning I settled myself on her curved stomach. She said, "relax." Surprised I did just that. She let go of me and I slid my body down. I felt her legs part and she fumbled as she tried to position me. I took over. "Here let me?" I whispered. And placing it before her vagina, she trembled as I pressed and entered her. A startled sound broke from her and I rested for a moment, inside her. I felt her swelling and then simultaneously we moved together. Lifting, pressing wet warmth of exhilarating moment. She was eager, enthusiastic. So much so I thought I could hold no longer. Vigorously she moved until finally she shuddered then, holding me tightly, gasped and I felt a hot tide meet my covered tip.

*   *   *

Wet, seeking breath, she laid by me, holding my hand. "That was heavenly." She whispered, as her breathing eased. We rested hand in hand, utterly content. As she rested I slipped my hand from her and under the sheet. My hand was on her stomach, fingering gently, her navel. She lifted my hand and put it on her left breast my hand cupped her. Her breast was inviting. I turned and held it between two hands, and pressed gently. The nipple expanded and she pulled my head down toward it. The movement of my tongue, the tugging of my teeth, the caressing of my hands inflamed her and she turned offering me both breasts which I took in turn. Now she was panting. I was stiff, hard, rigid. She lifted her legs and opened them wide. My hand left her chest. Seeking to increase her desire. My hand slid through her thick black hairs and hovering between her open thighs, now, gently rubbing the soft hot swelling entrance, Vanessa's eyes were wide, her breathing irregular. She lifted slightly, an invitation. I accepted. My fingers now inside her moved seeking, searching, for the tiny hanging gift she desired me to find and as I did so and gently caressed the wet tender suspended flesh she shuddered, her legs closed sharply trapping my arm. My fingers stilled. Then, slowly her legs parted. For a moment she relaxed as I gently resumed my seeking caressing.

This could not continue. Vanessa, shuddered again, pulling at me. Demanding me. I moved into position. She arched, legs wide. She was wet, enlarged. I entered her and she gave a sigh as of relief. She was hot. I entered her fully. She exercised a tightness against me, internally pressing, squeezing. Then as she relaxed her internal muscular grip, I moved further inside her. Slowly at first. She fell in a rhythm with me. Gently, gently, then as desire demanded, faster, faster. We exploded together. Vanessa cried out, shuddering, shivering with the ecstasy of it.

We stayed together, lost in each other. Then, it feeling like a punctured balloon I withdrew from the glorious wetness of her body.

CHAPTER NINE

We were in a local Market. Various shops visited. Shirts, underclothes, razor, toothbrush and a number of other male items purchased. Vanessa pulling me from one place to another was like an excited schoolgirl. Trying on dresses, tops and skirts. By lunchtime loaded with shopping bags we stopped off at a restaurant and ordered food and drink. I ordered a beer and she ordered the same. She was in a most happy mood. "What we should do Vanessa is after we've eaten, take this shopping to your place, dump it then spend the rest of the day in a park, at the zoo, seeing a film or whatever you want to do on a Saturday evening."

"Great!" She said. "My first Saturday night out in ages."

At her place I shaved, showered, changed into fresh clothes. Vanessa tried on a new top and skirt and we returned to the streets. I called a taxi and we headed for the West End. We were able to purchase tickets for a show and Vanessa was enthralled by Mama Mia and its ABBA music. When the show ended we found a drinking spot and settled down with drinks.

*   *   *

Back at the ranch – or rather Vanessa's tiny flat, I opened a bottle of wine I had purchased. I poured and handed her a glass. I was pleased she had enjoyed the day. Fulfilled, she was completely relaxed. We sat together on the sofa.

"I've been thinking," she said.

"That can be painful. What about?"

"This lady." She stated.

"What lady?"

"This woman who gave you advice. You must have been close?"

"We became very friendly." I said.

"How friendly?"

"As I said, very friendly."

"Was she good looking?"

"She is good looking, yes."

"Do you still see her?"

"We meet on occasions."

"Do you…"

"Vanessa, I can guess where this is leading! To cure your curiosity I will say just this. A very knowledgeable Indian lady of great charm who decided I was a fit and a competent person she could train and instruct to go forth and encourage happiness by being compassionate, gentle and helpful, particularly to women to find fulfilment and pleasure."

Vanessa stared at me then asked, "Did that include sexual instruction?"

"She taught me certain sexual positions as described by Vatsayana Mallanaga many years ago in his Treatise on the Provision of Happiness."

"Never heard of him."

"He wrote the Kama Sutra."

"Light dawned. "Oh! I've heard of that ..!"

"Thank goodness. Let's have another drink."

"We can take the glasses into the bedroom." Vanessa said

"Great idea," I replied, relieved at the change of subject.

"And you can tell me more about the sexual positions." Vanessa smiled.

*   *   *

We were seated backs against the headboard. Glasses of wine in our hands, sipping gently. Almost undressed I sat wearing boxers, Vanessa a bra and panties. Rather chaste.

"So tell me more," demanded Vanessa.

"About what?"

"About the sexual positions."

"We've had a few sexual positions already."

She snuggled up to me. "Oh I know, darling and they were lovely, but you have intrigued me, and well, I like you talking to me about them. You make me desire you more than ever!"

"When you think about it, love making is essentially a basic act. It is the entering of the man's lingam into the woman's yoni..." She sat up.

"The man's what?"

"The writer of the Kama Sutra, Vatsayana, possibly the earliest treatise on the subject refers to the male organ as his 'lingam' and the females as her 'yoni'. I rather like the use of these references. Gives a whole new meaning to the act of intercourse."

"Whatever you call it I love your big lingam." She snugged into me again, "Carry on."

"Describing the requirements of kindness, sympathy, compassion, gentleness and all the other essentials for the provision of happiness to sad unhappy or lonely people, he refers to basics of food, drink and also the demands of the fundamental desire for sexual gratification. He describes a number positions between male and female which help to obtain the necessary satisfaction." I shifted into a more comfortable position, Vanessa impatiently squeezing up to me again.

"Such as?" she asked.

"He describes different positions. Sitting, standing, rear entry, woman on top, man on top. I have to say that there is nothing new in the acts he described. After all, this was written two thousand years ago and millions of couples have been enacting these positions without ever knowing the name or numbers he ascribed to them."

"No matter, give me some names," Vanessa squeaked.

"Well there is the Dolita position, Samdamsha Position, the Madandivaja Position, the Dhenuka Position – can't remember them all, although I might know them." I continued "they are really very basic. Of course the end result is just the same."

"Explain the Dolita one to me," Vanessa requested.

I laughed. "Well it's not one we have used."

Vanessa looked intrigued, "Good. Perhaps we should, explore it."

"I will just quote this one. No more, understood?"

"Oh, okay. Understood." Vanessa replied.

"The Dolita Position, you face each other. You press your breasts hard against my chest. You lock your heels behind my waist. I lock my heels behind your waist. We both then lean back holding each other's wrists. We swing gently together."

Vanessa sat up looking perplexed.

"I forgot to mention that my 'lingam' is inside your 'yoni'. We rock back and forth like a ship on the sea. Except for the one difference."

"What's that?" Vanessa asked.

"Well a ship has a lot of rivets…"

"And?" Vanessa asked more puzzled.

"We have only one between us…"

She laughed. "But boy isn't it a big one! Let us give it a try. Now I put my breasts hard against your chest…stop laughing! Put my heels behind your waist...!"

*   *   *

Vanessa was in a gentle mood. Our act together had been hilarious with much falling sideways and recovering our positions. But the end result was inevitable as we settled into it. The "rivet" did its job and Vanessa's locked heels ensured her sensational shuddering finish.

We were lying back having recovered. Companionable in our silence.

"My bush is getting too thick!"

I was lying back my hands behind my head, quite comfortable.

"It's a nice bush," I said. "I like scratching about in it – never know what I might find!"

She giggled. Then, "it is too thick, becoming a nuisance. I'm going to cut it."

I reflected on her intentions. "Won't it be a bit difficult? You mean you want to wax it, or shave it off? Waxing can be painful, I guess. Shaving will mean it may become bristly."

She giggled at the thought. "I was thinking of just cutting it lower. Sort of trimming it."

"The way you are talking about it, one would think it's a garden hedge!" more giggling. "Not being personal, but with your -er- rather larger tummy to look over it might be a problem."

We sat silent.

Vanessa said mischievously, "You could do it."

I sat up. "You want me to wield a pair of scissors just above your-er-yoni?"

"I know you would be careful," she said giggling.

I considered. "I'll do it!"

Vanessa turned and gave me a hug. "You are a darling."

"This could be fun."

She slid off the bed returning with a pair of scissors and a comb. I clambered off the bed, wearing boxers. I said "I'll get a towel. Don't want hair all over the place."

I spread the bath towel on the edge of the bed. "On you get," I instructed.

She settled herself on the towel, put her hands behind her head. I pulled up a chair.

"Open your legs." I said all business like.

"What again?" she giggled, but did so. "Be artistic" she said.

"I'm a writer not an artist, but I will do my best!"

"I find myself in an unusual position," I continued.

She chortled. "I don't! With you! Get cutting."

I began. Fortunately, the scissors were sharp, the comb pulled easily through her hair. Steadily, carefully I reduced it to a flat surface mat. I was rather pleased with my work. Trimming spare hairs away at the edges. I produced a neat looking oblong of black half inch upright hair. A final combing and I said "Finished."

Vanessa sat up to view. She looked first at the neat oblong, then flushing at me. "It's lovely she said." Very neat. Much more convenient."

"Reminds me of a miniature garden lawn," I said. "A black garden lawn."

Vanessa laughed and kissed me. "Come and collect your reward," she whispered.

*　　*　　*

Afterwards we were lying close feeling the pleasant warmth of our bodies. My hand slid down to her neatly cut hair. Gently, as ever I ran my fingers through. "There are not any golf balls there now." She said smiling.

"Not searching for golf balls," I said as my fingers slipped over the edge. "But I've found a rabbit hole!"

*　　*　　*

It was time to go.

Vanesa said, "Ricci, you are a lovely man and you have given me a weekend to remember." She paused, then tremulously "Will I ever see you again?"

"Well, I'm not normally in this part of London very often but I have your address in my pocket and one never knows what the future holds. Your lovely smile makes me feel good fortune will look in our direction one day soon and our lives will cross again."

And with that cheerful thought we hugged, then I departed.

*　　*　　*

A couple of days later Vanessa was surprised to receive a slim cardboard box. It contained a dozen red roses. Entwined around the stems was a slim silver chain.

Extracting the chain, she saw it supported a silver pendant the size of an old penny. It's outer cover machine cut design sparkled as the light reflected. Vanessa sat with the chain in her fingers and found a tiny catch on the pendant, where it was supported by the chain. She pressed and the pendant fell open. She gazed in astonishment. A curl of black hair tied centrally with fine silk thread curved around a small circular card with the one word 'Ouch'. She stared uncomprehendingly for a moment. Then realization came to her. She giggled and as she fingered the circle of black coarse hairs she burst into pure uncontrolled laughter.

CHAPTER TEN
The Tailler Twins

I entered the waiting room to find I was not the only interviewee that morning. The regional broadcasting liaison chap had invited me to discuss my latest book and today was the appointed day. Being a distance from my home I had booked to stay overnight at a local hotel. Now facing me was a pair of young good looking females. Obviously waiting to be called in for a chat with the broadcasting jock.

They smilingly greeted me in unison. "Hi."

"Hello," I greeted in amazement. Absolutely surprised at the identical features of each. No question. Identical twins. Same identical shapes, same hair styles. Each a photo of the other. Each with a sexy look about them. Dressed as far as I could see in identical clothes. Even their mannerisms copied each other. "We are the Tailler Twins," announced the nearer one, with a delightful smile, speaking with a pronounced accent. "I am Alana". Her sister speaking in an identical voice, "I am her sister Aileen."

Again, another flashing smile. "We are to be interviewed and maybe sing our song," continued Aileen. The penny dropped. A Latvian pair of singing sisters. Currently something of a hit and touring Europe.

"I know you, I have seen you on a TV show. You have very good voices and are most charming." They were pleased to be recognized and chorused their pleasure. Probably in their mid-twenties. I also know something of a reputation of causing near riots with their uninhibited displays. Fun seekers, very popular particularly with the younger elements of their fans. There was no question - their perfect copy of each other - hair styles, clothing and all else was a unique and enchanting selling point.

"I am Ricci", I replied and was about to continue when the conversation was interrupted. The twins were called and were escorted to do their broadcast chat. I stood silently awaiting my five minutes of local fame.

Speakers broadcast voices from the interviewing studio and I listened to the laughing, giggling girls and then the playing of one of their recorded songs. I realized from the laughing comments the twins would be a handful to control both their conversations and their actions. Their session ended and they returned to the waiting room to pick up coats, still chatting, giggling whilst on their way out. Each blowing a cheeky kiss towards me as they departed.

Ten minutes later I was called into the interview studio

opposite a friendly announcer, faced the mic and a discussion of my writing began. I answered a series of questions, came up with a number of humorous anecdotes and before I was aware of it the interview was over.

*   *   *

I was seated in the hotel bar when the twins appeared. By the number of bags they were carrying they had been shopping. They saw me, waved and took the lift up to their room. Dumping their goods, they returned to the bar.

I was seated at a table with a glass before me. I rose as they entered smiling in my direction and said, "Can I get you ladies drinks?" They seemed pleased. "Thank you. Vodka and lemon" and made themselves comfortable at my table, as I collected the drinks.

Whilst they chatted to each other in their own language, I studied them. The cliché 'two peas in a pod' came to mind. Separately, I would be unable to decide which was Aileen and which was Alana. They seemed to be able to read each other's minds and often ended each other's sentences. It seemed natural for each to attempt to outdo the other in flirting. I took it all in good part and changed my drink to be the same as theirs, Vodka and lemon. The day passed pleasantly. We had bar meals at the table. Occasionally a person would realize the identity of my companions and join us briefly always sending over drinks following their departure. Conversation flowed naturally as did the Vodka. It was when I found difficulty in getting my words in the right order and people seemed to be gently floating I mistily realized I was getting quite drunk. One of the girls announced that today was their birthday. Had I been sober I would have dismissed it as untrue especially as I heard the other state everyday was their birthday. This caused even more celebratory drinking.

At some time or other the twins announced it was time to retire. Speaking to each other rapidly in their own tongue they both burst out laughing. I was too far gone to argue with them, as one on each side of me helped keep my stagger to a minimum as we headed for the lift. As we ascended I found each of the girls had an arm around me, they said to keep me upright. Foggily I wasn't complaining.

At my door I eventually found the door pass. The door opened, the light went on and the girls, ever giggling, staggered holding me towards my bed, blew me a drunken kiss and went on to their own room.

I sat unsteadily on the edge of the bed and vaguely became aware I needed to take off shoes, socks and all other apparel before I dropped into bed. This took quite a while longer than usual. Staggering into the bathroom I dipped my face in water. It cooled my face but didn't do much more for me. Drying, I moved back into the bedroom and flopped onto the bed.

I must have been drifting off when there was a tap, tap, tapping at the door. Blurrily I made it to the door. A smiling face above a pink fluffy dressing gown and hands holding a bottle of clear liquid and two glasses. "We have a nightcap just us two," announces the smiling face and pushing gently but firmly against the door moves into the room.

Seated on the edge of the bed she announced "I am Alana. We have nice drink together." There is no question I am too accommodating. Never like to refuse a lady, especially when I find it difficult to put my words in the right order. Groggily I realized the drink was something different to Vodka and two glasses insisted by Alana just about tipped me over the edge. Sitting there wearing nothing but my boxer shorts. Alana was definitely taking advantage of my condition, I became aware of the enchanting perfume she seemed to be bathed in.

"Aren't you going to give me a birthday kiss?" she whispered. So good natured as ever, I put my arms around her, more for support I think. That kiss became heated as it developed and became more so as Alana's hand slid down my body and her gown fell open. She was wearing nothing but a pretty necklace. Blearily I became aware of her hand becoming active.

With her lips still on mine she pressed my body until I fell back on the bed. Her body followed me down, her dressing gown slid off and her hand found the contents of my boxers. Inevitably and despite my drunken condition the reaction Alana was seeking came about. She lifted her body, my hand finding her hot inviting breast the nipple hardening quickly. Our hands sought various parts of each other's body and surprisingly the act of immediate interest seemed to focus my mind pushing aside some aspects of the result of my drinking.

Arching my body, I pulled of my boxers with some difficulty. The contents were engorged and taking up a lot of space. Now, except for two wrist watches and a necklace we were completely naked.

It was when I murmured, as you do, what a beautiful warm and fragrant body she had and she proudly lifted off me to show me even more, when she spied for the first time the member – waiting somewhat impatiently to enter her. She gasped, her eyes dilated, she pointed almost accusingly, spoke rapidly and briefly in Latvian and then so I could understand in English. "Oh my God!"

This gave me the opportunity to gently place her aside for a moment, reach into my long discarded trousers, and obtain a condom from its secret pocket. This may not be the appropriate moment to discuss the location of such articles but I can dispose of the matter quickly and to the point.

It was during an interview with a former soldier when obtaining details for one of my books that I became aware of pockets for condoms. It appears that during World War II the production of those rough serge khaki trousers included within the internal khaki dyed lining a slim double strip at just about waist level which provided an out of sight, available and reliable home for not more than three condoms. It was said that the idea was to help limit any sexual infections. Other stories suggested the lady workers involved in their manufacture placed names and addresses in these small pockets hoping to hear from the finders in the armed forces. Strangely it didn't appear to be a well-known fact to many soldiers, but, the elderly man I was speaking to assured me it was a genuine fact and stated he himself had taken advantage of it. This knowledge had quite intrigued me. Quite a sensible idea I decided. Conveniently out of sight, better than carried in a wallet which could cause embarrassment if it dropped out at the wrong time. Henceforth I had my tailor add a suitable pocket to the lining of my trousers and so carried contraceptives as a general precaution.

But to get back to Alana and her awareness of her imminent future!

After her sudden surprise at my larger than usual body part, Alana turned to me physically, as it happened, by pressing against me as I slipped on a condom watched by an interested and desiring companion.

The revelation as to what would inevitably be about to happen seemed to energize her and her cooperation became even more enthusiastic. Lifting herself above me, legs wide open she manipulated and encouraged the entry and our bodies became as one. Fortunately, I was able to maintain an erection long enough for a flood of hot shaking desire to flood her as she gripped me, calling my name "Ricci, Ricci!"

Finally, she slid off me. Turning her face towards me, she

whispered, "Wow!" pulled my head down and kissed me. We lie side by side. Her getting her breath back, me gazing vacantly at the ceiling. "I go get more drink." Standing, she retrieved her fluffy dressing gown, and despite my mumbled protest, left the room with the two empty glasses.

In my drink infused state I remembered the used contraceptive, awkwardly trying to knot and disposing of it out of sight.

For a moment I thought I was hearing things. Tap, tap, tapping on the door and densely realized Alana was back with more drinks. Staggering once again to the door, I opened to find her smiling face looking up at me once again. "I am back again," she said needlessly and followed me back to my crumpled bed. I didn't offer to take the drink out of her hands, her fluffy dressing gown fell open and once again I was looking at her lovely perfumed body.

This coming and going seemed to help blow a small gap in the curtain of my misty drunkenness, as once again we sat on the bed each with a glass of clear liquid. "This is not Vodka?" I asked my ever smiling companion. "No it is special Birthday drink from my country," she said and pronounced its name which was a bit of a tongue twister.

"It make you very sexy and happy." She waved her glass in front of my nose. "We drink, one, two all gone." She demonstrated by tipping her drink down her throat. "Now you drink, one, two!" she pushed my glass up to my mouth and without much choice I chokingly swallowed the lot.

She laughed. Taking my glass, she placed them on the side cabinet, slipped off her fluffy gown and placed her arms around my neck. This time I was more ready. Pulling her down with me, I rolled onto my side. We now faced each other. My hands either side of her face I drunkenly pulled her gently towards me and kissed her soft lips. She responded eagerly. Her lips parted and the tip of her tongue was seeking mine, as my hands found her breast. Yet there was some confusion in our love making. Something was slightly different. Yet love making is love making when all is said and done. Her hand moved eagerly into my boxers. Her finger slipped around my pride and joy encouraging its enlargement. Her eyes grew big and she was smiling with eagerness as she helped me slip off my underwear. She of course had no problem of this sort. Her hot silky fragrant skin responding to my every touch. I called a mild truce for a moment as I once again found my secret trouser pocket and retrieved a shiny square containing a condom which she enthusiastically unrolled placing it in its required position. The act of its placing seemed to heat her body even more for she rolled onto her back her hands seeking me, pulling me above her. For a moment my hand slid down between her thighs finding her enlarged entrance my finger gently massaging her clitoris.

Her breathing became uneven, erratic, her body twitching. She moved her legs apart even more and dug into my back and I finally lifted in line with her wet distended opening and entered her. Her body arched and I entered completely. It was surely those last mysterious Latvian drinks returning me completely to my drunken dazed state that excited her into her shuddering orgasm for as I felt the tide of her hot release, my personal contribution lost all interest and I flabbily, wetly, sleepily withdrew.

CHAPTER ELEVEN

The daylight shining across my face, the thumping of drums in my head, the unpleasant taste and the sensation my head was no longer a part of my body caused my eyes to open, close and squint open once more.

It was then the floating confusion during my second session, the slight awareness of difference in our love making dawned on me.

Discussing their singing on stage the Tailler Twins had mentioned they always adopted the same positions with Aileen facing the audience on the right of her sister and Alana obviously on her left. For a difference did exist between the sisters. Aileen was left handed!

The confusion cleared. I recalled Aileen pushing drinks towards my mouth, her left hand more active in bed, her unrolling a condom.

Now I realized I had been gently seduced, ravished (can a man be ravished?) not by one but by both of the giggling, laughing, sexy, fun loving Tailler Twins!

Vague moments of past activities flittered in my brain, as I tried to grasp where I was. Slowly things began to refocus. Carefully, tenderly I sat up. I was stark naked. Moving on to my elbows I looked down along my body. Things were not as I expected.

I could see writing on my stomach. The artwork was in red lipstick. With difficulty I deciphered. Around a red heart pierced by two arrows were the words 'Thank You' and the names – Alana and Aileen- with kisses.

It was then I saw my penis.

It was encircled by a neat pink bow!

CHAPTER TWELVE
Cassandra

The weather was good and despite the heavy traffic on the M2, I was in a good mood and looking forward to a weekend with John and Muriel. The invitation from my old Rugby pal said 'get out of London for a change of air. Come to the Garden of England and relax.' They lived near the Kentish coast and I was anticipating a weekend of beer and banter.

I was nearing the turn off onto a pleasant country route to my destination. The build up at the junction slowed traffic and I was pleased to finally get off the motorway. I was following a red open topped sports car. I could see nothing of the female driver other than a mass of blonde hair. The red BMW sports also turned off at the junction and as the traffic cleared, roared away.

Five minutes later, I turned onto a narrow country lane I had used before. It was a shortcut and would save me time. Warning signs indicated it was single traffic in a number of places and with it many bends and curves, required careful driving.

I was negotiating a bend when I braked sharply. Ahead was a stationary vehicle its emergency lights flashing, its bonnet up and smoke drifting away. It was the red sports car I realized as a blonde head appeared above the open bonnet. Turning on my own emergency lights, I approached the stricken car and its driver.

"Hi, what is the problem?" I asked.

"I have no idea. There was a sudden banging noise and the car slowed and stopped. I know nothing about cars and I have had no trouble with it before. Do you know anything about cars?" she asked.

She stood with a questioning look and for the first time, I saw her face. She was beautiful. No question. Natural thick blonde hair, deep blue well set eyes, flawless skin, and elfin body. Reluctantly, I dropped my gaze to the open bonnet.

"Not all that much. These days with modern computerized cars you need an expert." I took a look under the bonnet and studied the engines entrails. I shook my head. "Sorry, car engines and myself are strangers."

I looked at that beautiful face. "What must be done is to get your car off the road. This narrow road is dangerous. Thank God this part is a one-way street. But any car coming round that bend at speed could cause havoc. I've got a warning sign in the boot." I moved quickly and placed the warning sign on the far side of the bend. I returned to the disabled car.

"I can see a parking sign." I indicated the pole about thirty-five yards further along the road. I put the bonnet down. "If you would steer the car, I will push it to the off road parking."

I looked at the owner. I had the impression she had been studying me. She gave me a pleasant smile. She moved to the car door and I saw a flash of long silken covered legs as she slid into the driving seat.

"Make sure it's in neutral," I called and with my hands flat on the boot I gave a shove and the car moved forward. Once rolling, it moved at a good pace. She manoeuvred the car neatly off the road.

"I will move my car." I said and walking quickly recovered the sign from the bend and drove the car up behind the stationary sport car. "Danger averted," I grinned. I stuck out my hand. "I'm Ricci."

She smiled gratefully. "Cassie," she replied shaking my hand. Her hand was soft and her nails impeccable. I placed her around twenty-seven – twenty-eight, an immaculate business woman. A thin gold chain drew attention to her slender neck. She said, "you have been extremely kind. I don't know what I would have done had you not arrived." She smiled, "like a knight in shining armour."

"I will have to lift up my visor. We now have to work out what to do next. Where are you aiming to get to?" I asked.

"Melrose," she replied. Seeing my puzzled expression, she continued, "It's a tiny village, well, almost a hamlet actually. Near

Aylesham."

Then politely she said, "I hope I haven't caused you any inconvenience, delaying your journey over my problem." I replied, bending the truth slightly, "Delighted to be of assistance. Time is my own. Just heading towards the coast to have a break from London life."

"Two minds with a single thought," she laughed. "I'm heading for my country pile for a long weekend of doing nothing, also from London."

We fell into a general discussion. How to proceed. A 4X4 travelling at a good pace passed by. I said, "I am glad I am not in his way. That was built like a tank!" Cassie shivered slightly. "With these -er- expensive cars," I said, "You will require a main garage, and will need to be towed. Do you have breakdown cover?"

"Roadside breakdown cover," said Cassie. She phoned for assistance and thirty minutes later an RAC van drew up behind us. A cheerful mechanic came up to us. "Let's take a look at the problem." Making his inspection he said, "You are going to need specialist off road attention." After a discussion, he put through a call to a main dealer, then said, "I can put it on a rigid tow, you can accompany the car in my cab." I intervened. "Not necessary. We will follow you in my car." Cassie said, "you are an absolute kind gentleman." I smiled back. "At your service at any time. The pleasure is mine."

With the sports car deposited at the main dealers, Cassie seemingly and reluctantly turned to me and said, "I can get a taxi from here." I had a feeling, an imperceptible feeling she was hoping, just hoping.

We had been in each other's company for a couple of hours and an easy rapport seemed to have been established.

"I would not hear of it," I said. "I will run you home."

She seemed relieved. "If we could pick up a few things at the supermarket and thank you, you are a darling."

With two bulging bags we headed for Melrose, which turned out to be just a few miles away. Quiet, peaceful, a pleasant part of Kent. Hardly a dozen properties. "That's my getaway," pointed Cassie. A beautiful thatched elderly house sitting in its own square of land. I carried the bags into the kitchen as Cassie brought in her case.

"You must stay for a meal," Cassie said, "but first, we will have coffee." Conversation came easily between us. It was drifting towards evening. Cassie asked, "have you far to go?" "Twenty miles or so," I replied, "towards the coast."

Cassie thought for a moment and seemed to have come to a decision. "You don't have to leave. There is plenty of room here and you can tell me about the books you write, referring to a previous conversation. "If you are sure you want me around?" A thought struck me. "If I stayed it would mean I would be able to take you to pick up your car. As I said, time is my own. I was calling on a friend of mine but that is not important."

Cassie was smiling. "That's it sorted then," she rose. "I will whip up a meal for the two of us. We can open a bottle of wine." She returned from the kitchen with a bottle. "Just make yourself useful, then relax and make yourself comfortable."

With Cassie in the kitchen I wandered about the room with a glass of wine in my hand. A neat sofa with a bright coloured throw. Dark mahogany set of occasional tables, colourful, modern pictures adorning the walls. A pleasant mix of old and new. Background music played softly from a player Cassie had turned on before leaving the room.

Later, relaxed after a pleasant meal, conversation came easily between us. "Okay," I said, shifting into a more comfortable position in the armchair facing a relaxing Cassie. A fresh bottle had been opened. "Tell me about yourself. I have judged you are probably a successful business lady in a successful London business. Am I right?"

Cassie eyed me over her glass of wine. She stayed silent for a long minute. I felt I had intruded on a private matter. Cassie twirled the wine in her glass, looking at it, considering, thinking.

Cassie spoke. "When people ask what I do I usually give them a smile and give no indication of the true situation. But to you I will tell the truth. Don't ask me why, there is something about you. I can't put my finger on it but I feel compelled to tell you. You are such a friendly, attractive man," she sipped her drink.

"I am most definitely a business woman. A private hardnosed business woman. A one-woman business woman." Her face seemed to harden. "And it is all down to a man, a most unpleasant man. A good looking successful guy who raped me." She stopped and sipped her drink.

I stared at her. Uncertain I had heard the words correctly. "Sorry, I think I mis..." Cassie sighed "Yes, rape." She shifted slightly. "It was three years ago I was modelling at the time and he was, in a way, my boss. He was big, very rich and well, without going into details, with the aid of his friend, raped me. It was in a room in his house and other models were there.

Anyway, I screamed blue murder and swore I would take him to court and collected enough evidence from others. He was at the time involved in the production of his first film. To cut a long story short, he offered me ten thousand pounds to keep quiet then twenty thousand. As I said, he was loaded financially. At first, I would not even think of it. But then I started to give it some consideration. I had little money. I realized I could start a new life. The publicity would do him harm in the film world but he would surmount it over time. Money would see to that. I said forty thousand pounds and I would walk away. He paid it. From then on I decided if a man wanted my company, he would have to pay for it."

She stopped speaking, and stretched her legs. She smiled over her wine at me. "You may have heard of a certain model declaring she would not get out of bed for less than ten thousand pounds. Well, I thought modelling is not for me, they had wanted me to lose weight, become one of their stick type creations. So I came up with my own idea. The boss told me often my face could be my fortune and with nothing else to help me and knowing that one has limited time to remain the way I am, I set up on my own. Now, in certain circles, I am known and in demand."

I was about to speak. Cassie twirled her glass. "I'm in the Escort Business. I am a very high class, expensive and successful lady escort." I looked at her. Couldn't think of anything original to say. So I said, "Wow!"

Cassie laughed an attractive, tinkling laugh. "It probably isn't quite as bad as you may be thinking. There are many people in this world who, for one reason or another require a female companion to accompany them. Perhaps a business meeting, a public gathering, a high powered essential party that demands their attendance. You would be surprised at the number of men to whom money is no object and you may also be surprised at the many successful guys who are gay and for some personal reason do not want it to be known. Accompanying a man in public is a large part of my business whether he needs to attend a function in this country or abroad. In many cases his boyfriend also travels, but separately and takes a room in the same hotel. I, of course, have my own room."

I studied her beautiful face. Her lovely eyes gazed steadily at me. I said, "like I said before, Wow! Interesting!"

She replied with that lovely smile. "Wow, lucrative! I'm a companion, nothing more and in this tight private world, I am respected for reliability, keeping confidence and putting on a show, when required. You may be surprised how tiring it can be. For the last few weeks, I am temporarily resting. And so I am here to relax and chill out. To meet up with a lovely normal man on my way here is a nice unexpected bonus."

Cassie sat up. "That's my potted life story – now tell me about yourself. I know you have said and have confirmed you are a writer. What type of subjects? What part of the world do you come from? What interests you?" she looked at her glass and rose. "I'll get another bottle." She settled back again, glasses freshened. "So speak!" she commanded.

I took a swig, sighed. "I'll sum it up," I said. "I live in a household with my Grandmother, an Indian lady. She married my Scottish Grandfather who passed away a few years ago. She has a younger lady companion, a widow, also of Indian birth. Their only son Robin, my father, married my mother, a beautiful Italian. Both were killed in a road crash in Italy when I was fourteen. My grandparents were made the guardians of myself and my sister who is a few years older than me. They brought me up to be kind, generous and friendly- especially to ladies in distress…." I grinned at the cheeky face she pulled, and continued.

"Liked playing rugby but do little these days. Have had books published on modern warfare. My father was a well-known pianist particularly in Italy which was how he met my mother, a singer. I seem to have inherited something of his passion for the piano, although will never be up to his standard. So you see I am something of a cosmopolitan, with Scottish, Indian and Italian blood."

"You are an internationalist," she said intently, "What with -." She stopped.

"What with…." I teased.

She smiled. "I'm not saying. You are probably big headed enough! But I think you are a nice man." Then, as the music tempo softly changed, said, "Do you dance?"

"Ballroom, yes. Anything else, no."

Cassie scrambled off the sofa as I stood up. She moved into my arms and I placed a hand lightly on her back. As we slowly circled the room she moved closer and I could feel heat from her body.

"It's quite a while since I met a man like you," she breathed softly.

"It's quite a while since I met a hard headed woman who is so beautiful. In fact, it's never happened," I responded.

My phone rang. I was for ignoring it. I was preferably engaged. But insistence won. "Ricci, have you got lost? Where are you? John speaking." I hesitated with an explanation of my non arrival at my friend's place. About to speak I recalled

Rupinda's advice to tell the truth. "John, I'm really sorry and was about to ring you to explain. A friend's car broke down and I have been providing assistance. We have managed to get the car to a main dealer, but it will be a day or two before its back on the road. I've been providing assistance as my friend lives in a pretty out of the way spot. The way things are I'm going to have to apologize and cancel my trip to you. Perhaps we can reschedule it for later."

John replied. "Sure, we can do that. Muriel will be disappointed, but we were only lazing around the house and have nothing special laid on. When you have a free weekend to come down, give us a call. Hope your friend gets his car sorted okay."

"Good of you, John. Sorry about the weekend. I will be in touch shortly. Love to Muriel." I rang off.

I looked at Cassie. She was gazing at me, having difficulty in keeping a straight face. Her smile broke through and she laughed. "A friend's car broke down," she echoed. "John assumed it to be a male friend, I am helping out." I said, sheepishly. "I didn't put him right."

"So will you be staying the weekend?" Cassie moved towards me.

"Only if I am invited...?"

"You are invited! Having your company will be great." The music still providing background and the strains of a slow waltz, took Cassie's attention. "We didn't finish our dance," she said softly, moving into my ready arms.

"I am not really a hard headed woman." She said into my shoulder. "Only joking," I whispered. She raised her head, looking into my eyes. Her lips a few inches from mine. Soft full lips, slightly apart. She pressed closer her body merging with mine. We both moved, lips meeting. Her breasts tightened and she felt hardness against her thighs. The music ended. My arms moved around her. Her arm slid up and encircled my neck. She leaned into me. For a long moment we stood, tightly entwined. Cassie said, breathlessly, "It's a long time since I felt like this…"

As we slowly relaxed her face flushed. "I think perhaps I have had too much wine. I feel a wee bit tipsy." She moved to the sofa. Leaning back, she closed her eyes for a moment.

Standing before her I said, "You need a coffee. I'll make it."

Cassie, eyes still closed said, "thank you kind sir. Cream, no sugar."

I find where the cups and the coffee were. Put coffee in the percolator and a few minutes later returned with a tray. "Coffee is served Madame."

"Sounds like a TV advert, thanks."

I said. "Look Cassie. If you rather I left this evening…."

Cassie's eyes widened as she blew steam from her drink. "Good Lord, I don't want you to leave. I …well I really like you. There is something about you…" She looked directly at me. "What it is I don't know. It's indefinable. Almost an aura of goodness about you. I feel I can really trust you. You seem so honest."

I was embarrassed. "Dear Cassie, I'm just a normal human being."

"With human feelings?" She grinned.

"Sure thing!"

"Thank God for that!"

"So if I am staying, I have an overnight bag in the car I suggest whilst I go outside and collect it you finish your coffee and take a shower. Should clear your head." I smiled. "After all I wouldn't like to take advantage of a lady under the influence!"

"I think you are too polite to take advantage. In fact, I think you may need encouragement."

"If I'm thinking what you may be thinking…." I broke off. "I'll go get my bag. You go get a shower. Come to that I could do with one myself."

Greg MacBride

CHAPTER THIRTEEN

She was back on the sofa. Dressing gown, bare footed, long blonde combed hair, but dry. I dumped the bag on the armchair and slid open the zip. One by one I removed items placing them on an adjacent table.

First a long necked bottle. Cassie murmured, "Champagne!" Then, "White wine- two bottles. Wow and chocolate!"

"T'was for Muriel and John," I said.

Following out came a white dressing gown, usual man shaving items, shirts, sarong, socks, t-shirts, underclothes and a towel out of which slipped a leather type wallet. "What's that?" She pointed at the wallet.

"Mind your own business." I grinned pointing at her hair. "How can you have a shower without getting your hair wet?" I said trying to change the subject.

"Wear a plastic cap with my hair pushed under. Don't change the subject. What's in the wallet?"

I sighed. "Do you really want to know?"

"Yes. Open it!" She commanded.

I shrugged my shoulders, unfolded the wallet. Several enclosed strips of clear plastic tiny pockets. Each held a square silver packet. Cassie leaned forward, gazing at the strips, frowning. She suddenly realized what she was looking at.

"Condoms. Packets of them!" She glanced at me.

Unflustered I said, "Several Strips. Each of a different colour. White, cream, black, yellow, blue green and red. All carry out the same function but each has a different flavour."

Cassie, about to say, Why have they different flav… realized the reason, flushed and said instead, "Why, on earth are you carrying such items?"

I sighed, replacing the items returned them to the zip bag. Like somebody's motto 'Be Prepared'. "It's all part of a series of instructions I received from a person who had my welfare at heart."

"What sort of person would that be," she demanded.

"This is not the time to discuss it. Maybe later," I stopped. Smiling. "When we know each other a little better. Just let's say I don't want you to get the idea I am a weirdo or dirty old man."

Cassie sat silently. Then a big smile erupted over her face. "Promise you will let me know before you leave, cos I've just gotta know!"

"I promise. Now must have a shower."

* * *

Hair still damp I returned to the sitting room. A colourful sarong about my waist. Cassie slid off the sofa and stood eyeing me. "You have a lovely muscular body," she breathed. Jokingly I flexed my arms. "All the better to hold you with my dear," I teased. Cassie smiled sweetly her eyes sparkling.

In one deft movement she tugged the cloth around my waist, the twisting knot unravelling, the sarong slid to the floor despite my grab.

Cassie gasped, her eyes widening as they fixed on my manhood. "Wow! That is some thingy!"

I glanced down. I'm aware its larger than average. Presently at rest, more or less flaccid. I knew it wasn't going to stay that way much longer. Scooping up my sarong I held it before me. I grinned. "I've never had any complaints. In fact, just the opposite."

"Now you are being big-headed. Just like your -er- thingy." Then cheekily, "let's have another look."

I said, "Well in a situation like this the advice I was given was not to be shy, but with you so close there can only be one result."

I moved the sarong away. It stood proud, moving away from my body, hardening, engorged. She stood transfixed. It seemed a hot wave of passion encompassed her. Hot with desire she took my hand led me to her bed.

Music playing in the sitting room formed a backdrop of soft sound, drifting, enveloping our bodies lying side by side. Dance tunes had changed to love songs, muffled, yet seemingly so appropriate. Shyness, reluctance, nervousness, any reservation. All had fled before the on rush of submissiveness, of overwhelming happiness of desire.

I sensed the light perfume of her body. My hands cupped her face. Lips above her parted sensuous mouth. My tongue sought hers and she responded. Completely naked we were aware only of each other in the softly lit room. The gold chain around her slender neck rising and falling with her gentle breathing. My lips moved down to the chain brushing her warm smooth skin with the tip of my tongue and parted lips. A hand slid across her shoulders. Slim fingers caressing her breasts. Bending lips took her nipple, tongue circling the red base, lips gently sucked the hardened swollen teat causing a shudder which seemed to flow through her naked body.

I drew light tender circles on her skin as I moved my hand lower and in line with her hips, gently brushing fingers from side to side. She gasped and shivered, as my fingers continued their journey to the slenderness of her legs, and now brushing the inside smoothness of her thighs.

Her hand moved down my body reaching for the hardness she knew was there. Her hand closed about me, aware of the hotness, the stiffness and the size. Desire caused tremors throughout her body, as my fingers slid into her. First one, to be joined by a second, seeking, rubbing. Now a third pushing its way into her wetness, seeking her clitoris, gently caressing causing her to arch her body. "Please, please, now," she whispered. She moved her legs farther apart. My hand disengaged.

To her obvious unutterable unbelievable delight, I entered her, pressing aside her enlarged engorged vulva, distending and hotly expanding her tightness, entering and entering further. She sucked for air and her hands pressed tightly into my back yet being unaware of anything other than the glorious, heavenly, exquisite ecstasy she was experiencing. I slid further inside pressing, pressing. She moaned softly as my erection exploded into a hot spasmodic vibrating discharge, causing her to shudder as her own hot wet spasms of unbelievable relief, delightful sensation caused her to cry out. She clung to me, hair damp and eyes glistening. Her grip on me loosened as she rested. Then, "I want more," she whispered.

CHAPTER FOURTEEN

"Coffee or wine?" I asked.

I sat with a pillow supporting my back. Cassie looked at me quizzically. "My mouth is dry." I explained. "Fifteen-minute break so that I can become the man I was, and this," I indicated with my head, "returns to its former glory."

Cassie lifted her head and took a look at the limp item. "You get the wine. I need to wee." She slipped from the bed naked, and headed for the bathroom. I slipped on a pair of boxers and entered the kitchen.

I was sitting up in bed again, glasses of wine ready, when Cassie reappeared, slipping alongside me, her back against the headboard. I passed her a glass of wine. She looked down toward my shorts.

"I like the idea of a break. It implies we haven't finished yet." She looked impishly at the white covering.

"My tutor advised a break between interludes," I said.

"Tutor? Are you saying you have had instructions?"

"Er- Well, Yes!" I said.

"From a male or female?" she asked.

"Rupinda is female."

Cassie twisted round. "Rupinda? What sort of name is that?"

I sighed. I wrestled with the idea of changing the subject, knew it would never be easy. Tell the truth. After all that was what Rupinda had taught. "Rupinda is a young good looking widow of Indian birth. A friend of my grandmothers. When I was a callow youth she explained to me what Kama Sutra was all about."

Cassie screwed her face. "Kama Sutra. Isn't that the book written years ago with – er- rude pictures?"

"A treatise written in the third century by Vatsayama Mallanaga on the importance of how life should be conducted to obtain true happiness." I said sweepingly.

"But it has -er- rude pictures," insisted an interested Cassie.

"The sexual positions described are only one part of Kama Sutra which is viewed by many as of scholarly importance of the way life should be conducted."

Cassie sat looking at me, digesting this unexpected announcement. "And this Rupinda," she said finally, this lady informed you of the contents of this treatise?"

"Of the appreciation of attitude and requirements to obtain happiness and to provide it for others, yes," I replied.

"Such as?" Pressed Cassie.

"Such as good manners at all times. Kindness, putting oneself out for others. Providing assistance to unfortunates, helping the needy, avoid bad temper or anger. Always be courteous and encouraging happiness in others, and so on."

"What about these rude pictures?"

"They are not actually rude. They are providing drawings of alternative sexual positions of a man and a woman to encourage the seeking of happiness and pleasure. For Kama Sutra in translation means 'Treaty of Pleasure'.

Cassie hugs her legs.

"Rupinda was preparing me to seek and provide happiness in life. She was an excellent knowledgeable instructor and I became a willing pupil. That's it."

Cassie had a sudden thought. "How about this – er- moment of pleasure we have had. Did Rupinda teach you that?"

I smiled. "Let's be honest. I couldn't keep my hands off you and you didn't want me to. We wanted each other so much we did what most couples do in such circumstances."

She looked puzzled.

"We adopted what is generally referred to as the missionary position. Quick, urgent and comfortable. I've never been sure why it's called that, but nobody needs instruction in that position."

"So this Rupinda lady – or is that the wrong description of her …" I interrupted her. "She is a lady of good birth and manners. She is young, good looking and intelligent, and very knowledgeable. A pleasure to work with."

"I bet she was," said Cassie under her breath. "So," continued

Cassie impishly, "After we or rather you are rested are you going to introduce me to another way – another position?"

I said lightly, "If you want to, after all I am your humble servant in such matters. Some positions are really in the domain of athletic lovers. Others are – er- more relaxing. Of course in every case the outcome is the same." I stopped talking, looking at her cheeky smile. "I suspect those positions of the Kama Sutra," I said "were designed for couples seeking variation in their intimacy."

"I'm all for that," she said, "with you."

"These positions have all been named by Vatsayama."

"Give me an example," said a fascinated Cassie.

"Well, there is the Samputa Position. He states it is of advantage to males with a small penis for it gives required deepness of penetration and stimulation."

"That is certainly not one you require!" she snorted laughing.

"Well I have to say some of the comments are unconsciously humorous. He obviously studied the sexual activity of animals and explains the – er- requirements." I said.

"Such as?" inquired Cassie.

"I'm not going through a catalogue of animal methods, although most are pretty obvious which didn't stop Vatsayama applying names, some obvious, to them."

"Well, just give me one example of his -er- animal methods." Cassie pressed.

I put my empty glass on the bedside cabinet and snuggled up to Cassie. Her hand dropped gently onto my boxers. She was pleasantly aware of a slight movement. "One example, and that's it!"

She nodded her head, squeezing slightly.

"The 'Hirana Position'. Woman on her hands and knees positioned so the male can enter her like a male deer enters a female deer, he leans forward, grasps her hanging breasts to help penetration. He states provides maximum stimulation and enjoyment. He doesn't say whether he means the deer, or the woman, probably both!"

Cassie laughed. "I have seen a deer carry out the first part but not the second. But then," she slips her fingers under my boxers and murmured, "but you could complete the position."

I moved. She could feel heat and her breathing changed slightly. I moved my head and pressed my lips against her ear. "The Granya Position is far more exciting," I whispered. She squirmed and whispered back, "and what is that?" I smiled, kissed her gently and said "You are about to find out!"

Greg MacBride

CHAPTER FIFTEEN

Shortly after we had finished breakfast the phone rang. It was the mechanic at the garage. "We carried out a diagnostic check and have solved the problem. Your car is ready for collection."

Cassie put the phone down and said, "My car has been fixed and they say I can collect it anytime." It was then my phone went into action. It was Rupinda speaking and the news brought instant attention.

"Your Grandmother has been taken to hospital, Ricci. She had a fall, and has fractured her right hip. She banged her head and the doctors are worried about that too. I thought I must let you know as soon as possible for she is not a young woman."

I asked Rupinda which hospital she was in. "South Clapham Hospital, ward four," she replied.

"I will be there as soon as I can, are you with her?"

"Yes, she is sleeping at the moment. If she wakes I will let her know you are on your way."

I looked at Cassie, who had grasped the situation from my

conversation with Rupinda., "I must go," I said to her. "I can drop you off to pick up your car and then head back to London"

With my bag packed and returned to the back of the car we headed in the direction of the garage. Cassie looked at me. "I'm really sorry about your grandmother," she said. "but I'm really sorry, but understand why you have to go." Looking straight ahead she said, "you are a lovely man and if we can ever meet up again I will be delighted." I smiled at her. "You have my email and phone number should you ever want to get hold of me."

Her car was on the forecourt of the garage. I stood by as Cassie checked it was in good running order. She came back to me sliding her arms around me and whispered "Thank you for a lovely time – especially number 5!" She felt the tiny tremors of desire once again as I enfolded her in my arms. She breathed in the warmth and delight of my closeness. Her lips sampled mine one last time. Slowly I released her.

"Cassie you are beautiful. You are the most beautiful woman I have ever met. You move in a world where money is not that important. One day you will find a man of wealth who will love and adore you, and will make you happy."

Cassie laughed. Looking at me through misted eyes said, "Yes, but will he know the 'Granya' Position?" I laughed, "A man with that sort of money probably does. But if he doesn't, well, you can teach him."

A final hug. A final ardent kiss. A final wave and I was gone.

*   *   *

On my journey back to London my thoughts turned to Grandmother Kumari. I hoped she was not as bad as I feared.

But Cassie was not forgotten. The following day I entered a florist. Flowers for Grandmother and three dozen red roses for Cassie.

CHAPTER SIXTEEN
Kumari

I met Rupinda outside the room in which Grandmother Kumari was sleeping. The hospital in South Clapham had a good reputation particularly with female patients for it had been originally a women's only hospital in the past.

"She has responded well to treatment," Rupinda was saying. "There appears to be no damage other than a bruise when she banged her head, but because of her age the hip fracture will take some time to heal." I considered the immediate future. "They propose keeping her here resting for a few days but at the end of the week providing we can make arrangements for her as she has a comfortable home and we arrange some form of regular attendance we can take her home." Rupinda paused, then, "I know they, that is, the medical staff are urgently in need of bed space."

"Anne- Marie had made a quick visit and will be calling again tomorrow. She has suggested she meets you to discuss what arrangements can be made and will be at Grandmother's place sometime tomorrow."

Having received an update on Grandma's situation and checked with the medical staff I made my visit. Grandmother now awake, but looking rather frail her dark features outlined against the white sheets, looked up when I touched her hand. Her eyes opened and on recognizing her grandson her face lit up. I kissed her, saying "Can't leave you alone for five minutes without you getting into all sorts of nonsense." She smiled up at me as I continued with the usual enquiries in these situations. Seated on the side of the bed I said. "They are keeping you in for a few days to keep an eye on your progress, but by the end of the week we should have you back in your own bed and being spoiled by Rupinda, myself and everybody else."

Rupinda entered the room and after a general discussion assured Grandmother we would be returning the next day, giving her whatever comfort we could and departed.

* * *

The following day we discussed the situation. Rupinda came up with an interesting proposition. "I would be quite happy to move into the house whilst Grandmother requires care and assistance. I know you have a guest room near to her bedroom presently vacant."

"But you have your own property to consider," I said.

"Well it isn't any great distance and providing I can pop in to keep an eye on it there isn't a problem that I can see. I would be far happier being with her. She could have visits from a nurse to check how she is progressing and I am sure Grandmother would like the idea.

Anne-Marie and myself discussed it, thought it would be a good working arrangement, and accepted Rupinda's suggestion. She was, after all, virtually one of the family.

I drove her to her place to collect the more urgent necessities. Standing in her bedroom I said cheekily, "The two of us sleeping under the same roof. Sounds tempting. I may require an update in my instructions."

Rupinda smiling said, "Should any further information be required, it won't take place in your Grandmother's house." Hastily I concurred "Of course not, only joking."

Serenely, as though discussing the weather, she continued. "We mustn't overlook the fact I will still have my own place and once Grandmother Kumari is on the mend – Well you could always come round for supper - ?" I laughed. "I have always enjoyed your cooking."

And so, with Rupinda established in the house and Grandmother Kumari returned carefully to her own bedroom and feeling more cheerful, life moved on. A visiting nurse checked the patient regularly, Rupinda turned out to be a very good cook, preparing special Indian dishes for the pleasure of all concerned.

* * *

Anne- Marie now working on a fashion magazine, and despite a few arguments about clients and her city life lived happily in the North London area with her boyfriend. Her friend 'Pinky" had a current interest in a new boyfriend and I settled down to my writing once again, unaware of the change in my normal uneventful life about to take place.

CHAPTER SEVENTEEN
John Street

I was seated in my office when the phone rang.

"Hello."

"Am I speaking to Mr. Riccardo MacDonald?"

"You are, indeed."

"Mr. Macdonald, I refer to your advertisement in a military magazine in which you seek information on previous battles and incidents particularly of World War II. I am in possession of information which may be of interest to you from an older relative. It so happens I will be staying briefly at the Regent Hotel in Balham which I understand is a short distance from your location. If it is convenient I would be pleased to meet you in the lounge of the hotel at eleven o'clock tomorrow. I am here only for a short space of time but if this is inconvenient I could possibly make alternative arrangements."

I knew I had nothing planned for the day in question and advised the caller I could meet as he suggested. "Yes, I could manage that," I said. "May I ask your name?"

"I'm John Street. I look forward to seeing you tomorrow."

*　*　*

The Regent was a travellers' hotel. Not too expensive. An overnight stopping point for commercial salesman.

I entered the lounge. A seated solitary figure rose and asked quietly, "Mr. Macdonald?"

I confirmed and hand outstretched, "John Street. I'm pleased to meet you." he waved me to an armchair by his own. I noticed he faced the entrance door.

Seated we studied each other. A tall man, despite the sports coat and grey trousers I had the impression from the way he held himself, his definite movements he was or had been a military man.

He smiled at me. "Mr. Macdonald, I owe you an apology. The phone call was an excuse to make contact with you. for I am here to discuss a different matter." He broke off. "Would you like a coffee."

Surprised I said, "No thank you," then, "What sort of a different matter?"

Street uncrossed his legs, leaned forward. "Just say I'm from a Government Department which would like to use your time for the good of the country."

I stared at the man. "I don't understand," I said.

I'm from our Security Services," he began. "I have a detailed

122

knowledge of who you are, your background and your entire family back to your grandfather's Government service in India." He paused, "Let me explain what all this is about. You are a writer and will be aware of the present Terrorist situation existing in the world, particularly in this country. There is a continuous underlying threat to lives and our way of life. This threat exists and is getting stronger. So much so you may be aware our Security Services have publicly declared they are seeking another thousand plus agents to help combat the Terrorist threat. That is why we are having this conversation."

Astonished I said, "But I have no knowledge or experience of security work other than any I may have accumulated through my writings."

Street, "We are aware of that and I will deal with it in a moment. What we are seeking are eyes and ears throughout the land, but particularly in the London area. Reliable, capable, intelligent and most of all trustworthy. In our opinion you fit the bill. Your writing provides you with freedom of movement. You are observant like most writers. We can tell from your books you have a strong feeling for this country." He stopped for a moment, letting his comments register on me. Then, "I will be honest with you. we are not looking for heroes. We are seeking persons who will undertake what is often long, sometimes boring surveillance of people who have come to our attention. We are interested in their movements, their actions and who they meet with. This is not a nine to five job, seven days a week. It is sporadic often unconnected, with periods where we don't need your assistance. Pay is low and periodic. Expenses paid. Above all we want mouths that will keep shut. Go about their business until required. This is undercover work with the target hopefully unaware of your existence. Reports of interest are required and arrangements for that will be made." Street stopped talking then, "We could do with your help if you would consider what I have outlined. It would save lives."

I sat silently for a long moment, thinking about it. This was totally unexpected. Out of the blue. Yet I was pulled towards it. I appreciated the Service was having a tough time.

"But I know nothing about surveillance," I said again.

Street smiled, "I forgot to mention you don't do this on your own. You work in partnership. The partner for you has already been earmarked. She knows the business. Has spent years as a military counter intelligence operator. Surveillance is her bread and butter."

Surprised I said, "A woman. Is she still in the military?"

"She recently finished her tour of service and has returned to civilian life. You haven't yet given me your decision and I can't say more until I know."

"Is this employment open ended or for how long?"

"We propose an initial six months' trial period."

I decided. Seems it shouldn't interfere too much in my daily life, I thought optimistically. "Okay. I'm in. I agree to assist you."

He smiled. "Thank you." He drew some papers from his pocket. "A few essential details to sort out, such as the Official Secrets Act and a Positive Vetting of yourself which has been pretty well done already and a few other bits and pieces also requiring your signature."

I signed them all. "This partner. What age would she be?"

"I'd say middle to late twenties." Then, "She is nobody's fool. Seen service in Afghanistan, won a Military Cross." He rose as if to leave. "If you wait here, I'll send her in."

I stood in astonishment. "She's here? But you didn't know whether I would agree or not!"

Street smiled, "I've been doing this job for quite a while. An assessment of yourself was made and fortunately it was accurate." We shook hands. "You won't see me very often, if at all. Your partner will be provided with all necessary information as and when required. We of course speak on a 'Need to Know' basis and contact will be through her."

He moved towards the door, stopped and said, "One more bit of private information you can keep to yourself. She is a lesbian."

He closed the door behind him.

CHAPTER EIGHTEEN
Catriona

I stood awaiting this 'partner'. Everything was happening so quickly. In my mind's eye I visualized a thick no-nonsense woman in a tweed skirt.

The door opened and a slim boyish figure in jeans, blouse and short black coat entered. As she approached, my mental picture exploded into tiny fragments, as this brown haired, grey eyed smiling figure put out her hand.

"Hi! Catriona Hudson. Known to her friends as Cat."

"Hello," I replied. "Riccardo Macdonald known to everybody as Ricci." We shook hands and sank into armchairs. I noticed the firm handshake, despite her hand soft with neat naturally varnished nails.

"This has all come as something of a shock and surprise. Never ever dreamt I would be approached by such people and to be enrolled in such an undertaking has come out of the blue."

Cat laughed. "It's just 'bread and butter' stuff really. You may even find information later on which you could use in one of your books, for I understand you are a writer."

I looked surprised. "So what else do you know about me?"

Cat smiled. "Oh nothing very much I know something of your background and know where you live. That's about it."

I felt a bit miffed. "And how about yourself?"

"Oh!" she said. "I understand you know I'm ex-army and know something of this business. I don't live too far from you. not much else you need to know, really. As we will be working together we will see how we work out." She continued, "I will be the person contacted as to action required and will then fill you in. Which reminds me. We will need some sort of cover story to explain how and why we meet. Something simple that will satisfy your Grandmother who I understand you live with."

I looked at her. "You certainly know more about me than I know about you. I'm not too happy telling lies especially to my nearest and dearest."

Cat sighed. "I'm afraid sometimes it may be necessary. We will think of something that will avoid you using any terminological inexactitude…" I smiled at the phrase. She continued, "Perhaps we can say I'm your publicity agent or somebody from your publishers. Contact will be simple. I will just phone you, giving as much notice as possible. I presume you own a car?" I nodded. "Sometimes we will use yours and sometimes mine. I will take care of reports." Smiling cheekily, "Just consider yourself as my chauffeur! After all, we will be more or less observers."

I wasn't so certain about the establishment of our roles as described by this young lady, but decided to make no comment at this stage. After all, I was new to this game and Cat had the background knowledge. "How about we find a cafe and work out a story line over coffee?" she looked at her watch. "A good idea – I've got an hour to spare."

"You appear to be a busy lady."

She laughed. "Things to do, arrangements to make."

I had the idea Cat didn't give too much personal information away.

*   *   *

"This is not a bad idea of you being my storyline agent." We were seated in an alcove in a modern café. At this time of day business was quiet, few other visitors.

Cat spooned a latte. "You can arrange this with your Grandmother and anybody else in close contact with you. By the way what is Grandmother's name, just in case I meet her or she picks up the home phone – although most calls I will make on your cell phone. I'll slot your phone number now and I will give you mine now." She laughed. "Like a pair on their first date."

"How well do you know London?"

"I have a good general knowledge and know South London pretty well. So what part do you live in?" I asked.

"Wandsworth." She replied. "Not so far from yourself."

"So what is the procedure? What happens next?"

"Tomorrow I will contact you. It may be best if I call at your home and introduce myself to Grandmother and any other relatives, you may have. I will try to keep as near to real life as possible and as briefly as I can. We will work the story line out in a moment or so that suits the situation and both of us are happy with."

"There is one other person you will meet at my Grandmothers. She is an Indian lady who is companion to Grandmother Kumari. Name is Rupinda and is virtually a part of the family, for as you probably are aware Grandmother is also of Indian birth."

This opened some discussion of my own background, Catriona becoming aware of my dead parents, my sister and her circumstances.

She listened and asked relevant questions to which I gave appropriate replies. I noticed she gave no info on her own background. I decided such info may well be forthcoming when we were more used to each other. We moved on to the cover of our relationship. The idea of Cat being passed off as my book agent seemed shaky. For some time, a middle aged Hilary Thornton with connections to a number of book publishers had helped with my published books quite satisfactorily and was known to members of my family.

We gave some more thought to the difficulties arising from

making contact. "Of course there is one obvious way out of this problem." Cat was looking at me with a suppressed smile. "We could be dating."

I thought for a moment she was just joking but thinking about it I could see it would clear the way to simplify the reason for our meeting up.

"You could introduce me as a new girlfriend. We can work out how we met."

I was surprised at her comments bearing in mind her sexual tendencies revealed by Mr. Street. Yet it made good sense as a cover story. We sat discussing the possibilities. "Don't you have a – er- companion who might have something to say about this idea?"

She laughed. "Not at the moment. You could say I am free and available. After all it's only a cover for when we have to be in each other's company."

"When do you think we will get started on this commitment?"

"I expect in the next couple of days. I know they are under pressure and the quicker we get involved the better."

After more talk it was time to move.

"Tomorrow I will be in touch." Cat picked up her shoulder bag. "This should give you time to break the news of myself to you Grandmother."

So we parted. I was still confused to some extent. Not only was I now a small cog in the Intelligence and Security set up, I was also involved – at least on paper- with an attractive looking security agent.

* * *

Grandmother and Rupinda were tea drinking when I entered the room. "Just made fresh tea," Rupinda rose and I nodded my acceptance of a cup.

I settled into an armchair. "So how has been your day?" Grandmother enquired.

"Interesting," I began. "I have to tell you I have met a rather pleasant girl. She is calling round here tomorrow and we are going for a meal."

"That is interesting Ricci. So how did you meet?"

"Through a mutual friend. I dropped into a favourite café and by chance an old pal was having coffee with a couple of girls. We got talking and found one of them in particular was nice and we seemed to hit it off. When they were about to move out and the girls rose to go I asked if I could see her again. She seemed pleased to be asked."

"So what is her name?"

"Catriona. Although she likes to be called Cat. She is calling here. Normally, of course I would pick her up but she has a new car and wants to show if off. She was recently in the military and is now self employed as a Security Consultant. Anyway you will be able to say hello tomorrow."

Rupinda had been an interested listener to my piece of

information. "I believe this is the first time you have brought a girl home – or rather will tomorrow."

It was difficult to see what Rupinda thought of this news. Life was becoming more and more interesting....

*   *   *

Cat phoned me. "Have a job to start up. Be round to your place in an hour. Have you prepared the ground with Grandmother?"

Receiving confirmation, heard her chuckle "So I am on my way to our first date! This will be interesting!"

CHAPTER NINETEEN
West Croydon

An hour or so later a sleek black Audi slid into our short drive and I went out and met a smiling Cat. She looked stunning and I became aware of a pleasant perfume.

"Come in and say hello to two people who are dying to meet you," I said as I took her arm. As we entered the house, Cat looked around appreciatively, "A lovely house, much larger than I expected." "It's my Grandmothers. Since my Grandfather passed away a few years ago I and Rupinda are really her only companions. Although my sister who lives in North London visits when she can."

We crossed the floor of the large room to a smiling Grandmother Kumari and seated nearby, Rupinda. I made the introductions, and for the next few minutes they got to know each other. Cat was more forthcoming with the polite questioning that usually results from a first time meeting. It was obvious Grandmother was quite taken by this young lady.

I understand from Ricci you were in the Intelligence Corps. That must have been very exciting and interesting."

"It was certainly interesting and could on occasions become quite exciting." Cat replied smiling.

"Cat, apart from the other places, saw service in Afghanistan," I added.

"It's all behind me now, but I definitely enjoyed the time I spent in the Corps. Met interesting people in a number of interesting countries."

I looked at my watch. "We are off to have lunch. I'm keen to be chauffeured in that gleaming new Audi you have parked outside." We made our farewells and I took the passenger seat in her car which smelt of new leather.

"Your Grandmother is a lovely warm person and her companion is also very charming. Both seem to dote on you."

"They keep each other contented." The car moved quietly and I became aware of Cat's skilful driving.

"I have the information on our first job. It's over in West Croydon. We will take a look at the property as we take a run out to get an idea of it. The target, or person of interest- if you will, is a gentleman by the name of Hashim Algarabin. He is the older brother of Ali Beharin who left the country and eventually joined the Islamic State people. Apparently he was killed in an air raid. His parents, first generation settlers in the UK are considered respectable people but the sons seem to have been radicalized and the older one, our person of interest, carried out substantial fraud with his wife Saaiha and although she was given a suspended sentence he served time for this fraud. As a younger man he had tried a bit of glorified shoplifting. With the death of his younger brother it is believed he is an advocate of I.S. and has become radicalized more against the country in which he was born than anything else. A smooth, good looking talker our people are wondering what he might be up to. He supposedly works in a small corner shop run by his parents but seems to rarely be found working there."

She slipped fingers into a jacket pocket and produced a photo of the target. I agreed he was a good looking person. A clipped beard and tidy moustache, a smiling face. A second photo followed.

"This is wifey. We suspect she is just as bad as he is and they work as a team which is a bit unusual. She helps financially by stitching clothes." Cat carefully avoided a young cyclist, and the car purred away in the direction of Croydon. I noted the easy going relaxed yet careful driving style of my new companion.

"Nice car. I don't think you will need me as a chauffeur. You are doing okay as you are. Cat smiled, as she replaced the photos I had been studying.

"Early days. Early days."

We were close to the area where our suspect lived. "The idea of identifying their location and to familiarize the immediate area and also work out how and where we can park without causing suspicion." We drove slowly along the road where Cat identified the actual house. We continued and kept an interesting watch on the general area.

"They live in the top flat of the double flat accommodation." She pointed out where an old Land Rover was parked on the street. "Fortunately it is not one of the longer roads in the area and I've noted one or two points we can park and keep observation. Completing a circuit of the location, Cat returned and swung the car into a position where we had a view of the property. I watched with interest as she fiddled around in the car, her movements creating a slight hint of fragrance off her body. She was handling a pair of binoculars which she placed between her knees, as she busied herself with a hi-tech camera.

She looked up and saw my interested gaze. "Tools of the trade. If you don't mind, I'll run through the appropriate actions to make sure you know how to use it." I felt more of a novice then as she swiftly and clearly explained its use. Putting the items to one side Cat settled more comfortably into her seat.

"We will give this a dry run just to see if anything happens." Cat said

And so we sat, side by side, keeping tabs on the house. Silently, at first, interest keeping us alert. Then, inevitably my eyes began to wander. I was about to ask Cat some questions about herself when she suddenly sat up.

"Hello, who have we got here?" she murmured. She had idly watched a thick set man, in a white cap and wearing the long dress of an Asian, who had been one of several pedestrians over a period passing the house. This one had stopped and turned towards the front door, a moment later he entered as the door to the flat was opened for him.

A short time later the visitor re-emerged with Hashim Algarabin and his wife who was dressed in the usual long dress and head covering. Cat took a couple of camera shots as they all entered the black Land Rover. The car moved off and Cat eased the Audi a safe distance behind.

A short drive into the more commercial part of town and the black Rover drew into a parking lot which provided space for several supermarket type stores.

Cat parked, picked up a shoulder bag containing the binoculars and camera and slipped out the car indicating for me to do the same.

"We will just keep an eye on what they get up to. We separate but keep an eye on each other. When in doubt move back towards me and we act as a couple of potential purchasers."

So we moved, keeping the group in view who were heading for a particular store. A sign indicated 'Outdoor and Sports Supplies.' We looked at each other with raised surprised eyebrows. Rather unexpected. One didn't get the impression they were outdoor types. When they entered they grouped looking at the departmental signs until one saw the symbol they required and pointed it out to the others as they moved forward towards it we saw they were heading for the Angling section where a sign declared 'All Your Fishing Requirements'.

Showing no apparent interest in the group I inspected a line of landing nets, while they had moved to the 'clothing for fishermen' range. Here they inspected sleeveless fishing jackets, some with numerous pockets. Hashim took down a fawn jacket with two large pockets at the breast and zipped side pockets. They debated sizes and surprisingly held one up against his wife who decided their acceptance to purchase, for they moved to the checkout and made payment placing the jacket in a bag.

Cat was now ahead of them and I joined her. We watched as they left the store and headed for a general supermarket. Here we observed another surprising purchase. Candles! Two packs of them. Finally, they headed for the parked Land Rover and we moved into the Audi. Nothing further of interest. They returned to the flat and shortly after, the third person left the house and we noted he lived a street or so away in another flat, the address taken. The whole area had numerous dark shaven inhabitants. Nothing surprising, mixed nationalities here became the norm in all parts of London.

The following day we carried out the same observation of the house. We were in luck in that we had some sort of action. Hashim left the house alone. He was smartly dressed in a western style business suit. I was reminded of his history of something of a con-man.

He drove to an area of smart shops, parked in the street. A short distance and he was gazing into the window of a high class jewellers, apparently studying a display of good class watches. The shop was the type where two glass windows front the street with an opening between and similar glass windows on each side invite access to the single door at the far end of this short passage.

We watched him enter the shop. What followed and incidents of which we later became aware, I will now describe. We saw him visit and the visit we were to be informed played out like this:

Hashim smiled at the shop manager, a tall, rather smug pale faced Englishman and declared he was seeking a replacement wrist watch for himself. In addition to the manager the staff consisted of a young smartly dressed woman in her twenties and a more mature lady.

After an amicable discussion between the manager and Hashim and following inspection of a number of watches, Hashim declared he would purchase this rather fine watch which was priced at one hundred and fifty pounds. Announcing he would pay in cash he deposited the agreed sum on the counter which the manager carefully counted and checked the notes, placed the watch in a neat box and made out a receipt. In the meantime the two ladies stood at the far end behind the counter and smiled pleasantly at the smart, good looking purchaser.

About to depart a pleasant Hashim suddenly turned towards the manager and announced "I understand you purchase gold. My wife has a number of good quality gold chains and bracelets she has inherited and has no use for. I wondered if you would be interested in purchasing them?"

"I would be pleased to value them for you and give a good price," a friendly manager replied, mentally rubbing his hands together at making a pleasant profit. A man who paid one hundred and fifty pounds for a watch these days was a customer he would like to see more often.

"That's excellent. I will call back with my wife in a day or two." The purchaser smiled his farewell and departed.

CHAPTER TWENTY

It was two days later when Hashim and his wife revisited the jewellers. Of course we knew nothing of the transaction at this stage. We were fortunately in position to observe the unfolding events of the later visit and were informed of the full incident shortly afterwards.

The third person who had since been identified as a compatriot of Hashim's during his time in jail, came out of the house with Hashim and his wife. This time Hashim, who was carrying a briefcase, and his wife sat in the back of the Rover and Rashid the friend drove. Hashim was smartly dressed as before in a suit and tie, his wife, who seemed to have put on weight dressed in Asian form with head and neck covering.

Their route was in the same direction as before. The car stopping a short way from the jewellers. Hashim and wife alighted. A short conversation with Rashid and checks on watches.

Hashim and Saaiha, his wife entered the jewellers. Rather like a charade the manager and staff were virtually in the same positions as Hashim's last visit. Otherwise the store was empty.

The manager whose name was Rasport smiled his recognition of this person and his wife. "Ah, a pleasure to see you Sir."

Hashim greeted the staff, lifted the briefcase onto the counter. "I would like your opinion of the value of these gold items," he said. With the clips towards him he unlocked it, lifted the lid and as he turned the case toward the expectant Mr. Rasport, he retrieved an automatic pistol from it and with it directed at the smiling manager observed.

"Stand back away from the counter." He waved the pistol briefly in the direction of the astonished, not to say fearful female staff. "You also."

At the same time as he uttered these words Saaiha pulled aside the folds of her Asian dress. To the horror of two ladies and a manager they were staring at a jacket fitted with two series of narrow thin pockets from each protruded by an inch or so a tube of explosive. Like a chilling decoration two lines of wires, one red, one blue travelled her body joining each narrow tube with a connection. From those wires hung a cord which Saaiha was holding between thumb and finger. Hashim was speaking.

"Please have no doubt you are looking at the will of Allah the Blessed. You will have a choice. In these two plastic bags I am about to produce, you will fill with all the gold and jewellry before you, quickly. To avoid an explosion which is about to occur and which will blow this entire shop and its neighbours to hell. For it is the will of Allah these goods are to benefit the Daish. Or my wife and I will be assured of our place in Paradise and you all will find your place in hell as unbelievers will assuredly do. In three minutes my wife will be instructed to detonate the dynamite unless what I have requested is done. You have seconds to make up your minds or depart this earth."

For a frozen moment nothing. Then the fainting of the younger girl and her slumping to the floor galvanized the manager and the older woman into action. As Hashim held out the bags, a desperate manager and the older assistant threw in Matts of diamond rings, gold bracelets, as Hashim assisted. Meanwhile, her head and lower face covered, Saaiha stood immobile in the centre of the room, still holding aside the cloak exposing the explosive jacket. A terrifying figure of potential death.

Hashim kept glancing at his watch. His one hundred and fifty pounds watch. Suddenly he commanded "enough. No more time!" he spoke rapidly in his own language to Saaiha. The manager and the middle age lady froze hands in mid-air as Saaiha moved, with the gun still trained on them she backed towards the door still clutching the cord.

Hashim said "Allah the Blessed has been merciful to you." Now, quickly backing out of the store, two heavy bags of unknown value hanging from his hands they entered the black Land Rover as it stopped for a second and then moved away at speed.

Cat and I had been watching the Land Rover and at that moment the alarm sounded and the distraught manager appeared.

I sped after the Land Rover as Cat spoke urgently into her cell phone. The message was picked up immediately.

"Suspects number 47 and 48 involved in jewellry heist at - she gave details - two minutes ago. Travelling north in black Land Rover, 3 occupants – she gave vehicle registration- possibly armed. Two males, one female. We are following. Anticipate they will return to their Croydon address. Urgent police advised. Will stay on phone.

It appeared the shop manager had also recovered his wits and had described to police the actions of the hold-up particularly the gun and the suicide vest. The special armed police unit was alerted. Unmarked cars sped to a roundabout on the Croydon road where traffic was cleared and police blocked the roads. The black Land Rover heading for the roundabout was surrounded but police kept at a safe distance. The Land Rover drew to a halt Hashim realizing the game was up, stepped out with arms raised and shouted the explosive vest was a fake, dropped down to the ground instructing his wife and the second man to do likewise. There was a standoff for some time because of the suspect vest and consequent danger but eventually arrests were made and the vest turned out to be fitted with painted candles and dummy wires. And the pistol was also fake! By this time Cat and I had moved away from the scene, this surveillance job now over.

*   *   *

Cat was seated in an alcove as I returned holding cups of steaming coffee. Settled I sugared my cup. "Well, that was interesting. But not the brightest con-man is the world, I would have thought. They would have had photo shots of them taken inside the store, but I must say the dummy terrorist vest was a novel way to terrify the staff."

Cat blew on her coffee, and grinned. "Must have been a record arrest. Didn't even have time to hide the loot. Caught red-handed. That 'explosive vest' will certainly increase the length of jail sentence. The staff must have been terrified. It was a wonder the young girl didn't have a heart attack!"

I pondered on the day's events.

"Well it wasn't an outcome we expected. Not exactly potential terrorist activity."

Cat, "Well I hear police were grateful, from a word I heard from above." "So what will the team of Cat and Ricci do now. Without a target to follow?"

"We will just continue with our usual lifestyle, although I expect we will soon have another job passed to us."

I considered that. Cat was more in touch with the way things worked than myself. I felt a faint feeling of regret that we would be apart for a while. Yet I reflected these last few days had been pleasant being in her company. Still knowing little about her she had a clever habit of side stepping information about herself. I decided if and when we should be together again I would make a bigger effort to really get to know her. It was nice to think we were quite comfortable in each other's presence.

"When we are finished here you can be a nice man and drive me home."

I looked at her surprised. "You usually have me drop you off in town. I only know the general area of Wandsworth in which you live."

Well I know you better now. Perhaps I did overdo the 'need to know' aspect, but it is sort of ingrained in me. I realize it was rather silly of me, but then it was- and suppose- is – necessary for you to know, when we usually do all contacts by phone."

"I don't think many guys are unaware of where their girlfriend lives." She laughed at the dig. There is a lot about each other we are unaware of. She looked at me with her head dipped her eyes glancing from under her lids.

"May be its time to become more acquainted."

"I'm all for that, Miss Hudson."

*　　*　　*

For the next few days I was more often than not working in my study or mooching around the house.

Grandmother noticed. "So where is the beautiful young lady? Haven't had a tiff I hope."

"She is doing a survey of a house in Kent."

"I bet you miss her."

I was about to make a humorous reply when I suddenly realized Grandmother comment was accurate. "Yes, she is good company. But of course she has a life of her own and has to earn a living."

Greg MacBride

CHAPTER TWENTY-ONE
Maria

Nearly five o'clock. A Saturday. Shops about to close for the weekend. It was then I saw it. A Hairdressers. Still open. A chance to get my overdue haircut. I pulled up. Parked in front of the large plate windows. I could see a man moving from the chair and two women, through the glass. Hurriedly I moved to the door. The customer on his way out held the door for me as I entered. The two females were wearing blue uniform type coveralls with high collars. The older of the two was struggling into her coat. They both turned towards me as I entered.

Am I in time to get a haircut?" I enquired. The older woman glanced at her watch. The younger and prettier of the two was looking at me as I spoke. Her long beautiful hair was dyed almost white. The wall clock indicated three minutes to five.

"Sorry Sir, we are closing," said the now coated woman obviously the senior of the two. The younger one, still looking at me, smiled and turning to the woman said, "I will do it. It will only take a few minutes." The older woman hesitated, then obviously in a hurry, "In that case you can lock up and I will see you on Monday." Handing keys to her young companion she continued, "When you leave turn off the lights and remember to set the alarm." She turned towards the door. "Goodnight Maria. Enjoy your weekend." She smiled briefly at me as she left the shop.

Maria indicated a hairdresser's chair. With my coat removed I sat before the large facing mirror. She placed the covering sheet over me and secured it at the back of my neck.

"And how would you like it cut?" She asked

Giving her generalized instruction I appreciated her English was very good but was obviously from a foreign country. In addition to giving this young woman instructions on closing the shop in English the senior woman had spoken briefly to her in what appeared to be a Mediterranean language.

Maria was quick and deft with the scissors. She knew her business. I was able to study her as she moved behind me. Very light on her feet she almost danced as she moved around me. A heart shape animated face, a slim body. Very attractive. She had a light hearted air about her. She chatted away in the usual manner of hairdressers whilst shaping, trimming. As she finished cutting she ran her fingers through my thick hair as if providing a head massage.

"Nice hair," she said smiling.

I noticed her tendency to use the word 'nice' quite frequently. She ended her task at hand and with a flourish removed the cover. I settled the bill with a generous tip, asking "What part of the world are you from?"

"Brazil," she answered smiling.

I pulled on my coat, thanking her for taking time out to deal with my hair. She gave me a brilliant smile. "Not at all! Was my pleasure."

Closing the door behind me I walked up to my car. Maria wasted no time in setting the alarm and locking the darkened shop.

I settled into the car and watched her as she waved to me and walked a few yards to a bus stop, where a queue was beginning to form. I moved the car a few yards and slowed by the stop. The side window slid down as I called, "Maria!"

She looked up, recognized me and smiling came towards the car. "Can I give you a lift?" A red double decker bus was approaching at the rear. I knew I was occupying his slot as he flashed his lights. "Where are you living?" I spoke as she looked in the window.

"Balham," she answered in that attractive accent.

"I'm going in that direction." I continued.

She gave no hesitation. "Thank you." She settled in next to me as the bus driver flashed me again. I waved and moved away as he aligned with the now sizeable queue.

"This is nice," said Maria securing her seatbelt. I knew the

Balham area rather well and with just a few directions from Maria we drove close to Bedford Hill. We turned into a side street at the bottom of which behind iron railings stood a block of flats. Maria guided me to a numbered parking spot. "Number thirty-eight," she said pointing. We stopped. She gave me a huge smile. "You come in for coffee? Have much coffee." She laughed, totally uninhibited.

"Kind of you. Thanks." I followed her into the building to the lift, stepping out at the third floor. It was a comfortable looking flat.

"Please you sit. I get coffee. You relax." Another flashing smile. As she moved the mass of creamy coloured hair swung enticingly around her slim neck. It was certainly eye catching and enhanced her attractive features. Slightly oriental shaped brown eyes above a small nose. Her smile showed perfect teeth between full lips.

The coffee was delicious. We sat opposite each other, completely relaxed, as if we had known each other for years. About my own age, a lively countenance showing every emotion without any reservation. In the car I had introduced myself, "Oh, Ricci, nice name," she had smiled. "You give me lift. Very nice man."

"So tell me have you lived in England long?" We got into small talk I was interested in her background. "Maybe two years," she said. "My cousin - you see her in hairdresser shop, she send for

154

me to help her- nice lady. So my boyfriend and me came over. He also is hairdresser. But he not like this weather. Had no men friends, so he go back to Brazil, one year ago." Her face shadowed, briefly. "He not worry about me. He know I cannot go, must help my cousin. Me lonely. Have only work. Come home. No go out night time in dark. In Brazil always out late, many friends." She sighed, looked up at me. Her sparkle returned, "You nice man. Maybe you new boyfriend!" She laughed, peeking at me with those slightly slanted eyes.

"You are a lovely woman and cheeky." I like cheeky woman. I looked at my watch. She saw and looked alarmed, unhappy. "You no go. You stay for a while, we have drinks together. I make good drinks." She stood and moved into the kitchen. I sat comfortably listening to the rattling and clinking. Ten minutes passed and she returned balancing two plates of food. Delicious cold salads. She disappeared again into the kitchen. Returned with a tray of cutlery, condiments, two glasses and a beaker full of a white liquid with ice cubes swirling. "You drink. Very strong, very nice Brazilian drink."

She poured into two glasses, handing me one. She watched expectantly as I tasted it. Strong, not unpleasant, sharp tasting yet sweet and making the mouth feel clean. To me, unusual, but pleasant. "Nice. I could get used to this," I said and watched her face show delight.

"Pinga, I call it. Real name, Caipirinha. I like. Very nice."

I looked at my glass, "What is it made from?"

"Lime and white sugar. Mash together and Cachaca and crushed ice." She rose. "I must take off dress. It for saloon. I have shower and change. You sit, happy. You drink." She smiled her gleaming smile, and left the room. Half an hour later she returned. Gone was the high necked blue dress replaced by a man's button through shirt. Her hair tied back, bare footed. She had the same lovely smile. She dropped into her former seat opposite me. I reached forward and passed to her, her glass of Caipirinha – as I was preferring to call it, Pinga – being much easier.

It was then I noticed her. The man's shirt parted at the last lower button as all shirts do. Her legs were parted and she was clearly visible. All hair had been removed and there was no doubt she was all woman.

As my glance flickered to her face she looked at me over her drink. She was aware of what I had seen. "Oops!" she said quite unabashed and closed her legs. As though it was of no interest, she carried on chatting.

"What work do you do, Ricci?" she asked, "Where you living?"

I was explaining I was a writer, able to travel around and explained the part of London in which I lived. Unconsciously and quite unaware, her legs moved open and inevitably showed herself to me. Hair completely waxed away, the skin showered and shining above a closed opening seemingly awaiting the key to part an entrance. She was completely unembarrassed. The only thing I considered was to move!

"This drink is delicious," I muttered, looking into my glass.

She suddenly scrambled up. "I must oil." She said. Bare footed, outline of her body against the shirt, she entered the bathroom, returning with a bottle of scented body oil and a large towel. Placing the towel on the floor she moved to the darkening windows, glanced through them, shivered, and closed the curtains. She returned, stood on the towel and slipping out of the man's shirt, smiled at me sweetly.

"This body oil, no greasy, dries quickly, nice smell." Now completely naked proceeded to oil her body. Pouring oil into the palm of her hand she slowly, gently rubbed her throat, breasts, arms, past her navel continuing onto her thighs. Bending she oiled the inside of her thighs and down the front of her legs before straightening again.

She smiled at me as I stood transfixed. "you not see lady's body before?" she teased. She stepped towards me, proffering the bottle of oil. I saw her breasts were hardening. "You be good man. Oil my back, yes? Please?" she stood again on the towel now with her back facing me.

I began at her shoulders. She held her beautiful off white hair away from her body as I began, her breasts lifting as she raised her arms. Down her slim body, into her curved narrow waist. Oiled hands now reached the twin halves of her rear. Daringly I slipped my fingers into the parting. My hand travelled down to the shiny spot where she had been waxed. She shivered slightly. She whispered, "Don't forget legs." My oiled fingers slid down to the backs of her slender legs to end at her ankles. I stood up.

She turned towards me, breasts glistening. "Thank you. That nice." She took the bottle from me, placed it on the floor and again that teasing smile. "Now we oil you." Before I could make any comment she was undoing the buttons on my shirt. We tugged it off. She picked up the oil, turned me. "First I do back." She proceeded to massage oil into my shoulders and arms. Oiling neck muscles she muttered something I didn't understand. Her fingers slipped round my waist undoing my belt. I stood still wondering where this was going. I soon found out. Her fingers nimbly unzipped my trousers and with a tug they slipped to my ankles with my boxer shorts. Once again her fingers worked. Undoing my shoes, she slipped them off. I bent my knees and pulled off my socks. I stood wearing nothing but my wristwatch my back still towards her.

She continued oiling my back at the waist and humorously, as if reminding me, as she oiled my backside her fingers slid into my cleft. As I had done with her, fingers now continued to stop between my legs. She paused pulling back slightly now rubbing into the backs of my legs her hand smoothing round the front up to my knees. She stood straight.

"Back finished, very nice. Now I do front." With that smiling remark she turned me. She gasped. Spoke rapidly in Portuguese. "Mio Santa…!" staring down at me she said, "You big man. Very big man'"

Recovering from her surprise a broad smile crossed her face. "You big, lucky man. You big to happy woman." Then, "Maybe me lucky woman tonight?" she lifted the oil. "Now I do your chest and front."

She began rubbing into my chest, my stomach to my navel. She slowed. She looked down at me, smiled, and teasingly said "Now I anoint your penis." She did so. Oily fingers gripped harder than necessary and it rose, firming, enlarging. Maria seemed fascinated. She gave a final squeeze and said "I finish now. All oiled," releasing me. She looked at me. Then said quietly, "You nice man, Ricci. I am on pill. You take me to bedroom, Yes?"

*   *   *

It has always been accepted that language is no barrier to intercourse and so it proved. Maria spoke rapidly in her own language breaking into her form of English when required. Enthusiastic, uninhibited. Embracing heatedly and uncovered on her bed she whispered in my ear. "Me no man for long time – one year!"

"How did you manage?" I said, for want of reply. "Me have to use many things," she giggled, totally unconsciously. "I put inside me, I get hot and whoosh! She exclaimed throwing her hands forward in demonstration. "Nice. But much better you inside me."

*　　*　　*

It wasn't our first time when she excitedly leapt up and fondling me addressed her desire to my lower part, "Please now, for Maria, get bigger." Inevitably it responded to her kissing and fondling. She sat above me her knees either side of my body. She lined me up at her swollen shining entrance and with her fingers holding herself apart she slipped over its hardness, sighed happily, "It's so big," and lowered her body until it filled her. Her movements now continuous she rose and lowered her actions quickening as she realized she could hold back no longer and with a shuddering ecstasy she cried out as she flooded and flopped onto me.

Recovering, she smiled and kissed me. "Very nice. Lovely." Her arm came forward. "Whoosh!" she demonstrated happily. Her arm came round me. She pressed her breast against me. "You great lover!" she whispered.

*　　*　　*

Maria had been right about the oil. Non-greasy, it had been absorbed through my skin. Now once again dressed and on my interrupted journey home I had a faint feeling I had been seduced. Not complaining, you will understand, but this young beautiful Brazilian with long white coloured hair, totally unselfconscious, uninhibited and carefree was certainly in no need of instruction.

*　　*　　*

A substantial bouquet of roses was delivered to her during working hours. With a note, hopefully in good Portuguese. 'To a Beautiful Lady. R.'

Greg MacBride

CHAPTER TWENTY-TWO
Alexandria

I spotted the studio as I passed out the far end of the village. Isolated, ancient bricks warm in the sun, wisteria around the entrance and a profusion of blooms in the small front garden. An island of unfussy calm. The intricate carved sign board invited passers-by to enter and inspect the work of 'Alex Walters- Professional Wood Carver'.

I had, for some time been considering a gift for Rupinda for the care she bestowed on my Grandmother. A vague thought hovering at the back of my mind of perhaps a religious symbol.

I drove into the small clearing at the front of the studio. Alighting, I looked around, taking in the air and smells of the country side, listening to a distant bird call. Except for the lilt of the far songstress there was total silence.

I walked towards the entrance. Pushing the door, I entered a large room. Surprisingly large I realized and then appreciated the rear wall had given way to an extension providing the room with an airy feeling of space and the smell of various woods gave a pleasant fragrance.

Around the walls, on tables, in glass fronted display cabinets were examples of the carvers art.

I stood looking around. Complete silence.

"Hello," I called loudly.

A moment later a side door opened and a figure appeared. My immediate impression was of a slightly built female with wood chips in her hair, wearing an apron. As she came fully into view I saw she was a youngish woman, short cut brown hair, a pleasant face and a quizzical expression.

"Hello can I help you," she enquired.

I said, surprised, "Would you be the owner who carves wood?"

The woman smiled at my enquiry. Yes. I am the owner and I carve wood."

I noticed how her face lit up when she smiled. I stepped towards her, hand extended. "I'm not normally so stupid," I said. "I really came in by chance. I noticed the sign outside and as I am looking for a gift for a friend I thought I may find something suitable here."

The young woman brushed a wood chip from her hair and shook my hand. She appeared to like the friendly immediate confession, my open easy candour. I sensed also an indefinable, almost sensual awareness I would be hard put to define.

"Please, take a look around. Take as long as you like. I will be back in a moment and will answer any questions you may have." With that and again a pleasant smile she re-entered the side door. I turned towards the items on sale.

Inspecting each item as I passed slowly I appreciated the amount of detail. Animals in various poses, carvings with a pronounced Asian and Far Eastern influence, quirky pieces and a number of carvings displaying a sense of humour. One that caught my eye was a representation of Moby Dick with a glass inset on one side showing a sailor figure at the table having a meal, in the stomach of the whale. Heads and busts of several well-known personalities, representation of various fish. A group of three reclining lions, elegant and shapely females, some in religious poses others more given to artistic license.

The side door opened and a refreshed Alex, apron removed, hair brushed free of wood chips re-entered the display area. At her side totally obedient to her quiet commands strode a German Shepherd. "This is Ben," she said, "My companion and protector."

I nodded. "In a quiet rather remote area like this I find that very wise."

"Have you seen anything that may interest you?" she enquired. "Most of my work is commissioned and so obviously not exhibited."

We slowly walked with Ben keeping pace at the side of Alex. "What commission work have you done recently?" I asked.

"Well a gentleman from Malaysia requested a replica of the Railway Station in Kuala Lumpur which was rather interesting and something of a challenge. I have recently completed a pair of replacement carvings of an ancient royal couple."

"Replacement Carvings?" I repeated.

"The original carvings were most beautifully done in Bali of a prince and his female consort. It appears they had been side by side on a wall for many years but unfortunately over time each developed unsightly cracks due to years of central heating and the owners were sufficiently upset to ask if I could replicate the features precisely in identical carvings. I am pleased to say they were delighted with the results. One of the figures had hair formed into an elegant pointed knurled bun and the other's hair drawn up and surmounted by a carved miniature decorative tiara. I was never certain which was the prince and which was the consort. When the gentleman came to collect them I asked him, and do you know he smiled and said they had been in his possession for over fifty years and he had never been certain which was the prince and which was the female!"

"I am quite impressed with the intricate carving, particularly of the heads. I have in mind a bust of Lakshmi for an Indian lady. Would that be possible?" I asked.

Alex Walters wondering for a quick moment who would be the recipient of such a gift, said, "I would be delighted to carve such a figure. I can show a number of designs, drawings and perhaps you may see one you like particularly and also show you samples of the wood on which perhaps I can advise you. if you would like I could show you photos and drawings of similar type commissions now if it is convenient."

"That would be great," I exclaimed.

"Please take a seat," she indicated an empty table, "I will get some samples." As she turned she said, "Would you care for something to drink? Tea or coffee?"

"Love one. Tea, please," I said smiling.

Again Alex disappeared, to return with tea, sugar and milk. Depositing the tray on the table, "Please help yourself," and again vanished, this time returning with a bulky folder of photographs, drawings, sketches. On the front was a photograph of an elderly man proudly exhibiting a carving of a sailing ship. Placing the folder on the table she said, simply, pointing to the cover, "That was my father, Alexander Walters who taught me all I know about carving wood."

I studied the picture which had obviously been taken some time ago. "He looks a proud dedicated man," I said.

"He loved his work and as he had no sons, in my teens I became his assistant and protégé. When he passed away I continued with his studio and work. I had been christened Alexandra so it was unnecessary to change the sign outside the workshop."

I drank tea, studied and considered sketches and the like.

Listened to advice and suggestions and placed a commission for the representation of Lakshmi.

"It will be a while before I am able to tell you it is ready for an individual piece should not be rushed," she said.

During the lengthy discussion on the merits of one design against another, we had sat next to each other and I had become very much aware of this lady, sensing her friendliness and something pleasing but yet less definable between us.

Finally, we stood up both satisfied with the way things had progressed. "Good Lord, how the time has passed," I murmured, looking at my watch. "Is there a hotel or such nearby?"

Alex replied, "There is no hotel in the village. The local pub used to let rooms but that has closed down through lack of trade." She looked at me. "The nearest town with a hotel is nine or ten miles away, I'm afraid."

"Ah! Well, so be it. I'll drive there and take a room and have a meal." I stopped, looking at Alex said, "Forgive me asking but would you care to join me for dinner?" I smiled. "I know I'm something of a stranger but I promise I am an honest upstanding man and can confirm it. I would be delighted if you would accept. I will, of course drive you back, and if you would prefer to take Ben along he is very welcome too."

Alex surprised at the invitation, hesitated. I sensed her life in this out of the way place had been uneventful for some time. Later I was to understand the reason.

Still undecided she said, "Well thank you. but I'm not dressed for a meal in public, and it's time for me to take Ben for his evening walk."

"I'm in no hurry," I replied. The thought struck me. "What if I took Ben out for half an hour or so, would that give you time to change your dress and comb your hair?"

She smiled. "if you would take Ben give me time to shower and become presentable, I would be delighted to join you."

So it was arranged. Ben came eagerly. I was given his lead and advice on a nearby field and pathway in which to take him. "You can let him off his lead in the field and he will come when called."

"I'll take him out for forty minutes." I said.

"I will be ready and thank you for taking Ben."

We headed for the door. "You will need these," Alex pressed two brown plastic bags into my hand. "The bin for dog poo is at the end of the lane." She grinned, mischievously.

*   *   *

So following forty minutes of walking, playing with Ben and disposing of the results of Ben's activities I returned, to find a surprise. The working carver of wood was no longer about. I was presented with a demure, slender elfin woman with darkened eyes, lightly powdered silken skin, a touch of lipstick, a cleverly shaped hair style in a black clinging dress which showed her figure to great advantage.

"Wow!" I said appreciatively, then remembering, proffered a

169

filled brown plastic bag to this smartly dressed young lady.

Confused and delicately accepting, she said "Why on earth did you not put it in the bin?" She then realized the contents were totally different. Opening the bag, peering, she gasped. I stood smiling as she pulled out a neck chain of clear crystals supporting a carved capital 'A' of the same material.

"I happened to follow Ben into a small clearing of rough ground, stony, with long grass. As I bent to deal with – er- Ben's actions I noticed something glistening in the grass. I picked it up and when I saw what it was I guessed it belonged to you."

Alex clutched the chain. She was overcome. "I found it missing last year, lost, whilst out with Ben. I searched for ages. Couldn't find it. It was given to me by the man I was going to marry." Her eyes glistened. "I just can't thank you enough for finding it."

"Just a repaired clasp and it will be as good as new. I'm pleased I came across it." I grinned, "Sorry about the bag, I didn't want to lose any part of it, and so the bag came in handy. If I can use a bathroom to quickly wash my hands, we will be off."

Later, with Ben on the back seat, Alex alongside me we headed for the nearby town. Ben promptly went to sleep. The light perfume of Alex made the car interior pleasant and in a relaxed atmosphere we were each aware and enjoyed each other's presence. Presently Alex giggled. I looked at her enquiringly.

"I thought you were giving me Ben's-er-contributions, and

couldn't understand why. I should have realized you are too much of a gentleman to do such a thing. I think you did it because you have a crazy sense of humour."

I grinned. "It was sort of retaliation for suddenly thrusting the bags into my hands, but I shouldn't have done it."

She squeezed my arm. "Don't be silly. It was just unexpected, that's all."

So the chatting continued, steadily enhancing our friendliness.

CHAPTER TWENTY-THREE

The hotel was a busy place. With Ben asleep in the car with a window half open we entered the foyer and I enquired about a room. "Sorry Sir, there is a convention on and we are fully booked. You may find a vacancy at the Travelodge but it is unlikely." To further enquiries the manager was much more cheerful. "A table for two? No problem Sir." He indicated the dining room and we were soon comfortably seated, a waiter placing menus in front of us. "A drink?" I asked Alex. "Perhaps white wine. I would think ninety percent of ladies start drinks with white wine," I mused.

Alex said, "I think it's time you told me about yourself. What do you do? Where do you come from? Tell me all," she laughed.

"I'm a writer. Recently published. Interested in Modern History." I reached in my wallet and placed a business card before her. She read it with interest. "An author! I've never met an author before."

"I've never met a female wood carver before. Keep the card

although my books are probably not to your taste, such as analysis of a war general's decisions."

Alex looked at the name.

"Riccardo MacDonald. Is that a made up name?" she asked

"It certainly is not! My Grandfather was a Scot who married an Indian lady, my Grandmother, who I live with in South London. My father, their only son was a professional pianist who met and married an Italian singer. They were killed in Italy, a road accident, when I was fourteen. Since then I have lived with my Grandparents, although only my Grandmother is still alive. I spend my time writing, play rugby occasionally, although not so much as I used to, some travelling. I also play piano, but not to the standard my father did." I looked keenly at Alex. "What are your interests?"

Alex looked up and shrugged. "Come to think of it, not very much. When I close the studio I return to my little nest of rooms, take Ben for walks, do a lot of reading, like to cook – that's about it." Her eyes looked into her past. "At one time we would go dancing, see films. The usual things, but that all changed when Sam died."

"Who was Sam?" I asked.

"He joined my father and more or less became an apprentice, like myself. Over time we got to like each other and were going to marry." She paused and looked down at her plate. "He was a Territorial in the Army and he was called up or volunteered, I'm

not quite sure which now, for six months' active service in Iraq."
She stopped and then quietly, continued. "He was killed.
Apparently by what they called friendly fire!"

I said "I'm so sorry, it's heart breaking."

Alex gave a deep sigh. "It was a few years ago now and the
pain slowly fades. But the memories remain. Since, I've had no
great desire to mix with people, and as you can see I don't exactly
live in the Metropolis. I just get on with my little world."

I gently moved the conversation to a lighter plane with one or
two anecdotes of incidents on the rugby pitch and stories passed
in interviews with war veterans or their descendants.

As we finished our meal, Alex said "I must let Ben out for a
moment." We found Ben fast asleep. He stretched, yawned, did
what was required of him, jumped back into his seat and settled
down again. We moved out of the car park and headed for the
studio. Dance music played softly and in companionable silence
we sped through the evening darkness.

*   *   *

Pulling into the small parking lot, I said "I'll take Ben for a walk
if you like."

"That's kind of you," said Alex, handing me the dog's lead, "It's
beginning to get chilly."

Five minutes later we ambled back. "Come in," called Alex as I
stood undecided in the large room. At the side door a hall gave
access to rooms. Standing, silhouetted against the light of the

sitting room stood Alex. Ben brushed past her heading for his personal blanket in a corner. "Tea, coffee or something stronger?" enquired Alex indicating a comfortable armchair.

With my preference for tea she moved to the kitchen, I looked around. A few feminine touches. Vases of flowers, rugs on the carpet, several photo frames on a side table. A substantial bookcase heavy with a miscellany of books. The inevitable TV set faced a large cushioned sofa and a music centre stood against a far wall. A door to the kitchen, others presumably to bedrooms and to a family bathroom.

Alex returned with a tray of drinks. Depositing them on a side table she picked up Ben's water bowl which he had noisily emptied, filled it, returned it to Ben's corner and finally sat on the couch curling her legs under her.

I sipped hot tea. Then it hit me. "Darn it. I've forgotten to ring the Travelodge." I reflected a moment. "Still, no harm done. I'll drive to Brighton where I was going to spend the weekend anyway. Sure to find accommodation there."

Alex looked at me over the rim of her cup. "If you would rather stay here tonight and continue your journey tomorrow, there is a spare room available." She smiled impishly. "I am sure you are a gentleman and won't steal the family silver – that is if you can find any of course."

"Are you sure? That is most kind of you. I do assure you I am a gentleman of high degree!"

She smiled, tying to ignore the warm feeling. "And there is always Ben to protect me."

"Totally unnecessary," I protested. "My word is my bond."

"So that's settled. Later, when we are finished here I will show you the spare guest room which is actually quite comfortable."

"I have my overnight bag in the car, thank you." I said.

"So tell me, don't you have any commitments or people to consider?" she asked.

I laughed. "I'm in the advantageous position of having no responsibilities, at least that I can think of at the moment – I am financially independent, footloose and fancy free, other than my writing of course."

Alex, continued asking "No relatives?"

"Well, I have a sister who has a partner who she alleges she doesn't trust and both of them knock sparks off each other. But I happen to know he thinks the world of her and she knows it." I said. "There is of course my Grandmother but at the moment she is being looked after by her companion, Rupinda."

"Rupinda. That's an unusual name. who is she?" Alex asked.

"Rupinda is a very interesting woman. Indian by birth as of course is my Grandmother. She is Gran's companion with the same interests. A much younger woman, a widow, well-educated and intelligent." I paused. "Has a lot to do with my attitude to life and people. She is the lady for whom I seek a gift."

"The God of Love," mused Alex.

"Yep!" I smiled.

The next hour or so was spent in friendly conversation. The radio playing softly in the background. Alex unsnarled her legs and rose from the couch. She said softly, "I must thank you for a lovely evening. It is a long time since I have so enjoyed myself." For a moment I thought she was about to kiss me, but sensed her shyness and the moment passed. "I'll turn your bed sheets back whilst you get your bag," she said briskly and moved from the room.

On my return she indicated the family bathroom. "It's all yours," she said. "I have an en suite in my bedroom. Sleep well and I will see you at breakfast." With that she was gone.

It was a pleasant room with a double bed, crisp white sheets and duvet. I slipped into bed, noting the bottle of water and tumbler on the bedside cabinet, the soft pillows. Enjoying the comfort, I closed my eyes, wondering about the woman in the next room and her quiet life as I drifted off to sleep.

Lying still, Alex, awake, listened for the small sounds of the usually unoccupied room. She had no reason to be afraid of this man who, until only hours ago had been a complete stranger. She visualized his broad shoulders, steady brown eyes and knew it was not just his friendliness or good manners that so attracted and warmed her body. There was something infinitively about him that brought out a hidden yearning, a desire, a need for him to be close to her, his hands to be on her. She tingled. It was a while before her eyes closed and she found sleep.

I woke to the smell of bacon cooking. I rose, showered, shaved and dressed casually before entering the kitchen. "Hi," she said. "How did you sleep?"

"Like the proverbial log. And you?" I asked

"Very well," said Alex, ignoring the truth. "How do you like your eggs, boiled, fried or scrambled?"

"As there is a choice, I'll take scrambled."

Later seated and munching toast I asked, "What do you usually do on a Saturday?"

Alex shrugged. "Nothing much. With the studio closed I relax and if the weather is fine as it is today I'd maybe sit out in the back garden with Ben and read a book. Other than take him for a walk not much else."

"How would you like to spend the day mooching around Brighton? I could buy you a stick of rock, an ice-cream or if you are good, both. We could look like a couple of tourists, walk the pier. I believe there is still one left. It's a while since I was on that part of the coast. You could have a paddle, or I could sing 'Just One More Cornetto' to you on the boat pond. Then have lunch. Pick up a couple bottles of wine – because I can't drink if I am driving."

Alex's eyes widened, "But don't you have to get back to London? Could you stay another night?"

"As I said, I'm a free spirit. My time is my own. If there is somewhere else you would rather be, regard me as your personal chauffeur!"

Alex felt her prayers had been answered. "Oh! I would love to spend the day with you at Brighton, that would be terrific."

"How about Ben? Does he come with us?" I asked.

"No. I'll take him for his walk before we go and he will be quite comfortable here."

"We won't stay late in town. I expect the traffic will be quite heavy as it's a weekend and with this T-shirt weather." I stood up. "We will walk Ben together. Don't forget the brown bags!"

She giggled. "Is that all you can think of?"

I laughed, "I can think of a lot more than that."

Alex secretly wondered if he was thinking what she was thinking.

It was late morning by the time we moved off. Dressed in a white cotton top, slim jeans and minimal make up, Alex was like an animated teenager, inhibitions evaporated. She suddenly thought to herself this is like being on a date. She felt surprise at the realization. Well it would be a second date really. I glanced at her radiant face. It raised my own awareness of happiness. She caught my look and squeezed my arm intimately not really knowing why other than she just had to touch this man.

Arriving at the outskirt of Brighton I began to wonder whether this trip was a good idea. The traffic congested, movement was low. But it seemed nothing was going to dampen her happiness.

Finally, with good fortune I managed to legally   park. We headed for the promenade and beach area. The sun shone. The younger women had a tendency to shed more items of clothing resulting in hopefully witty remarks by me and giggles by Alex.

In due course many of the promised pleasures outlined by me came to pass, we licked swirls of ice cream, sucked sticky colourful sticks of rock. I found a wide brimmed hat for Alex much to her liking. We giggled our way into a numbered boat on the lake and duly rendered a couple of lines of 'O Sole Mio' to a helplessly laughing embarrassed Alex. Walked the length of the pier halting at the many amusements and sat for an hour in deck chairs on the promenade. Relaxed.

"We could change the ambiance of our wanderings whenever you wish and seek out a quiet country pub, have a late lunch and a glass of wine if that tickles your fancy." I suggested.

"That sounds lovely," breathed Alex.

Greg MacBride

CHAPTER TWENTY-FOUR

When finally moving back to the car Alex put her arm through mine and smiling pressed her arm against my side.

Enjoying the fine weather, the sound of Brighton behind us we headed for Hurstpierpoint. We found an olde worlde pub with few customers and settled down to a meal and drinks. Replete we took a leisurely ride finally ending back at the studio.

Relaxed, with wine I had purchased in town, Ben at our feet, comfortable in each other's presence, Alex experienced a glow of happiness and an unusual warmth.

"It's been a lovely change for me today," she began. "I can't thank you enough." Whether it was the wine which caused a feeling of light headedness, of a sensation of floating in a sea of pure joy, she continued. "You will stay over tonight, won't you?"

"I have nothing to race home about. I will be pleased to stay until tomorrow."

"But won't Rupinda miss you?" she asked shyly.

"Rupinda, my friend, confidante and tutor is always delighted to see me," I replied. "So does my grandmother."

"Confidante and tutor," she mused, "Unusual way to speak of a young lady."

"Rupinda guides me with her sayings, warnings, and other utterings, through life's journey. Particularly with companionship of the fairer sex."

"You mean women you meet during your life's journey?"

"Exactly. To think only of their welfare, their happiness, their desires."

"Crikey!" said a smiling Alex. "a Samaritan for lonely ladies."

Ben stirred. I said, "Although he is no lady I am quite willing to think of his welfare and walk him."

Alex jumped up. "Let's take a stroll together and so you will be providing welfare, happiness to us both."

I laughed, "And what about desire?"

Alex coloured. "Perhaps that can be provided later. Maybe he is not that interested."

*   *   *

"Can I re-fill your glass?" I asked.

Night had brought darkness. Alex closed curtains, Ben snored, sleeping in his corner. Alex looked at her empty glass, undecided. "I must make it my last one. If you don't mind, I'll first take a shower. I'll enjoy it better, afterwards."

"Good idea," I confirmed. She left the room. I stretched comfortably in the arm chair.

Alex returned. A dressing gown about her, rubbing her short brown wet hair. I stood. "Would you mind if I do the same and take a shower?"

"Good Lord, Ricci, of course I don't mind. There is a pile of towels in the drawer. I'll show you." she headed for her own bedroom. Use this shower. The other one has not been used for quite a while." Dutifully I followed her past the double bed into a comfortably sized en-suite, still wet and warm from Alex's use. She pointed out the soap, creams, shampoos and pulled a drawer to show a neat pile of white towels. "Enjoy!" she said as she left.

Steam rose as I lathered and shampooed and ended with a cold shower. I felt refreshed as I dried myself. Dressed in a pair of boxers, a large bath towel around my waist I re-entered the lounge.

Alex sitting stiffly upright now rose, moved towards me, slid her arm around my neck and whispered, "thank you for a lovely day." And kissed me. As her lips pressed harder her body tightened against mine. My hands moved up her shoulders, her breasts pressing into my chest as I returned her kiss. I was aware of her body perfume. She sighed, "It must be the wine. Stay with me tonight, please." I lifted her body, arms still tight around my neck and took her to her bed.

CHAPTER TWENTY-FIVE

We were side by side looking up at the ceiling in the half light. I sensed she was troubled. It happened. Eyes filled, she tried to stifle her sobs. I turned towards her. I felt her tears. Placing my arms around her I lifted her slight heaving body onto myself. Her face buried into my chest, my hands stroking her hair. Her body shook with silent sobbing. So we remained. Gradually sobs subsided, her tight grip on my shoulders relaxing.

Alex raised her head. "Sorry," she said tearfully.

I smiled. 'Memory is a funny thing. Can catch you out anytime." She looked gratefully at my face below her.

"I think I was closing a chapter on long ago. Thank you."

A few moments she rested. I said, "I need a towel. I think I have a swimming pool on my chest."

Alex laughed as she eased her body off me, "I feel better now."

I climbed back into bed. "Where were we?"

She turned towards me. "I was on your chest."

"Then it's my turn." My body came down on her, my lips

seeking hers. She responded, her mouth parting, our tongues seeking each other. I lifted my head and nuzzling her ear I took the lobe gently between my teeth and breathed softly into her ear. Her body surged as my lips lightly touched her neck, breath warming a gentle track down to her shoulder and moved toward the rise of her breasts, seeking the swelling hardening tips. My tongue circling, teasing, gently sucking. Her breath caught as my teeth tugged, the hardened swollen teat. She gave a soft moan as I lifted my head to between her warm perfumed breasts, my hands compressing them against my face before I lifted and took her other breast into my mouth. Her hands tightened on my shoulders. Lips moved from her engorged breasts and slowly lightly touching, moved down and across her body until they found her navel where they slowed kissed, licked and sucked. Her body shook, I felt her fingers dipping into my skin as my mouth continued a seemingly rambling journey, my body had moved down in concert with my movements. My hands on her hips, her hand now on my head for a moment. My hand now moved as I lifted my head and my fingers brushed her dark coloured bush. She jerked, her legs moved slightly apart, I moved again her eyes opening wide as my hands brushed her inner thighs and then parted her legs. As my head dropped down her eyes widened. "Oh! No!" she whispered. Her swollen entrance seemed like a barrier but as my tongue pressed the wet portals parted. Alex gave a violent shudder and a moan as it slipped between them seeking and finding the soft tissue of her clitoris. I tasted her as the tip of my tongue touched, withdrew slightly and then fondled her clitoris again and again. "Please, please," she whispered, "I so want you!"

I moved from her to slip off my boxers. It was then Alex saw. It was stiff, hard and large. "Oh my God," she breathed. "It has been a long time…"

"I'll be gentle," I said softly. I moved onto her.

My hands traced across her perfumed silky skin under her breasts, along the inside of her raised arms, moving slowly again towards her hips and stomach. From her left hip I brushed the tips of my fingers below her navel to her other hip. She shuddered. Stroking the outside of her thighs, fingertips gently returning to her waist, pausing, returning on a different line now touching caressing the inner sides of her thighs. For a moment my hand was still. Her breathing irregular. Heavy with anticipation.

She moved her legs apart slightly invitingly. Still I fondled her thighs. She was silently begging me. She was hot, burning, wet swollen. My fingers slid, entering, parting, seeking into her. How she wanted me! Now I was moving up towards her. At last! Her legs parted and stiffly I sought her entrance. Parting, pressing my hard glans found entry and led the hardness, stiff, rigidity into her and she was distending, enlarging, stretching until joyfully it was inside her, massaging, pressing, titillating her clitoris. Her eyes wide with the wonder, the delight, the exhilarating fullness. As I moved further inside her she gasped. Shuddering waves of exultation enveloped her a I moved gently, pressing, releasing, pressing – she pulled at me and moved in concert with me aware of nothing but the fire inside her, the all-consuming waves of passion. Heavenly. Her whole body vibrated as a final thrust travelled through her. Waves of ecstasy engulfed her causing her to cry out as she orgasmed, flooding as I joined her.

Her mind disorientated. As I withdrew she had the sensation of a train leaving a station.

CHAPTER TWENTY-SIX

Alex lay back relaxed, she sighed with the contentment her fulfilled body granted. Her hand sought mine.

"You okay?" I asked.

"Oh, yes. I haven't felt so happy in ages." She squeezed his hands. "I feel full of life."

I smiled, "Er, I don't think so."

Alex raised her head, puzzled. "What do you mean..." then the double entendre hit her. "Oh, my God. I'm not on the pill, I haven't bothered with it for some time. You er-didn't use anything?"

I said, "in that moment of bliss, no."

Alex fell silent. I lifted myself on one elbow. "Relax. You don't have to worry, Alex. I would have taken precautions had they been necessary. It can't happen."

Alex, perplexed. "I don't understand."

"I am presently unable to cause you to conceive. I had an accident whilst playing rugby some time ago the result, to put it crudely, I am unable to provide the necessary sperm."

Alex sat up. "You mean it is not possible for me to conceive?"

"Not with me, at the moment you can't." I said ungrammatically. "But I would advise taking precautions. After all you have, after some delay, become sexually active."

"That is something of a relief," she sighed. "I love children, but this would be the wrong time."

I flinched. Alex noticed and said, alarmed, "Oh, Ricci I didn't mean to insult you."

I curved my shoulder. "Don't be silly, it isn't anything you said. The muscles in my shoulder sometimes give me a sharp pain. It is due to an old rugby injury. Don't worry about it."

She said, relieved. "This rugby thing sounds a dangerous occupation." Her eyes glistened and she jumped up. "You need a massage. That will help. I'm good at massages. Lie on your front and I will massage your shoulders."

I demurred. "It's okay. The pain is going now." But Alex insisted.

Mumbling I turned on my front. Alex was naked. "I love to look at your breasts," I said, "Now I can't."

She smiled. "They are small."

"They are pert," I said.

"I'll get oil," replied a happy Alex, and moved to the en-suite bathroom.

The oil, pleasant smelling, a small amount cupped in her hand, her warm legs either side of my body, was pleasant as her fingers pressed into the locked muscle of my shoulder. Fingers and the pads of her hands eased and relieved. "Ah, this is great," I acknowledged.

Finally, she said, "that's done. You can turn over." I did as instructed. It was as Alex glanced down, she again said, "Wow!" Then remembering, breathed, "Now I know why!"

"Why what?" I asked.

"Why I thought of a train leaving the station and entering a tunnel," she smiled. "Can I touch it?"

"If you must." She held it and it responded to the warmth of her oiled hand. Fascinated she released her hand to allow it to return to its original position. It remained steadily, firmly erect.

She slipped next to me, our bodies responding to each other's sensations, her hands went around my neck, mine to her hardening breasts. "They are pert." I breathed. She pushed them towards me.

"I'm pleased you like them," she whispered and once again my lips covered them, tongue caressing their hardened tips.

It may have been the awareness of the information imparted by me or perhaps the exertions of massaging but any reserves of shyness had now vanished. Alex slid onto my body. I released her encaptured breasts as she bestrode me. She moved slowly backwards until she felt my erection against her naked back. She raised herself until she was above me then slowly wetly her legs either side of me she lowered herself, her hand between her legs holding me steady as the hot throbbing apex entered her enlarged wet lips filling her, swelling her as she slowly gently relaxed onto me until we were joined as one, she curved her body from her waist not disturbing our union, her breasts again in my shaped hands.

"You look like a jockey!"

She pressed her knees into my sides, her feet trailing. For a long moment we remained still. Then, as I raised my knees behind her back she straightened her body, leaning against my knees. Placing a hand each side of my thighs she raised and lowered herself, the stiff hardness heating her vagina as it slid inside her.

I reacted. With her knees still tight against my body I turned her until I was above her. We were still as one. Alex feeling again the sliding deep penetration. She sought my lips with hers and tightly entwined could no longer hold back the pleasure, the ecstasy caused by waves of pure lust filling her whole arching body. A sensation of drowning in a sea of exquisite unutterable pure bliss.

CHAPTER TWENTY-SEVEN
Tom

Alex sent an Email:

COMMISSION COMPLETED. PLEASE ADVISE
DATE/TIME OF COLLECTION
ALEX.

I sent a reply:

REGRET UNABLE TO MAKE JOURNEY MYSELF.
SENDING EMISSARY. WILL ARRIVE 5 PM FRIDAY
EVENING WITH LETTER. SUGGEST YOU WEAR
BLACK DRESS.
RICCI

*   *   *

Receiving notification, the commission was ready I began putting a little plan into action. I phoned an old friend, Tom Barford.

"Hi Tom. Thought it time I phoned an old pal. So how are you doing?"

"Ricci. Hi, man, pleased to hear from you."

"Tom, I've got an interesting proposition I thought I might put to you. have you any plans for the coming weekend?"

Tom, surprised. "Nothing planned – yet! So what sort of proposition would this be?"

"Tell you what," I said. "How about meeting up for a pint and a chat this evening at the usual pub. Then I can explain all!"

"Never have much to do evenings, yeah, be pleased to meet up."

"Say eight o'clock okay?"

"Fine, sounds interesting. See you later then Ric."

I arrived at our usual haunt to find Tom sitting at a table with two pints drawn. We had been friends since school rugby days. He married early and had the incredible bad luck of losing his wife of just a few years to cancer. A tall friendly man we got on well together.

I shook hands, taking a seat as he pushed a pint towards me. An old style pub with no pretensions to modernity, not many customers weekdays except a few regulars. I lifted the glass. "Cheers!" Tom did the same. We talked rugby for a while although neither of us had played for quite some time.

"Getting older and wiser," reflected Tom. He looked at me. Took a drink. "So what is this proposition you have been on about?"

I studied his interested face for a moment, collecting my thoughts. Of the many friends I had made over the years Tom was one I really liked. I knew quite a lot about him. An ex-soldier having served several years in the Army. The death of his wife had hit him hard. A steady presence, reliable, straight forward. Now I was about to ask a favour.

"How would you like to drive into darkest Sussex this Friday and collect a valuable package for me from a very pleasant young lady?"

He looked at me astonished. "Why can't you go yourself?" he asked.

"Other commitments." I answered.

"A valuable package," he said. "You are not into drugs?" he grinned.

"I'll explain all," and told him of the gift I was having made. "It is a particular religious symbol for an Indian friend. It is being specially carved by an experienced wood carver who I met by chance. Her name is Alexandra, a young woman who was about to marry her soldier boyfriend several years ago when he was killed in Iraq. Since then she has lead a quiet life in her studio which is rather off the beaten track."

I stopped talking, took a drink and studied Tom. I continued, "As I said we met when by chance I was passing her studio, stopped and went in. It was closing time for the weekend. We got on well. So I took her out to dinner."

I decided to tell Tom like it is. "Tom," I said. "I'll be straight with you. Alex is a lovely lady, lives a lonely life, is very talented. Because of commitments I can't do the trip myself. I will explain all in a letter I want you to give to her with some flowers I will send. It's important I have the gift for my Indian friend collected, undamaged. It's a pleasant part of the countryside where she lives and, as I say, a pleasant woman!" I grinned. "If by chance you both hit it off – well it would do no harm."

Tom narrowed his eyes. "You are not by chance trying to set me up on a blind date?"

I laughed. "Tom," I said. "I need you to do me a favour. Just consider. A pleasant journey into the countryside – I can give you full details of how to get there. A meeting with a pleasant woman – I'm making no comment on how you should proceed, if you wanted to relax for the weekend there is a hotel a short distance away." I grinned. "They have a great dining room!"

Tom thought about it. "Sounds like a bit of an adventure. Make a change from built up London."

"I'll pay expenses." I said and realized my error when he said. "Not necessary, Pal!" and then, "Okay I'll do the trip for you."

"Thanks Tom, I appreciate it. I've contacted Alex and said my friend will be visiting at 5 PM on Friday evening, so she will be expecting you. The studio is closed weekends." I went on to outline the best route and precise location of the wood carving studio.

"I'll call round at your place Ricci and pick up the letter and blooms on Friday," said Tom on our parting.

I purchased a bouquet of roses and written the promised letter to Alex on the Friday. As I handed them to Tom I said, "Whatever you get up to don't forget to collect my commissioned gift!"

Tom smiled, "Wish me luck."

CHAPTER TWENTY-EIGHT

Tom stood in the large room hardly noticing the wood carvings around him. "Hello!" he called out. The side door opened and Alex appeared. Beside her Ben, the German Shepherd.

"Good evening," said Alex, noticing the bouquet of roses and the letter held by a rather nervous Tom. "You must be Ricci's friend, come to collect his commissioned work."

"Hi! Yes, Tom Barford at your service," he said and proffered the flowers. "From Ricci who regrets he was unable to make the visit himself." Alex smiled and accepted the flowers saying how lovely they were. Tom continued. "I am instructed to give you this letter which I am to recommend you read immediately."

Alex placed the flowers on a nearby table and opened the envelope. She read:

Dear Alex,

I very much regret I am unable to collect the carving personally. An old rugby friend has kindly agreed to journey out to darkest Sussex on my behalf.

May I introduce Tom Barford and a number of facts about him.

Single man since the passing of his wife several years ago.

Often said he would like to shake the dust of London and move to the countryside

Self-employed in a similar profession to yourself

Have known him many years to be a quiet, reliable, unassuming guy – rather like myself! –

His time is his own.

Should the foregoing not be of interest to you, kindly give him the carving and he will go on his way.

On the other hand, should you agree and obtain the impression he is a friendly, pleasant person, the following should be noted:

a)   He drinks coffee

b)   He likes dogs

c)   He would like to ask you out to dinner!

P.S.   you have my permission to read this letter out loud in his presence if you so wish!

Your Very Good Friend

Ricci

XXX

Alex carefully read the letter for the second time, then studied the well-built ex-soldier who stood before her, looking at her steadily.

"Ricci says you are self-employed in a similar profession to myself. So what do you do for a living?"

"I'm a self-employed carpenter," said Tom.

Alex smiled, "So we are both 'chippies'!"

Tom smiled and nodded,

"So we have something in common." Alex decided.

"Ricci says here that I have his permission to read this letter out loud in your presence. But I think it's your permission I really need."

Surprised Tom said "I don't quite know why he would write that, but I have no objection. It is after all your letter and your decision." Alex eyes twinkled.

"I will read it out," and commenced.

"May I introduce Tom Barford and a number of facts about him...." Alex read on, inwardly smiling at his embarrassment. She looked up from the letter. "Last paragraph," she said, and continued. "Should you agree and obtain the impression he is a friendly pleasant person, the following should be noted: a) He drinks coffee, b) He likes dogs, and c) He would like to ask you out to dinner." Carefully she replaced the letter in the envelope

Tom said "A, B, & C are correct."

"In that case," smiled Alex "May I offer you a drink – Coffee perhaps?"

"Thank you." Tom said. "And I truly like dogs especially German Shepherds, and may I ask whether you would care to join me for dinner?"

"As a friend of Ricci's, that would be lovely. Thank you."

CHAPTER TWENTY-NINE
Lakshmi

I removed the packaging enclosing the statue and gazed in pleasurable surprise. Beautifully carved. Against a background of designed sky a lake in which elephants and birds stood knee deep in slightly disturbed water from which rose the figure of 'Lakshmi' the Goddess of Wealth and Purity, the consort of the God Vishnu and one of the most popular gods of Hindu Mythology. The shapely female figure rising on a lotus leaf from the water the stem of which barely touching the slight waves. In the traditional way a profusion of bare arms extended, lotus flowers on the palms of the two forward hands. Beautifully carved in polished brown wood the features sharply defined, the whole triumphant efficacy.

I carefully removed and placed it against the wall on a side table. As I did so I noticed another, smaller package. Slim, oblong shaped. Mystified I removed the wrappings. About two inches deep, and eight inches long with a curved carved top of overlapping leaves I was reminded of a sepulchre.

Holding it in one hand I slid an overlaying cover slowly towards the other. As I did so a shaped wooden face and bare chest of a naked male with painted black hair, red cheeks, a wide toothy smile slowly sat up. I slowly retracted the curved cover which returned the smiling wooden figure to its horizontal position. At the same time the second vaulted cover moved slowly open, revealing in sequence the feet, bare legs, bare thighs of the male figure and as the opening increased a large wooden carved circular, red tipped penis rose vertically into sight. This object also returned to its horizontal position as the cover was closed. Again, beautifully carved I realized as I made the man sit up, lie down, penis raised, the sense of humour of Alex!

CHAPTER THIRTY
Lindsey

It was a pleasant day, a Sunday and I had decided to take a stroll in the local park having taken lunch at a local restaurant. At the side of the path were occasional benches. I was about to pass a seated solitary female when she glanced up from the book she was reading. We recognized each other. She smiled at me and said, "Hi!" I walked over to her. "Hello. It's the first time I have seen you in this part of the world. How are you?" she patted the seat indicating, and at the same time quickly closed the book and placed it in a shoulder bag.

"It's such a pleasant day I decided to sit out and read my book in the sunshine, and thank you, I am very well."

Now like all writers I am a devoted reader of books. Convenient to my home was a Public Library. Well, actually a Sub-Public Library. An off shoot of the main branch in the centre of the council area. It had the advantage of being near a medical centre with its weekly stream of visitors and patients as well as local inhabitants withdrawing and returning books. This library is competently run by my present companion, a pleasant helpful and quietly spoken woman, the librarian Lindsey. Over time and with her helpful smiling assistance we had become quite friendly in a sort of way.

So what are you reading?" I enquired. She laughed, I thought rather nervously, "Oh! Nothing special. Just a romance." She changed the subject. "Haven't seen you in the library lately."

"No. Well I am quite busy scribbling away."

"I admire you, a published author. I don't think I could ever write all those thousands of words, despite being surrounded by books and having so much time on my hands."

We chatted easily. The trees threw long shadows and the air chilled slightly. Lindsey pulled her coat tighter around her shoulders, "Time I headed for home."

"Do you mind if I walk with you, I'm heading in the same direction?"

"That would be nice, thank you."

As we began our walk a thought struck Lindsey. "How did you know which direction I was taking," she said in surprise. I smiled at her.

"I confess all. I didn't mind which direction I was being led into. My time is my own and I was interested in continuing out conversation. If you would rather I buzzed off I will of course do so." I didn't explain I had the impression she was lonely.

"Well, that is kind of you," she smiled at me. "I would hate you copying the bees and buzz off!" she placed her bag over her shoulder and seemed delighted when I placed her arm under mine.

Her place was a maisonette in a long road of maisonettes all built in the last few years. As I was about to say goodbye, she said "Come in for coffee," and assuming I would do so unlocked the door and entered. She paused for me and I followed.

The rooms were light and airy, quite pleasant. Lindsey headed for the kitchen and soon I could smell coffee.

I plumped for a comfortable armchair and smiled to myself on noticing the couch against one wall faced the television on the opposite wall. A book case was stuffed with books. On a small side table were several holiday brochures. In came Lindsey with coffee.

"Have you lived here long?" I asked, making conversation. Lindsey sat on the couch putting the tray on an adjacent table. "About two years it must be," she replied.

"Must make many friends here. I get the impression it is mostly young couples who are buying their first home."

"You are quite right. But in my case I'm renting. Could never manage the deposit to purchase. Yes, they are nice enough neighbours. Yet have little contact. I know the name of my immediate neighbour, I may say 'good morning' and 'good afternoon' to some of them but that is about it. They all seem to work hard. In the evening they return home and everything closes up. As you may have noticed there are no shops in the area."

Lindsey paused.

"Same with myself. After I close the library, I return and spend the evening quietly on my own."

"Don't you have brothers or sisters visiting you?"

"I have two sisters, both older and both married but neither lives nearby. We occasionally phone each other to keep up to date with family news but not much else. They have families to worry about."

"But surely you must have or had boyfriends, you are such a pleasant, intelligent and good looking woman."

Lindsey laughed, "I don't know about intelligent or good looking." She hesitated, then spoke quietly, "it is quite some time ago now. I had a relationship- I might add – a very short relationship- with an ever smiling man from Ireland. What captivated me was his voice. An engaging manner of speech with a lovely Irish lilt. Think Terry Wogan as a young man. At first I was enchanted. He did all the right things. Attentive, brought me flowers. I recall it was before I moved to this flat. I knew he liked to gamble, bet on horses, football, anything that moved. He moved in with me, saying his digs were filthy. We had only been together a few days when he told me he was in trouble over money he owed. He said they were hard men and had threatened to break his legs if he didn't pay up and soon. He looked really worried and asked me if I could help and if I did so he would stop gambling, get a contractors job with some friends and repay me. I went to my bank and gave him the five hundred pounds he said would clear his debt." She stopped talking. Then quietly continued. "The following day I went to work as usual. He was seated having breakfast. I remember he smiled when I kissed him. "See you later," he said. I returned home at my usual time. The breakfast things were in the sink, unwashed. I was thinking he may have gone to arrange to clear his debt. It was getting dark and I had an unusual feeling. I went into the bedroom and opened the drawers he used. They were empty. I checked the wardrobe where he hung his coat. Empty. Of course I then realized. He had gone. Probably back to Ireland. It was then I felt sick and knew I had been stupid." She looked at me sadly. "I have always been shy, rather introverted. I feel that affair made me more so."

We sat quietly. "That must have been awful. You haven't met anybody since?"

"Not really. Actually I am content with my life although there are occasions when I feel lonely. I read a lot, as you know." She laughed, "Sort of Busman's Holiday!"

"You don't mix much with people, other than within the library?" She thought for a moment, "No. I'm not good with small talk-"

"That surprises me," I interrupted. "We've been chatting for quite a while." Lindsey smiled. "I find you easy to talk to. You seem to be genuinely interested in what I say. There is something about you I find attractive. You are yourself quite an interesting man."

"So how will you be spending the remainder of this Sunday evening?" I asked.

"Probably read my book. How about yourself? What will fill your evening?"

"Well, I live with my Grandmother and would normally be spending the evening with her, but my sister has taken her home for a few days to give her a change of scenery. So I'm rather at a loose end. If you don't object to my company, I can stay for a while yet."

"I'd like that. We can open a bottle of wine. Obviously you don't live far and haven't your car to worry about. It will be lovely to have company for a change. Especially a nice young man."

I said, 'I see you have holiday brochures. Are you thinking of taking a holiday?"

Lindsey looked at me keenly. "You are quite observant – part of being a writer I suppose. I like to look at them. I've never been abroad, but then, I haven't done much of anything really. I am not very adventurous."

"I don't believe it." I said. "You read a lot. You enjoy books. Your imagination must take you along many channels. Including romance as you were reading today."

There was a sudden quiet rolling noise. I looked at Lindsey. "Was that your stomach or mine?" She giggled, "It was mine.

I've just realized I haven't eaten since a sandwich at lunch time." I stood up. "How stupid of me to take up your time like this. I will call a taxi, and we can go off to some eatery or other." I pulled out my cell phone. She put her arm on mine. "Ricci hold on a minute. No need to go out. I can rustle up a meal in no time. How do you fancy 'Mee Hoon'. Ready in half an hour, with wine, followed by coffee and biscuits?"

I returned my phone to my pocket. "What's Mee Hoon?" I asked. "Chinese dish of chicken and fried rice with soya sauce and side dishes," she answered. "That will be a meal I will owe you," I said. "Anytime," she said pleased. Sudden activity seemed to cheer her. "I will give you a hand in the kitchen." She looked doubtful for a moment, then smiled. "You can stir the rice. That should keep you out of my way."

The meal ready as promised within thirty minutes. We sat at the kitchen table. Pieces of chicken breast on rice with a salad on the side. Lindsey seemed a surprisingly good cook. "All those books on Chinese food," she laughed, "Simple dishes, really." With the meal ended and everything cleared away, we returned to the sitting room, with glasses of wine.

"We were talking holidays," I said when we were settled. She laughed. "oh, yes. Those holiday brochures." "And I was disagreeing with you, saying your imagination must take you to all sorts of places." She coloured slightly and then smiled. "Well it is true about imagination. I have a confession to make. The book I was reading wasn't strictly romantic. It was exotic." I said, "It was about another country?" The coloured deepened. "I didn't want to say it but, well, it was an erotic book." I grinned. "And you found it-er-interesting." "In a way. It takes me in a sense, to a different world."

I considered her words. "In the book world there has been a monumental groundswell of change, reflected in the overwhelming success of that book by E. L. James. I don't know whether it is a broadmindedness or a new acceptance of what are frank or erotic publications, but when you see what is now available to everyone on the internet, particularly the sexual content, not much is left to the imagination. It is a long way from Lady Chatterley's Lover. The comments from readers particularly from women of all ages, makes one wonder if we have been suppressing our urges, over the years, particularly lonely or unfulfilled women, or come to that, unfulfilled married women."

We sat for a moment, digesting my comments. "Being a librarian I tend to find a lot of truth in what you are saying." She fell silent for a moment and then smiled to herself as the thought passed through her mind.

I noticed. "What is it?" I asked. "the book," she said, the, "I was just reading about a tall good looking man putting his arms around this shy, lonely, woman when you approached and said 'hello'. I thought it an amazing coincidence. It was my imagination working overtime."

"How do you mean – your imagination working overtime?" We were looking at each other. I saw the blush starting at her throat, flood her face. Her gaze dropped to her hands. Softly she spoke. "I was imagining I was the lonely woman being kissed." Muted music from the kitchen radio switched on by Lindsey at the commencement of our meal drifted in. Yet there was a stillness. A silence, then. "And would you have liked my arms around you and kissing you?"

Lindsey looked up. Face pink. She whispered, "Yes!"

I stood. Moved to her. Placed my arms around her. Kissed her. She stood rigid. I kissed her again. Now her lips pressed mine, her arms moved around me. I placed my cheek against her hot flushed face. "Just relax." I whispered. "I'm not going anywhere." We stood together each enfolding the other, silent.

Gradually the pink of her embarrassment or nervousness faded. Gently we released, now a small distance apart. We looked at each other.

Softly I said, "What do we do now?" Lindsey smiled. "I would like you to continue what you are doing, but let me get my breath back, first!"

With drinks, we sat together on the sofa. Both aware of a momentous change in our relationship. She held my hand, shyly she said "As you rightly comment, these sexier books have become more popular. I have often wondered how it would be between a couple if, instead of reading such a book to herself, she read the descriptive passages out loud and her partner physically carried out the actions…" She stopped. Shyness overtaking. I looked at her smiling broadly.

"Some imagination! I can imagine it becoming extremely sexy or extremely hilarious!" I stopped talking. Then, "We wondered what we would do next. This seems like the answer." Quietly I said, "Would you like to try it?" She giggled "With you? Oh, yes."

CHAPTER THIRTY-ONE

We were in the bedroom. Lindsey had demanded I be elsewhere whilst she slipped into bed. She had pulled a sheet up to her neck when I joined her. I pushed pillows behind her so she was half sitting, half reclining. I could smell the heat from her body and the mixing perfume heightening the atmosphere. She was naturally nervous. She looked desirable but I wanted to be sure.

"Look Lindsey. If you are happy about this, then I am pleased for you. But I want to be sure I am not taking advantage of you." She stared at me clear eyed. Then once again she giggled. "I get undressed, my blood pressure increases, I'm looking forward to a heavenly bit of storytelling with a lovely man, who is asking me, are you sure! Ricci, I think you have been sent from heaven to take care of my dreams. I know I am terribly shy normally, but at this moment I couldn't be happier. To tell you the truth, I've always fancied you." She pulled me towards her, the sheet slipping and kissed me, her mouth opening as she did so.

"That's settled then," I said. I looked around. "So where's the book?"

She put her hand over her mouth. "It is still in my shoulder bag. Other things were on my mind. We could leave it in my bag for a while," she finished, the thought taking her.

She snuggled up to me. She put her lips to my ear. "Make love to me," she breathed.

"You can twist me round your little finger," I joked, my hands on her body. "It's not my little finger I want you to be twisted around," she whispered. "Such imagination!" I said. She was hot, physically. My fingers slipped over a smooth slim body. Her breast now in my cupped hand. She pushed towards me, hardening. Her teat swollen. I took it into my mouth, my tongue gently pressing. She pushed harder and I pulled and stretched it with my teeth. I released as she let out a low moan, my lips at her throat, kissing licking down towards her breasts, a hand cupping her sore teat as I found its partner, it becoming hardened, swollen, delightful. My hand travelled south brushing her skin lightly skimming slowly across her body. Her body jumped sharply as my fingers touched and brushed her hips. "Please," she whispered, "Please," moving her legs. I had forgotten something in the heat of the moment. "Hold still a moment," I muttered. "Don't go away!"

I slipped from the bed picked up my trousers and recovered condoms from the lining. I slipped off my boxers. That was when she spied my lower body. "What...?" It had risen, hardened enlarged. "Oh, my God," she whispered, fascinated. "Is that all for me?"

Contraceptive in place, I returned to her. Placing my arms around her body she could feel me against her inner thighs. She was wet and swollen even before my finger gently massaged her clitoris. Her breath was now irregular as though difficult to breath. "Please," she implored. I lifted above her, her legs now wide. With my fingers holding her swollen lips apart I entered her. The tip touching the soft suspended mound I moved just inside her, making small movements caressing her clitoris. Her eyes wide, lips apart she pulled at me.

She was whispering continuously, almost silently. "Please, please, please." I entered her completely. She rose up, nails digging in my flesh as she jerked savagely, calling my name, suddenly, as the force of a continuous orgasm racked her burning flooding body.

CHAPTER THIRTY-TWO

Lindsey was in the bathroom. I could hear the shower on. Still lying in her bed I was thinking of how her shyness had been replaced by a fierce craving, a want, the satisfaction of which had provided a renewed happiness. I was pleased for her.

As I heard the bathroom door close, I hopped out of the bed wearing just my boxers, and headed for the steamed up bathroom, passing Lindsey dressed in a bath towel. "Can't stop!" I said. "I'm bursting!" A moment later my requirements urgently met, I turned, and decided a shower would do me no harm whatsoever. Finding a large towel, I stepped under the shower and stickiness, perspiration and whatever else was on my skin became a thing of the past. Refreshed, I returned to the bedroom to pick up my trousers. Lindsey was sitting upright in her bed, sheet across her waist, breasts encased in a bra on show. Mentally I thought 'So what's happened to the demure, shy, retiring, quietly spoken librarian I once knew?' As I picked up my clothing, she frowned, tapped the sheet at her side, and said "Here."

"I assumed it was time for me to go," I said. "We have unfinished business," she demanded sternly but her face broke into a grin. "We do?" I replied.

"I haven't read to you. I thought that was our intention."

"We were side lined," I said keeping a straight face.

"It had been a long time; I desired you so much." She whispered.

"Are you saying you want me back in bed with you?" I asked. "Of course – be a darling, and get the book for me." So with the book and more prepared this time I returned to my appointed place. Lindsey leaned over, kissed me and took the book. "Remember this may turn out to be hilarious," I warned. "Perhaps I should get you in the mood first."

"And how will you do that?" she impishly replied. "Like this," I said, pulling her towards me, taking the softness of her ear between my teeth then with the tip of my tongue tickled the cavity. She squirmed, laughing. Pulling away from me, she settled herself and opened the book.

"So you read, I act. Is that it?"

"Yes."

" So it will be all in your imagination?"

"Er, well not exactly. We will see."

Half lying, half reclining Lindsey began reading. "His lips snuggled her ear, taking the lobe between his teeth."

"I've just done that!" I interrupted

"You must be psychic," she smiled and continued. "She felt his warm breath as his lips brushed her face following the angle of her throat, moving towards her parted, expectant lips. He enjoyed the smell of her, his kiss, demanding, exploring." Lindsey looked up. I complied with instructions and my lips reached hers. She responded to my kiss whether the kiss was demanding or exploring was difficult to judge, for both gurgled with laughter as our lips met.

Lindsey resumed her reading. "His head low over her body, lips sought her breast..." "Hold on," I said touching her bra. "This shouldn't be here." "Oops" said a laughing Lindsey, sitting up. "Allow me," I said slipping my hands behind her. The bra fell away, showing the indented outline. Lindsey fell back laughing. "Read that piece again," I said.

"His head low over her body, his lips sought her breast..." she lifted the book out of the way as my head came towards her. The laughter left her as my head lowered. My lips covered her nipple and a rush of desire ran through her whole body. Her breast swelled, the teat enlarging, hardening.

I raised my head. "What follows?" Her voice slightly higher, she continued, no longer laughing. "His hand moved lightly, slowly brushing her warm skin above and gently, below her navel...." "Yup! Done that," said I. She was having difficulty with her breathing, breasts gorged, hard. My fingers seemingly a delight, causing all sorts of sensation.

Her hands shook as she tried to continue. "His hand reached the rise above her expectant entrance, his fingers brushing the edge then curved, entered her hot wet…" "There is a small problem," I interrupted, as my finger slid beneath her panties. "Be better if I remove these first." She arched her body as I kneeled and slipped the damp panties down her legs. I took this diversion to remove my own boxers. About to slip on a condom, Lindsey sat up. "Let me," she said, holding out her hand. Realizing, I moved to the side of the bed, put the rolled circle on the tip, her fingers replacing mine as she sheathed the one thing she desired and bending, kissed it. Returning to her original position, she picked up the book, seemingly strengthened by the intermission.

She repeated the interruption. "His hand reached the rise above her expectant entrance his fingers brushing the edge then curved, entered her hot wet swollen labia, his head following pushing her thighs apart his tongue…" she dropped the book. My head pressed against her "Oh! No! I didn't reali…" her hands on my head pulling me as my tongue moved gently, across her clitoris seeking, moving… she moaned, widening her legs, hands now behind her, supporting her. She arched, calling my name, whispering, confused as the total unexpected delightful sensation diffused her burning body. With one last firmer pressure on her clitoris I lifted my head and moved up on her hot wetness. My hardened tip a nudging replacement pressed heightened delight against her sensual clitoris causing her to cry out. Tightening her hold on my arms, pulling, pulling. Slowly, gently at first I entered her fully. Gasping as I pulled back and then re-entered. We moved together quickly, urgently. Shudderingly unable to resist any longer she came, hot violent waves rocked her. Slowly her shaking spent itself and I pulled out.

"I hope you have finished that chapter." I said. "It's exhausting!"

CHAPTER THIRTY-THREE

Lindsey sat, a dressing gown pulled around her. I sat in shirt and trousers opposite. Each holding a cup of hot coffee.

"Do you have a passport?" I asked. Puzzled, she said "No. I've never needed one. I told you I've never been abroad."

I had been giving a lot of thought to Lindsey. Under all that shyness was a sexy, intelligent, humorous woman, who I think desires a little more out of life.

"How would you like to spend a week in Southern Italy?"

She looked at me astonished, "I don't understand."

"My sister's boyfriend owns a property not too far from Naples. He and my sister spend time there quite often; I know I can always use it when I wish," I said. "My parents were killed in a car around that part of Italy when I was a youngster and I have never returned there, but it was over ten years ago now. My sister who is older than me has been over there several times and keeps pressing me to go. To soften the memories, she says. So I repeat. Would you like to spend a week in Southern Italy? Doing nothing or whatever you would prefer."

Lindsey's face showed excitement. "How I would love that!" she exclaimed.

"Then you must apply for a passport. You may not need this in Europe but it's useful and it will last ten years. You will never know what the future holds, but with a passport you will always be ready. Should have it in a few weeks," I said. "Then we could fly out, rest up, see the sights."

Lindsey sighed. "Why would you do this for me – or are we now girlfriend and boyfriend?"

I knew this might come up. "Lindsey, a much as I wish I could, I'm afraid it can't happen."

She looked at me "You are not married, are you?" I laughed. "No. I'm not married."

"You have a girlfriend!"

"No." I laughed again. I have lots of friends many are girls but no girlfriend. The fact is I'm so busy with writing, the responsibility of Grandmother, much travelling in U.K. interviewing and talks to writer's forums. I'm pretty busy."

Lindsey sighed again. "Just my luck. Meet a lovely man. Probably never see him again."

"Hold on," I said. "I thought we were going to Italy."

She cheered up. "That will be lovely."

I said, "Although I haven't seen it, I'm told by my sister and the owner it is in a lovely secluded spot, a low slung bungalow type casa, with grapes in abundance. It has several rooms and a verandah. Of course you go with no strings attached. You have your own room and what you want to do is entirely up to you."

Lindsey looked at me archly. "Ricci after last night and the things you did to me you may have to lock your door." I laughed. "Well it is a romantic spot."

"This is extremely kind of you," she said quietly.

"My absolute pleasure," I said. "All you will need will be clothing for the week. I'll arrange flights and everything else. We will keep in touch."

"Now I must get dressed and wander home. Once you have your passport, contact me and I will set the ball rolling. Don't forget your sunblock!" Dressed, I walked over to Lindsay. She held me tightly, kissed me.

"Thank you for everything," She whispered.

CHAPTER THIRTY-FOUR
Colliers Wood

It was nearly three weeks later when a phone call from Catriona came through. "Hi Ricci, still busy with your scribbling?"

"Hi Cat. Nice to hear your dulcet tones again. So what is happening? Has some more come in?"

"Yep. Received info this morning- same bread and butter work. How about you, pick me up at my place? Ill fill you in on the job then. So how is your Grandmother these days?"

I gave her a quick update on Grandma's health and arranged to be at her place in an hour or so. Despite the long periods of boredom occasionally experienced I looked forward to this type of diversion. I batted away the immediate thought of Cat's presence having something to do with it.

Arriving at the house in Wandsworth, I gave a toot to make Cat aware I had arrived. I saw the door open, two female figures gave each other a hug and Cat strode over and seated, said, "Forward, MacDuff. Find a nice café, buy me a Latte and I will fill you in with our next job."

It was a clear spring day. Cat chatted about the security survey she had been doing. The owner of a rambling property – some big wheel in the business of a company studying illness in dogs, had been the subject of alleged vivisection in several red tops and had been the recipient of harsh, sometimes threatening comments on social networks and letters. An elderly man, despite protests of innocence, he had received death threats. For this reason, he had been advised to have a detailed check of his personal and property security which is where Cat came in.

"So how did it go?" I enquired.

Cat said "Oh, I carried out a detailed examination of each potential threat – security of access, security of location, property, person security and all the rest. He was a nice old boy with a couple of sons in the business who disagreed with just about everything. On my suggestion that perhaps their father might be better off living elsewhere with members of the family, each had excuses why they couldn't have their father with them, each saying the other son had more suitable circumstances. I suspect a lot of bad blood had been between family members in the past but it wasn't part of my contract to get involved."

We parked at a café with a reputation for decent coffee. Seated I studied Cat as she gurgled down a Latte.

"So what is on the cards for us this time?" I asked.

"Well, observation of some guys, is the key, once again" she said, as she wiped milk off her lips.

"Two friends who have radical ideas. Our people in high places had them under review but contact was lost when they changed accommodation. They have re-surfaced in our area and having been provided with what little is known of them we are a fresh team to write up details of their activities"

"So what is known about them?"

"Well they are originally from Luton. Usual story of decent parents and tearaways who disliked discipline. Suspected of being radicalized in a questionable mosque. Seemed to have got wind of being watched or something else, they decided to disappear, and for a short while our people lost track of them. They were found to have surfaced in our part of London. They have rented what had been a long closed shop in the Colliers Wood area. The frontage is on a sub main road. They have second hand furniture and household goods for sale. They have a Ford van and buy up the contents of houses they think will make a profit. Mainly when the inhabitant dies and the family want to be shot of the old furniture."

"So what brings them to our attention?"

"They were suspected of preparing to cause a bit of mayhem when in Luton, and as persons of interest we would like to know what they are up to since contact was lost."

"So when do we take a look at their set up?"

"When you have finished your coffee," announced Cat.

There was little traffic on the road when we reached the shop with second hand furniture on show. A single glass window with items for sale- most pretty ropey sprawled on a small forecourt. Adjacent was an antique shop, presumably so called because the items on display were ancient. Mostly low value, the type sold at boot fairs. As we passed we noticed the scruffy dressed owner of the antiques, perched on a rickety chair in front of his shop, reading the sports page of a newspaper with the aid of a large magnifying glass. Of the owners of the used furniture store, there was no sign. Further along the road having passed the block of shops, Cat said, "Take a turn off so that we can see the back of the shops." So turning into a side road we drove slowly, returning in the direction we had come. Ahead of us was a parked white van at the front of an open garage at the rear of the shop. Two bearded Asian males were lifting an armchair from the van and between them entered the garage which provided entry through to the shop front. Parked further up the road, keeping the van in view in our mirrors we saw them return to the van, pull out a large cardboard box which one balanced on his knee whilst his partner closed up the rear of the van. They moved out of sight into the garage.

"We should have no trouble keeping an eye on these guys," said Cat. "We can park in this rear road at several places for they would need the van if they leave the shop. In the meantime we can singly or in pairs take a stroll now and again along the main road and keep an eye on the front of the shop."

"So who are these two fellows?"

The older one who is probably the one who makes most of the decisions, the one with the thicker beard, is Mohamed Hanjook. The other guy, probably a couple of years younger is Nawaf Al-Mindhar."

Over the next few days we kept the place in view. Nothing of interest. Then the day came when the younger man came through the rear, entered the truck and moved off. At a sensible distance, we followed. He drove into the carpark of a Garden Centre where he took a trolley and loaded two of the bulky fertilizer bags each of thirty kilos, paid for them and loaded them into his van. He moved off but instead of heading back to the Colliers Wood store he parked in a branch of B&Q and again with the use of a trolley provided, purchased another two bulk bags of bagged fertilizer.

Returning to the store and under the gaze of two interested erstwhile shoppers he bought a roll of thick steel wire, a large pack of four inch nails, a strong pair of wire cutters and a pair of heavy duty gardening gloves. These also were dumped in the rear of the van.

As we followed on the return journey to the store. I said, "So what does he want fertilizer for? They don't have a garden." Earlier surveillance had confirmed that they both lived at the rear of the shop. We had watched as they purchased supplies of food and watched as each evening they moved the items on show back into the shop proper, closed up and we saw no evidence of subsequent departure other than a visit to a local mosque.

"I'm not quite sure what they are up to yet, but it looks as if things are becoming interesting," murmured Cat. As time passed we changed from my car to Cats and vice versa. Parked in various places, sauntered along the high street singly and together.

They didn't appear to do a great deal of sales so it was a new development when another larger white Ford van made its appearance at the rear of the shop. An old second hand purchase, with a small amount of rust it never the less became a matter of interest particularly when the fertilizer was transferred to the larger van.

Almost daily now, one or the other would drive the smaller van away, always to a different location, a garden centre, a 'do it yourself' store, wherever fertilizer in bulk could be purchased. Always just a few bulk bags would be purchased. Over the course of a week or two the fertilizer now transferred to the larger truck became a substantial amount.

Catriona had voiced both of our opinions, "Could be the basis of a dirt bomb," she announced. We needed to find out more of the situation. Difficult to do without forewarning the conspirators. What was really needed was a check inside the living quarters of the couple.

We had received no instructions to do so but this didn't stop us sitting in the car considering possibilities. In the meantime, a movement by the Asians became of interest. With the older of the two driving the smaller van they moved off in the direction of Tooting and Balham. Expecting them to be on another fertilizer purchase we followed at a safe distance.

Heading in the direction of Balham they passed the two adjacent open fronted markets in the Tooting High Street on their right. It was a weekday and the area was not particularly busy. A few side roads later Mohamed Hanjook turned the van and returning past the markets, slowed at the kerb, the pavement only between the vehicle and the open market fronts. The van then continued towards the Broadway did a left into Mitcham Road and left again, coming up to the rear entrances of the markets in Longmead road where market stall holder's supplies were unloaded. Again it stopped briefly, before moving away and took the route back to the second hand store, where they parked the van in its usual place and entered the store by the back entrance.

Parked further along the side street, I murmured, "Now what was that all about?"

Cat had no doubts. "I think they were doing a recce of a possible target area. It seems they may now be getting into a serious situation." Cat continued, "We really need to have a quick look inside their store. I think I may know how we can manage it."

I looked at her with renewed interest. "And how do we do that?"

Cat explained her thinking. "What we need is the two targets away from the store together, with us knowing where they are and how long they will be away. One of us will sneak into the store and take some shots if there is something unusual in there. Two minutes should be enough time. In! Take picture! Out! Simple!"

I wasn't so sure about 'simple'. "How about the old boy in Antiques? He may be half blind but he would know a potential customer in the forecourt if he spots somebody."

Cat considered the situation. "Okay. Think along these lines. The second hand furniture shop get a call about a home clearance offer, with limited time factor. It sounds profitable enough to take the two from the store. When they have taken off, having let the old boy know they are away for a short time, the phone in the Antiques shop rings and the old boy goes in the shop to answer it. This is the opportunity for you, say to enter the target's place, take a couple of pictures, and be out and gone before the old boy has finished the call. May be a 2-minute window of opportunity!"

I considered. It made sense, if it went well.

"I'll be the potential phone caller purchasing of something or other in Antiques, and keep him on the phone as long as is sensible. Earlier you phone and can be the nephew of a Grandmother who has passed away and you want to be shot of the furniture A.S.A.P. to enable the house to be sold. You are only available for the next two hours today and would they be interested. There are some valuable things available, such as inlaid tables, silverware, glass cabinets, etc." Cat paused. "There is one factor that puzzles me. If they propose to blow up their trucks with themselves in, why would they be interested in making money? They can't take it to Paradise with them."

I thought about it. "Perhaps their intention is to station the vans each end of the market, light fuses which would enable them to walk away and be clear before the material exploded. If they got away with it they could do more damage to the country at a later date."

"Is there a potential date of causing mayhem in the minds of these two, I wonder."

I said, "If the markets are their target, to do maximum damage would be at the busiest times." We looked at each other. "A Saturday," we chorused. Which would be in a few days' time.

"Let's try out your plan with the phone calls," I said.

CHAPTER THIRTY-FIVE

On the sign boards above each establishment naming the type of business conducted was printed the phone numbers. I picked a real road about ten minutes distance by van that would be known to the targets and allay any suspicion the call was bogus, but gave a number which I hoped would provide some confusion on their arrival. Making the call the older man answered. I went through the spiel as arranged, quoting, silver items, inlaid tables and the rest. He was interested. I mentioned I was pressed for time, he said no problem they would be there in 20 minutes or so, and would give a good quote. Putting my IPhone back in my pocket, we watched as the two men, had a word with the old boy neighbour and both drove off in the van. As soon as they were out of sight. Cat phoned the number above the antique shop. The owner put down his paper on hearing the buzzer and entered his shop. This was my cue to move fast. Crossing between armchairs and other pieces of second hand furniture I entered the shop proper. It was gloomy, but I could see in front of me a closed door leading into the rooms. It was locked. For a moment I was baffled. It was a normal internal house door which would normally require a larger type standard key. Not a front door or similar key. From experience I knew it was left either in the lock or certainly nearby. I ran my fingers across the door lintel above. With relief I felt a solid type old fashioned key. Fitting it in the lock, I pushed the door. It swung open. In the brighter light I saw a miscellany of items on the central table. Bottles of coloured liquid, wire cutters, a pile of wire segments cut into two inch lengths each, cut at an angle to provide point ends. Two cheap alarm clocks. Strong smells of hair bleach and acetone and diesel oil were very prevalent.

Standing in the doorway I used my phone to take shots of the rooms contents. I stepped forward and took one of the wire cuttings, slipping it into my pocket. Time to go. Relocked the door. Returned the key to its place on the lintel. Returning to the open front door I peeped out. All clear. Within seconds I was gone, walking casually down the street.

Cat looked at the shots I had taken, I passed the wire cutting over to her. "Nasty" she said fingering the sharp pointed ends. I also described the smells. Diesel fuel, acetone and peroxide.

"All these point towards bomb making in progress." Muttered Cat. "Their apparent recce of a potential target indicates to me action is not far off. Time to send all details and set up a safe arrest."

As we moved off I said "They may already have everything prepared and it's only a matter of setting things up. Maybe tonight. For they will need to prepare things while the streets are quiet."

"Good thinking," said Cat. "we will return this evening after I have passed on all information. I think there is sufficient evidence to hold these people. We will be back as soon as it is dark. Drive me home now. After I've passed on all info I will use my own car to return here and you do the same and I'll meet you here in this street." We checked and agreed a time to return. Having dropped off Cat I headed home, stopping briefly on my way to pick up a quick meal and a few other items.

*   *   *

When later I returned to the side road I found Cat already there. I parked nearby and joined her in her car. She had a pair of night glasses on her lap. "So how do we play this?" I asked. In such situation I acknowledged she was the boss.

"Assuming their original target is the Tooting Markets I think tomorrow, Saturday, would be their target times. I thing they would synchronize their watches and from what I surmise, I think they will use both trucks, the largest van at the front in the main road, pretending to have a break down and the smaller van at the markets rear entrance. There they will take the final act to prime the bombs with detonation to take place. Some minutes after they leave the vans, for I don't believe they intend to be around when the explosion takes place."

Cat had given a detailed verbal report to the Security Services with a full written report to follow.

The report was not understated, content of the rooms, the substantial bulk buys with no other evident explanation of their purchase, the recce of the markets all led to a legitimate conclusion. The information was acknowledged and immediately passed to the anti-Terrorist group of Special Branch. We, the surveillance team was instructed to keep watch.

In the dark early morning, two mini buses appeared, each with a full complement of police armed and in full kit, helmets, breast plates. One vehicle on the main road entrance, the second entered the side road at the rear. An unidentified car and two marked police cars also silently made an appearance.

Cat had provided details of the access door and kitchen door, explaining locks are run of the mill, and the room with the bomb making kit had doors on the far side to bedrooms which were unlikely to be locked. Every detail had been passed on. Well trained, operating efficiently, the group at the front of the store move into position, the leading cop ready to swing the heavy duty door opener.

On command they burst in smashing both the front door and kitchen door locks, crossed the room and charged through bedroom doors, and had the two bemused potential terrorists facing automatic weapons.

Into handcuffs. Fait Accompli!

At the rear, the second group of armed police surrounded the two vans. As the light improved two army members of Bomb Disposal arrived and proceeded to carefully examine and enter the vans. The detonators had yet to be connected, nevertheless everything was checked and rendered safe. A strong smell of diesel oil was noticeable when the back was opened, the whole operation had been conducted low key, with minimum of awareness by local inhabitants. Later a small crowd gathered as the two vans were hoisted onto transporters to be taken for forensic inspection. Several police remained at the scene, but the armed anti-terrorist element left as quietly as they had arrived.

Suddenly it struck me, "I'm hungry." I announced.

Cat immediately replied, "Me too, let's find a decent restaurant and have breakfast."

Greg MacBride

CHAPTER THIRTY-SIX

Later, seated and with full stomachs, we sat with coffees before us ruminating on the eventful morning.

"If this had been a film and not true life the director would have had the vans each with a mobile bomb outside the entrances to the markets, with lot of people milling around and the terrorists about to connect up the clocks to the detonators giving themselves time to vanish, with the hero guy stopping the explosions at the last minute with a subsequent chase and arrest of the bad guys. Typical cliff-hanger situation!"

I nodded my agreement. "But this is real life and such an operation must be nipped in the bud before any dangerous situation can arise. The safety of everyone is paramount."

Cat said, "I understand this operation is the eleventh this year stopped in its tracks by the Security Service and Special Police before death and destruction could take place."

I said, "I think this calls for a small celebration." I hesitated, then, "How about I take you for a meal this evening? A slap up dinner at one of the best restaurants." Her reply surprised me. "I thought you'd never ask." She laughed, "I'd be delighted."

*　　*　　*

Seated at a corner table I gazed appreciatively at Cat. As a dining companion she was enchanting. Dressed in a rather low cut dress, silver drop earrings swinging slightly guarding her smiling face, she was a long way from the original assumption of a dumpy lady in tweed.

I lifted my glass, "Here's to a successful bit of observation." Raising her glass Cat said. "It is nice to think we may have saved somebody's life."

Over a pleasant meal we discussed the events of the last few days. "I'm still in the dark more or less over what and how they used and devised this type of bomb," I said.

"The fertilizer was the key ingredient," commented Cat. "Strangely, as I remember from a lecture on bomb making the sales are banned in Northern Ireland and the Republic, but not in England. To be effective, it requires a substantial amount to be compressed. Diesel oil is added to improve the blasting effect. I recall a half ton bomb of this type was used in Oklahoma which killed a hundred and sixty-eight people and scores of injuries. A similar type truck bomb killed over two hundred in Bali. Most are killed by the blast but the addition of cut wire, ball bearings, nails and other bits of metal can substantially increase the effectiveness."

Cat picked up her glass of wine, took a sip and seeing I was interested, continued. "In Palestine normal light bulbs were used for making detonators." I raised an eyebrow, "How did they do that?"

"You break the glass, coat the elements with inflammable material. When heated, it can instantly explode a bomb. TNT requires real detonators. Many originate from thefts of ex IRA stores. Then there is Acetone Peroxide, widely used and available for its use for bleaching hair and acetone for nail polish, but is dangerous to make up. But it has the advantage of not being discovered by dogs. They can identify ammonal, plastic explosive, hydrogen, but not AP." She stopped. Smiling she said, "That's a quick course in bomb making ingredients. The guys we were tracking were preparing a real humdinger. Had it been used, it would have blown masonry and the market entrances sky high apart from the death and injuries which was the intention."

As I cut into my steak I pondered on our immediate future "So what now, I wonder?" I asked.

"Well, I don't know what or when we will be called on again," she said. "I expect we will have some free time for a while. You continue writing. I continue surveys!"

CHAPTER THIRTY-SEVEN
Lindsey

My laptop pinged.

I found a short but informative email.

'PASSPORT ARRIVED! PURCHASED S.S.S. (SEXY SWIM SUIT)

HAVE YOU BOOKS TO BE RETURNED?

LINDSEY'

With no great distance to the library and no immediate commitments, I called on this working lady. Pleased to see me, we discussed dates she would be available. She would be free in a week or so time. I promised to make the necessary arrangements in good time. Returning to my room I phoned Anne Marie. "And how is my charming sister these days?" I enquired.

"Good Lord, Ricci. And what made you call your beloved sister?" A thought struck her "How is Grandma?"

"Enjoying all the attention she is getting from Rupinda and yours truly," I replied. "I want to ask a favour. I wondered if you would ask Peter if his Italian 'get away' is available and if so could I rent it for a few days in the next week or so."

"Of course, darling, I'm sure he has no plans at the moment for us to use it. I will check with him tonight and get him to phone you back." She paused, then "I'm pleased you are going over to Italy. As you know from my previous description it really is a lovely restful place. I will get Peter to send details of the best way to get there and so on. He has a local old Italian friend who lives nearby and keeps the place in good condition. He will speak to him and also send you a key to the place. I'm sure you will love it."

"Anne-Marie, much appreciate it. I look forward to hearing from one of you."

In due course I heard from Peter, Anne-Marie's partner, received details of the best way to travel from the airport. "You will presumably rent a car at the airport for your time in Italy," explained Peter. "There are two road routes to Paestum. The best, more interesting but slightly longer road is the Litoranea road which follows the coast. Has signs to Paestum. You can't miss it. When you get there just west is a small hamlet called Campani, sign posted. You go through this place and enter a short dirt road which ends in the place you are looking for. A single story brick building, the front door facing you, fruit trees either side and vines along the side of the dry road. I'll contact my Italian friend, an old boy who keeps an eye on the place and arrange some food and drink to be delivered. You will enjoy it. Anne-Marie tells me you've been working too hard, have hit a writing block and feel a change of scenery will do you good! I will post a key to you tomorrow. Good Luck Ricci."

I had been away from Italy for over ten years, and to refresh my memory I purchased a book on Southern Italy with a good map enclosed. It gave details of places which, should be of interest to Lindsey. Whilst in the book shop I made other purchases of reading material.

The days passed. Lindsey informed of times and place. I ensured Rupinda and Grandmother were happy with my absence. So, with bags packed, passport ready, cash converted and an excited Lindsey, we took off.

The weather in U.K. was warm and pleasant when we left. The flight was relatively short and arrived on time. Leaving the plane was the first taste of a different land, particularly to Lindsey. The heat was like a buffer and took a while to become used to. A car booked, cases stowed and we were away.

The journey along the coastal road was the beginning of an enchanting journey. The smell of the sea, the white houses, vineyards on our left. I glanced at a delighted Lindsey, and smiled at my pleasure in her happiness. We passed by Paestum and turned as directed to the few houses of Campani. Passing through we hit the dirt road. Here I slowed to observe the line of grape vines on either side, and there in front of us was out destination.

Almost lost in a profusion of olives, mulberry trees and hanging grapes, its attractiveness was complete. Wide eyed Lindsey stood by as I unlocked the entrance door. A large room, cool and inviting beyond. Peter had made it a pleasant, comfortable hide away and it was now ours to enjoy. Kitchen cupboards yielded fresh fruit, bread, coffee, other drinks and food. Lindsey couldn't hide how charmed she was. Standing at the rear she could see a swimming pool although no great size it looked with the sun gleaming on the blue water most inviting.

She turned to me and throwing her arms around me said, "Oh, Thank you so much for this. I am overwhelmed," her eyes watered, I hugged her.

"I am happy when you are happy." I released her. "You get a cold meal and drinks ready, I'll get the bags into the bedrooms."

Taking a look at the bedrooms I decided to be greedy and take the larger one with the open window spaces taking in a view of the shimmering pool and a fantastic scene of hanging grapes and hills in the distance. Placing my bag in this room I then carried Lindsay's into the other room, just as pleasant but without such an attractive view. Each with a double bed, each neatly prepared for occupation. I noticed Lindsay's eyebrows raised at the distribution of bags and cases, but she made no comment.

In the warmth of the day we sat in the kitchen, quite large for the size of the property I thought. Then I appreciated this was Italy, its occupants well known for enjoying much sitting, eating and drinking. Lindsey had prepared a pleasant meal of cheeses, grapes, ham, Italian bread and various condiments. Long necked bottles of the local wines had also been provided.

Returning my glass to the table, I said, "this is the life. As a young lad I used to think this was my spiritual home."

"I can understand that. This is a beautiful place I think it is a wonderful, generous thought you had to give me this introduction to a foreign land." Lindsey squeezed my hand in thanks. She continued, "Apart from seeing the sights of the surrounding countryside I am going to relax, eat, grow fat and dream."

I laughed. "I would like you to enjoy the first and last, not so sure about the second." I paused. "I must take a trip to Naples whilst we are here. It will be an act of homage to my parents who were killed there in that street accident."

Impulsively Lindsey squeezed my hand. "Oh, Ricci. I'm so sorry, saying how happy I am, when you are thinking of your lost parents. It is so sad."

I stood up. "It happened. Some ten years ago. It's in the past. We are here in the present. Talking of present, I have something for you. Don't go away!" I said, breezily.

Entering my room, I unzipped my bag, picked out a couple of items and returned to an anticipating Lindsey. "Sun block." I said, placing a bottle before her. Also three books. "First book entitled 'Forbidden Desires!'" I placed it before her. "Next book entitled 'Enraptured'. And finally, a book entitled 'The Horse Rider'."

Astonished she picked up the top book. "I think you may find them of interest," I grinned.

"All for me?" she asked surprised. Then as she realized, her face reddened. "They are sexy erotic romances."

"Yep. Not only are they of a certain genre but are purchased for a purpose." She stared at me uncomprehending. For the second time I entered my room. Returning, I placed before her a thick writing pad, a notebook and a set of biros.

"I don't understand." Lindsey said, puzzled.

"Let's take our glasses outside and sit and relax by the pool and I will explain," I said filling our glasses.

We sat in the shade by the pool, the air heavy with a pleasant aroma of grapes. "You may think this too presumptuous of me," I began, "but over the last few days I have been given your circumstances some thought."

"You have been thinking of me?" she interrupted. "Why?"

"It was the thought of your evenings and perhaps how they might become more rewarding."

"My evenings?" she said puzzled.

"Lindsey," I said. "Let me put this in my own way, without being interrupted. You can kick me, tear me to pieces or tell me I must be stupid, but let me explain first."

She hesitated. Then, "Okay,"

So I began. "I've known you on and off for quite a while. Changing and discussing books over a period – and then, er-spending time with you at your place confirmed what I had always known. You are a kind, thoughtful, intelligent sensitive human being. Essentially shy, somewhat retiring, but underneath the shyness is a vibrant, humorous, sexy woman. A woman who is a first class librarian, knowledgeable about books but, perhaps being unaware of it herself is frustrated for she could be doing more with her life." I broke off looked at a silent, attentive Lindsey, and continued. "Being an intelligent, knowledgeable woman, I am surprised you hadn't thought along the lines I'm thinking?" I looked up at the blue cloudless sky.

"You should become a writer. Surrounded by writers works of every description, imaginative, well read. Bored with television programmes, each evening you could sit and reflect. Keep that notebook beside you wherever you are. Jot down reflections, thoughts that pass through your mind. At any time of the day. You love romances. A popular genre. You enjoy erotic novels. Let me tell you the popularity of such have soared in recent years. So write a romantic book with carnal knowledge. Write it just for yourself, if you like. Millions of books are started but never finished. But these days of self-published publications you can complete a book and see your name on it. You are an author! The book good or bad. You are an author! Something to be proud of." I stopped talking.

"But, like I once told you, writing thousands of words is too overwhelming." She was obviously considering my comments.

"In the course of a day dealing with different people you may not be aware but you will have used hundreds if not thousands of words. Seated at a desk you invent characters, often based on real people, with whom you discuss all sorts of matters. You have the advantages of deciding what you are talking about. I'm not saying writing is easy. It can be damn hard. Confidence wanes. You think you are no good. You hit a mental wall and so on, happens to many writers. It's a challenge. But I think it's got to be better than watching old boring movies on the TV."

Lindsey sipped her wine, reflecting.

"Just think," I said with a smile. You can sit and write a story line of a romantic, erotic novel using your – er- knowledge or knowledge you acquire."

"Plotting would be a problem," she murmured, "Without any knowledge of writing."

"I'm not so sure," I replied. "Your own experience could provide a basic story line."

Her brow screwed as she cocked her head. "How come?" she enquired.

"A romantic story line. The main character, the protagonist, is badly treated in some form or other, think of your Irish boyfriend, which shatters her confidence and she avoids relationships. Then a tall handsome stranger is met under unusual circumstances, which opens an interest. Which she plays down. Other characters support or undermine her thoughts of this person. So you have the beginning of a plot! It could be either a pure romance or develops hot sexual events, depending on your desires or intentions. Anyway, don't let my thoughts on your future disturb your enjoyment and relaxation of this place. But give it some thought. You will be surprised at the amount of assistance in plotting and so on that is available." I stood up, went in the kitchen and came back with a green and black swollen plateful. "While you are thinking, you can peel me a grape!"

*　　*　　*

The sun dipped below the hills. We had moved back into the sitting room, where I had dozed off. It had been a long yet interesting day. The driving in the warm air must have been more tiring than usual for I was now weary. "I'm tired!" I yawned. "I'm off to bed." Then "Is there anything you need help with." Lindsey shook her head. "I'm off to bed too." I ambled into my bedroom, removed t-shirt, trousers, shoe and socks and fell into the soft wide bed, comfortably weary. Within seconds I was asleep.

I have no idea what time it was when I became aware through broken sleep I was not alone.

"I've been thinking on what you were saying," she whispered, as her arm began to encircle me. "I thought I had better do some research!"

Greg MacBride

.

CHAPTER THIRTY-EIGHT

The heat of the day was beginning to circulate through the room as I drowsily re-awoke. Yet it was not the sun making my body damp with perspiration. Carefully I edged away from the naked, still sleeping form curled up by my side and slipping from the bed headed for the shower and its cooling clear water.

Shaven and refreshed I found eggs and ham in the kitchen and prepared breakfast for two. I was confident that my companion was in need of sustenance after carrying out her somewhat extensive 'research'. It would seem my comments of the previous day had sparked an interest in acts erotic- and she had yet to become conversant with the books on the subject. I remembered the lines I had read somewhere or other of the passion often hidden behind the shyness of ladies!

I heard the shower in action and greeted a damp haired cheerful Lindsey. "Buongiorno, come stai?" Good morning, how are you?"

"I'm fine, thank you. and how are you?"

"Considering my slumbers were demolished and my attention directed into another direction by a beautiful enthusiastic young woman I'm very well, thank you."

She giggled. Slipping into a seat as I served coffee and ham and eggs. "I had been considering the unexpected speech you had made of my possible future, as a writer. I wanted to show my appreciation of you thinking of me."

"Oh! So it was not any desire on your part to investigate my body parts?"

"That too!" she spilt coffee as she tried to control her shaking body and endeavoured to suppress her laughter.

Light hearted banter over breakfast moved into what we might do with the day.

"We could take the car and visit the famous temples and monuments of long ago Greek influence. A few miles from here. Why I think of it I might mention it is always advisable for ladies to have a head and shoulder covering of some sort. If at any time we intend to enter a house of worship respect is traditionally shown."

Lindsey nodded her awareness of the traditions. "I looked up advice on visiting," she said. "I would be embarrassed if it was indicated I was incorrectly dressed."

"Later we can find a place to have lunch and perhaps drive down to the beaches." The suggestion pleased Lindsey, and so we moved off in the direction of Paestum and its treasures of earlier dynasties.

And so the long past history of this part of Italy, its world famous Greek and Roman temples including the 6th century BC

Tempio di Cerere, (Temple of Ceres) and the Temple of Neptune (c 450 BC) which is the longest and best preserved of the temples and finally the Basilica. A 6th century temple to the Goddess Hera – oldest surviving monument, a fantastic twenty-seven stone columns reaching to the sky, were impressively observed.

On departing we found a charming restaurant run by a whole family and enjoyed a fabulous meal of freshly caught fish piled with zingy lemon washed down with a popular house wine.

By the time we had finished we agreed to leave the visit to the coast for another day and taking a pleasant drive returned to the welcoming vine covered accommodation. With a wine bottle accompanied by two glasses we relaxed in the shade of the house overhang beside the pool.

"It looks very inviting," said Lindsey a short time later, nodding towards the pool. "So dive in and enjoy," I replied. "Both of us," she insisted. It took just a few moments to change and slip into a pair of swim trunks and I was back at the water's edge when Lindsay re-appeared. "Wow!" I said appreciatively. "So this is your treble's purchase." Dark blue- almost black- about as brief as safety and respectability allowed she was stunningly gorgeous. Pleased with my reaction she raised her arms and dived in. I joined her. The water heated by the sun swirled around us. Inevitably, not being the biggest pool in the world we were close to each other – but Lindsey considered not close enough.

She dived, came up in my immediate front and drew me to her.

Anticipating a damp kiss, I moved closer to receive a spurt of pool water from a teasing laughing Lindsey. She turned away as I dived after her. My hands entangled in her bra support and unexpectedly they slipped from her breasts. She made a grab to save her modesty as I came alongside and cupped them in my hands. Like an eel she slipped round and her arms slid around my neck. Now we were standing the water at our chests. We kissed. Kissed again, her bare breasts hard against my chest. Dipping my head, I transferred my kissing to her nipples. Her hands around me tightened. Her breast hardened. I brought my head up. "Must be time for coffee." She whispered.

* * *

Acting like tourists which for the most part I suppose we were, we followed the trails visiting the many attractions of this part of Southern Italy. In addition, we made the journey to inner Naples in honour of my deceased parents. It was an anti-climax. Standing at the covering of a busy section where it occurred, watching the ever intermingling traffic, the disregarding taxis, I recalled the driving opinion of Italians as dare devil impatient brake/ accelerator drivers. We turned away recovered the car and left the noise, fumes and non-stop hooting for the peace of the sun lit countryside.

The days passed. Visits to Pompeii to see the amazing preserved presentation of ancient life with its Roman streets buried under the magna of molten lava of Mount Vesuvius. Trips past small villages and towns each with its own unique character to Salerno with its beautiful cathedral and mix of medieval churches, more of interest to myself possibly than my companion for it was virtually destroyed in 1943 when the 5th Army of Americans during WWII fought desperately, to maintain its landing just south of the city, with thousands of casualties before the landing was secured.

The days seemed to pass quickly. Towards the end of the week, seated at a local restaurant, cracking lobster legs, I said "Well tomorrow is our last day here. Have to start packing and hand in the car at the airport."

"I have had a fantastic time. You have been an absolute darling. I shall never forget this time in Italy." Said Lindsey.

"Have you given any thought to becoming a writer?" I asked. There are some excellent books on the subject.

"Yes, I am definitely thinking this could be the answer to my long lonely evenings. I would appreciate reading advice on how to start."

"Advice will always be available. I can hear your laptop burning up already. You could just give thought to creating a romantic fiction and see how it works out."

After a final romantic evening we made an early start. Unusually everything went smoothly. No queue at the car check in, not too long a wait at security and the plane left on time.

I dropped off Lindsey at her flat, promising to be in touch

shortly and returned home to be greeted by a smiling Rupinda and an affectionate Grandmother. "Darling, so pleased to see you."

Then the time bomb. "You secretive young devil. You hadn't mentioned your young lady was accompanying you to Italy." Anne-Marie had told us all about it." It transpired the old Italian friend of Peter had confirmed our arrival and had made typical Italian compliments about the unexpected female companion. It appeared all interested had assumed I had taken Catriona with me.

I stood there, smiling as if over a guilty secret. My mind whirring away. For I realized if I dared to mention my companion was not Cat I would be causing confusion in these ladies, with much explanation required. By good fortune my phone rang. It was Catriona. "Hi, I wondered if you were around. Need to have a chat. Can we meet up for a coffee?"

Temporary relief provided in front of Grandma and Rupinda. "I'll be round straight away," I answered. Closed my phone. "It was Catriona," I said knowing it was an unnecessary comment. "Can't stop now, we will speak later," and I hastily left their company.

CHAPTER THIRTY-NINE

We are seated in this smart café sipping coffee. Cat is animated by describing a TV programme she'd watched.

"Nice to see you again," she had said on meeting. I showed interest in the described TV programme until she had finished chatting and had her head over her latte.

The subject I was to bring up was rather delicate. I wasn't sure of its reception. I plunged in. Cat," I began. "I'm in an awkward spot." She lifted her head surprised.

'Sorry. What did you say?"

"I'm in a bit of a bind and I am hoping you can help me out."

"I don't follow."

I sighed. This was going to be tricky. "I've just returned from a week in Southern Italy."

"Lucky you!" she said. "So what's the problem?"

"I took a friend with me."

"Yeah? Man or woman?"

"A woman. Therein lies my problem."

She looked vaguely disappointed. "So?"

"My grandmother, sister and Rupinda have become aware of this companion. Because of our story of being a couple, they assume the companion was you."

She stared at me. Hastily I said, "I didn't expect them to be aware I had a companion. I hadn't thought it necessary to mention it for I was just helping her out. An Italian who looks after the accommodation, which is the property of my sister's boyfriend, mentioned a lady there in passing, to my sister's boyfriend."

I reflected, remembering the surprise I had felt when they had mentioned it and assumed Cat was my companion."

"So, who is this woman? Why did you take her with you to Italy?"

I tried to give an easy going picture and circumstances of having Lindsey with me on a holiday in Italy. "This lady, Lindsey, is the librarian at my local library. I had known her on and off for quite a while, when I accidently bumped into her in the local park. We chatted and I walked her to her place as it was in the same direction of my own. Unexpectedly she asked me in for coffee, I then discovered, although an intelligent woman she led a lonely life and because of an incident some years before, didn't trust men."

"What a shame!" said a cynical Cat. "Carry on."

I had the feeling this explanation wasn't being greeted with a great amount of sympathy. "I recalled the advice and other points Rupinda had instructed me about helping sad and lonely ladies."

"This is getting more and more interesting!" Said a catty Cat.

"To cut the story short, she said she had never been abroad. I said I was considering popping over to Italy and seeing the place in Naples where my parents had been killed in the car accident and, well I offered to take her and bring some interest into her life."

Cat sat silent looking at me. "How old is this woman?"

"Lindsey? Probably in her middle to late twenties." I replied evenly.

"Of course she is," said grim faced Cat.

I tried to move to the request I was needing. Cat beat me to it.

"You said you wondered if I would help you out of this 'awkward' situation. How?"

I tried to word it as carefully as possible. "The family holds the assumption that we- that is- you and I are an item. For that is what we came up with when we were hammering out our acceptable story line for out surveillance work together."

"So?"

I swallowed, and then, "I wondered if you would agree to letting them assume that it was you with me in Italy."

Cat's eyes, unblinking were fixed on my face. "Why?"

"Because otherwise they would know the story of us being boyfriend/girlfriend is not true if they knew it was another female with me in Italy."

"So this woman- What's her name, Lindsey? Is she your actual girlfriend?"

"Oh, no. in fact, I don't actually have what you would call a girlfriend. She is just somebody who I thought needed a helping hand."

"So you took her for a week in Italy!"

"Er- yes. As I said she had never been abroad before."

"Now I am confused. What was this you were saying about Rupinda advising you on sad and lonely ladies? That needs some explanation."

"I have never had to explain conversations with Rupinda to anyone before and indeed they are private and personal. You mentioned 'Need to Know' practice which is one of the reasons I still know very little about your own life. I will try and keep it as short as I can. As you know Rupinda is of Indian birth as is my Grandmother. We, were at one time discussing things Indian and we got onto the subject of the Kama Sutra and the reason for it being written. Despite the general thoughts of this book it is actually written on the subject of universal happiness. This book as you know was written several thousand years ago and many of its meanings are still being interpreted by scholars. However, the essence of happiness is providing same to others. Those suffering sadness or loneliness particularly ladies. The conduct of a gentleman towards such was described extensively by Rupinda covering good manners, compassion, attitude, sympathy – the necessities and desires of life- food, shelter, companionship, warmth, the fulfilling of desires and so on. Rupinda had explained that she believed I was a compassionate, generous and sensitive person who should be instructed in the art of providing happiness where it was required." I stopped talking. Catriona pondered.

"Let me get this clear. You took this twenty something Lindsey woman for a week in Italy because you found she was living a lonely life despite being a librarian and you felt sorry for her."

"More or less." I agreed. "But of course there was a bit more to it than that!"

"Such as?"

"Because of a swindling Irishman sometime before, she had retired into herself, so to speak. Had no confidence outside of the library, no social contact, extremely shy and withdrawn."

Cat gave it more thought. I had the feeling I wasn't doing too well.

"Did you sleep with her?"

I knew the question was going to be asked inevitably. "To be completely accurate she slept with me."

Cat had asked. Hadn't expected a direct reply it seemed for she looked shocked. "Have you done this before?"

Have I done what before?"

"Endeavoured to bring happiness to lonely ladies."

"Yes."

The frown on her brow increased. "How often?" She whispered.

"On several occasions."

"And members of your family have been unaware?"

"Yes."

She flushed. "What are you! A dirty old man? A con-artist? A stud?"

"None of those things. I have a clear conscience. On every occasion I have acted as an honest helpful person. I believe each is happier following my assistance."

"So you are not a rapist, then?"

"Don't be ridiculous. I have never forced my attentions on anyone. That has never been my intention!" I paused. Then continued. "The main reason I am proposing the idea of it being you with me in Italy is to preserve the cover for whenever we have a surveillances job to carry out."

Cat considered. "You may not be a pervert or whatever, but I have to say your 'hobby' if nothing else is certainly unorthodox."

"It is not a hobby," I said indignantly. "I help people when they need it."

"Whatever. Okay. So if somebody in your family asks me what I thought of Italy what answer do I give? First- time holiday abroad. Fascinating. We were near Naples. Can't remember name of places. Had a lovely restful time. Sorry to have to come back. That sort of thing?" she stopped, then continued "So I am to lie for you to cover up your friendship with this woman!"

"Cat," I said. "This is only to ensure we can carry out the special work we are doing without fuss. I am sorry if you think the less of me because I helped a woman to find a happier life."

She pondered my comment. "So if I was a sad, unhappy lonely woman, would you come to bring me happiness?"

"If I was aware that situation existed I would be delighted to come to your aid. Not that I can see it ever happening."

"Why not?" the question threw me for a minute.

"Well you have a companion. You are comfortable in your own skin."

"What makes you think I have a companion?"

"I saw you hugging her when I drove up to your place."

Cat looked surprised. Then she laughed. "My cousin. Who I live with. I was hugging my cousin! I think you have got hold of the wrong end of the stick there."

I flushed. "I just assumed it was your female partner. Naturally, having heard of your female tendencies." Her head came up sharply.

"What female tendencies?"

"Well I don't make anything of it. But you are a lesbian."

She glared at me. "I'm a what? Who told you that?"

Confused, I said, "John Street warned me."

She stared at me. "Good Lord. He was having one of his jokes." She grinned. "Is that why you have never made a pass at me?"

"Could be." I said.

"To think I was beginning to think you were something of a cold fish or liked men or something!" she giggles. "All this time you have been a companion to lonely women! I will have to look at you in a whole new light now!"

CHAPTER FORTY
Vernon

He is sitting in a wheelchair, a blanket around his legs, eyes shining as he recalls those days of over 75 years ago. He won't see ninety again. I've always had a soft spot for those who fought at the sharp end of World War II. With his son, nearing sixty, seated nearby, I had been noting down recollections of the old man's service now talking of Tunisia and the Battle for North Africa.

He was on about superstitions. "We had taken quite a few casualties. Been knocked about a bit. That's when I remember two particular things that were verboten!" He savoured the use of the German word, then continued. "There had been a time when some blokes had tried to make pets of tiny land turtles they picked up. They would carry them in their small packs. Don't know how the word got about but a number of guys killed were found to have these little darlings crawling out of the dead men's packs." The old man stopped talking. His eyes pitched on the past. "The word got around that having dealings with these turtle things could bring bad luck. So there would be a row in the section if anybody had one." He reflected on what he was saying. His son gave him drink. He then continued. "There was another thing considered to bring bad luck." He twisted the edge of the blanket between thin fingers. "Danny Boy! Don't know how that came about but the men wouldn't whistle or sing it. Certainly never when they were in the frontline!" As though talking to himself, he muttered, "I still wouldn't sing it."

I could see he was tiring. I rose, thanked them both for their time and an interesting conversation and took my leave.

Seated in the car I reflected on the talking of the old boy. His mind had seemed to be still sharp but I did wonder about the land turtles, and whether he had his facts right. It was the first I had heard of them. I would have to check the facts before I could use them.

I drove off. I was nearing Stockwell when I saw a builder's truck parked outside a row of houses. Two men were loading ladders on the back. The younger one was securing the ladders at the cab end but it was the man leaning casually on the rear of the truck that had my attention.

I parked, got out and walked towards the truck.

"Hi! Verne!" I shouted.

Tall, well built, he straightened up, turned, surprised on hearing his name. A big wide grin greeted me.

"Ricci! Well I'll be dammed!" He came towards me shaking

hands and punching me on the shoulder. "It's been a long time no see," he said smiling.

A thought flitted through my brain. "You got time for a beer?" I asked pointing to a pub across the way.

"Man, I sure have. A drink with an old mate." He turned towards the truck calling to the other worker. "Take the truck and leave it parked in the yard," he instructed. The younger man nodded and moved to the cab. As he drove off Vernon and myself crossed the road and entered the pub.

Once we had drinks before us, Vernon stretched his legs, saying "It's quite a while since we were drinking with the gang. So what have you been doing with yourself since we last met up? Do you still play rugby?"

"Haven't played for ages," I said. "I meet up with a few of the boys for a pint now and again but now spend a lot of my time writing- I'll have you know I've become an author!"

"Man! That is good news. Always knew you were interested in the written word!"

I lifted my glass. "And how about you- How have things been. If I remember correctly, the last time I saw you, you were going through a bad patch?"

Vernon sighed. "You are right about that. Split up with me partner when money got tight and little work coming in." He reflected for a moment. Then his dark face split into a smile. "All behind me now. Started up again with a new team and right now

I'm making good money. Have several teams of building guys working for me now with plenty of work coming in." He chuckled. "the only problem I've got is being buried under piles of paper and invoices since my secretary got married and moved to Birmingham." He laughed again, "Don't know any good looking blondes who are any use in an office and don't mind visiting working sites with me, do you?" He chuckled.

I looked at him in surprise, "You know, it so happens I know someone I think might be the very person." I slumped in my seat. "Maybe not, cos she's not a blonde. Actually the woman I have in mind is from your part of the world. Single woman in her thirties working for a firm in London and bored to tears." I looked at an interested Vernon.

He said, "A blonde- I was only joking! I'd be much happier having a woman with a mutual background. You say she's single?"

"And with a great sense of humour." I add.

"You say she's already got a job, though?"

"You know, Verne, without beating about the bush, I think you would like her and she would fit in nicely with the type of business you are running!" I paused, then, "If you are interested I could contact her and set up a meeting with you. She's a friendly straight speaking type and let's face it- your single and she's single. I don't think opportunities like this turn up all that often."

He nodded slowly, thinking. "Well I'm in and out of the office. Don't suppose any chance of meeting up with her tomorrow afternoon, is there? Tomorrow's Saturday. I got to be somewhere in the morning but if she could get to the office in the afternoon we could have a chat."

"Can't see why not." I replied. "Give me your phone details and I'll give you mine. I can ring you tonight and let you know. What time this date – sorry – appointment you want?"

So we chatted on for another half hour when he had to get away. He seemed very interested in what I had said. So when we moved out I ran him to his office and dropped him off taking the address as I did so. Shaking hands, I said, "Be in touch shortly," and drove home, stopping at a florist on the way.

It happened to be once again a Friday evening and getting dark, when I make my way to Vanessa's flat. I rang the bell. I could hear movement, then heard the safety chain go on before the door was pulled ajar and eyes peeped around the door.

"Good evening Vanessa! Remember me, Ricci?"

Her eyes widened in surprise, then a delighted smile. "Ricci!" Hastily, she pulled the door open and hugged me, beaming all the while. "Ricci!" she repeated.

"Lovely to see you again," I smiled as she opened wide the door. I entered, handing her a bouquet of mixed blooms.

"Oh, my God," she breathed. "These are lovely."

"Vanessa," I said. "I'm afraid I'm in a bit of a rush – have to see someone in an hour or so. Depending on your situation at the moment you may be interested in what I have to say." I looked at her, "Must say you are looking great – still that lovely smile- and I'm sure you've lost weight!" She was pleased with my remarks. "Put the flowers down for the moment," I continued. "We need to talk."

"About what?" She asked sitting on the sofa as I took the armchair opposite."

"Two quick questions. Are you still working in the bowels of a company, as you once told me, and do you have a boyfriend?"

Surprised registered. "Yes. Still in the boring job. No – no boyfriend."

"Right," I said, "I'll explain why I am here. An old friend of mine, parents from Jamaica years ago, is looking for a woman to run his office. He is in the building game and his secretary got married and moved out of the area. He is looking for a replacement. Says he is disappearing under a pile of paperwork. He says he needs someone who is adaptable, reliable and easy going who now and then will need to accompany him on site visits. He was telling me all this over a pint and I immediately thought of you! Another thing. Before we got to talking about the job he was telling me he split with his partner a while back and asked jokingly if I knew any blondes looking for a single guy. I told him no blondes but I know a cheerful, cheeky woman around his own age who might be interested. He perked up at the idea and even more so when I said she could be the one to sort his office out." I stopped talking. Vanessa was hanging on every word.

"And what is this guy like?"

"I've known him for years. A decent, hardworking friendly man whose had a few knocks and came through still smiling. As I said a few years older than me. First knew him through rugby. I honestly think you would both get on very well. Having told him about you and if you are interested in having a chat with him about the job – and maybe something more – he will be in his office tomorrow, Saturday at about two o'clock." I looked at her animated face.

"If you are interested, I said I would confirm the appointment."

"Oh, yes," she said. Could be my chance to get out from this boring job."

"And meet a nice man," I grinned.

"That would be interesting," she smiled.

I looked at my watch. "I must be off." I gave her details of the address and confirmed it to be in reasonable distance. I stood.

"I never thanked you for this necklace," she said fingering the thin silver chain about her throat. "Or your previous visit."

I smiled, ready to leave. "I don't think it will be necessary to mention our pleasant weekend together," I said.

"Perhaps not," she whispered moving towards me. We hugged and with a kiss and my wishing 'Best of Luck' I was gone.

* * *

She sat intently staring across the battered desk piled high in files and unfiled invoices. He looked across at her, her gaze fixed on his. "Well, I've told you about the job, something about myself and you have filled me in about yourself." He leaned back, the chair creaking with his weight. "So what do you think?"

Vanessa, with a straight face, "about the job as secretary or about a date?"

"Both," he answered.

"Sounds good to me," she said, "Both!"

*   *   *

It was a couple of weeks later seated in my study I was able to check out the old soldier's story of the tiny land turtles and was pleased he was pretty accurate. He had been talking of his experiences of a long time in his past. Where he got the names of the creatures as tiny land turtles is impossible to say, for he had been referring to tiny tortoises, possibly the spur-thigh Tortoise (Testudo Graeca) one of the smallest yet with a life span exceeding his own! An example of things that can remain in the memory!

CHAPTER FORTY-ONE
Pinky

We were in a pub near Cat's accommodation. I was on soft drinks whilst Cat cuddled a white wine when my iPhone buzzed. It was Anne-Marie in a troubled voice. She spoke urgently. "Ricci, can you help me out? I'm worried about Pinky."

"Why? What's the problem?"

Quickly Anne-Marie filled me in about her best friend. It seemed Pinky had been besotted with her boyfriend- really taken to him. But now Anne-Marie was telling me they had split.

"He had been two timing her and she only recently found out. He then told her he preferred the other girl and was dumping Pinky. She is heartbroken. She has left her job, was living in his flat and has now gone to live with her older sister in Southfields. She seems completely lost," says Anne-Marie. "She is hitting the bottle despite pleas from her sister and seems to have gone crazy. Her older sister, Sandra, does two jobs to bring in enough to pay for the two bed flat. Evenings she works in a pub in London.

Pinky spends a lot of her time in bed during the day and the evenings in a dodgy singles bar near Sandra's flat, getting drunk."

Anne-Marie stopped for breath. Cat was watching me. Anne-Marie continued. "She keeps ringing me in tears and she has just told me she is in this bar and she really is sounding in a drunken state." Anne-Marie stopped, then, "I'm too far away to get to her but I know you are much nearer and wondered if you could see if Pinky is okay. I can give you the address of her sister."

Cat leaned over, having heard me repeat the address. "I know where that is. No distance from here."

I checked with Anne-Marie. "Do you know the whereabouts of the bar?" I asked my sister.

"I only know it's not far from where she is staying and it's called 'The Crocodile."

Cat said, "I know it."

"Okay, Sis. I'm with Catriona, it's not too far and we are on our way!"

"Thanks Darling. Let me know how she is, later."

With Cat giving me directions I drove to the bar.

In the darkness we walked towards the bright lights. Pushing open the door we entered immediately noticing the warmth and fugginess. It was late evening. I looked around. A number of men were chatting up several of the woman. But no Pinky. I spoke to a middle aged barman. "Do you know a girl named Pinky who was in here tonight?" The barman was polishing a glass. "Pinky? Yes, I know Pinky! You have just missed her. Left with a guy I've not seen in here before. She was in a bit of a state. Said he was seeing her home."

Returning to the car we headed for Sandra's flat. We were walking towards the door when I heard a scream from the flat. It seemed to fade away into a gurgle of nothingness. We approached the front door. Simultaneously it was yanked open. A heavy breathing, squat, red faced middle aged man was confronting us. I saw the bloodied muscle of the hand holding the door edge had torn blooded skin. Three parallel blooded scratches on his face. For a second he halted, then charged at us in a bid to leave. I cannoned into Cat before moving towards him.

"Not so fast," I said. He raised a fist. I saw it coming and punched hard to the pit of his protruding stomach. The breath hissed out of him. I connected with his jaw. He tripped as he went down his head hitting the step.

Cat bounded past me as I pulled his unconscious body into the hall. I heard a cry of dismay through the open door of a bedroom. "Ricci! Quickly!" Called Cat.

Pinky was sprawled across the bed her skirt pulled up, blouse torn. It was then I saw her face. Her left eye was closed in the centre of a purpling bruise. Blood in rivulets marked lines from her nose and a split lip. The right side of her face was bruised and swollen. The only eye with which she could see stared up at me as I lifted her head into my arms.

Cat was on the phone, angrily calling an ambulance and the police.

She took another horrified look at that beaten face, found the kitchen and come out with a large bladed knife. Squatted by the recumbent form of the thug whose eyes were flickering open. She placed the point of the knife on his throat. "You move and I will f**king kill you!" she said, and meant it.

CHAPTER FORTY-TWO

The ambulance was on its way to the hospital when Sandra arrived confused to see a police car outside her flat. We were detailing our knowledge of the assault to an elderly policeman when she entered the sitting room. I had never met Sandra and the shock of seeing her place full of police and strangers dumfounded then petrified her. "What's happened? Where is my sister?" she asked, lost in confusion and dread.

I stepped forward, introduced myself, explained my connection with her sister and then the news of the attack. For a moment she seemed about to faint. Cat took her arm and seated her before she fell. She sat, white faced as the police gave up to the minute information.

"I must see her," she trembled.

"Of course," I will take you to her," I said. And with an agreement to provide a written statement to the police the following day, Cat and I took Sandra to the hospital. I had given an account of the situation to a horrified Anne-Marie who said she would take time off from her job the following day and visit her friend and give support to Sandra, who was staying the remainder of the night by Pinky's hospital bed.

At some point, and with no further assistance required of us, I returned Cat to her home and drove myself to Grandma's house.

*   *   *

The following day I picked up Cat and we visited the hospital. There we found a tired, exhausted Sandra and my sister, Anne-Marie. Whilst Sandra sat by the sedated puffy faced Leona as Sandra correctly referred to her sister, we sat with Anne-Marie in the passageway holding machine produced paper cupped coffee, hearing the outcome of the previous night.

'The staff say her cheek is fractured, but fortunately her eye will be unharmed once the swelling has reduced."

Cat asked quietly, "Was she raped?"

Anne-Marie replied, "No. It may have been a near thing but she was actually menstruating and had a tampon in place. It was as she was drunkenly fending him off that he realized it. Probably what made him so furious."

"What about the thug?"

"Seems he has been done for assault before. The police are charging him with attempted rape, aggravated violent assault and other charges. Should go down for several years!"

A passing nurse was asked if we could visit Pinky. "For a short while and just two of you at a time," she replied and stepping into the room had a word with Sandra who came out, joining us. Anne-Marie re-introduced Cat and myself and Sandra recalled our earlier meeting. I asked if we could see Pinky for a few minutes and we left Sandra in the company of my sister. We stood by her bed. I took her hand in mine and felt her squeeze my fingers. The staff had done a clever job of bandaging her face where possible. One eye was still closed but the other gazed at me as she smiled through her damaged lips. "Hi!" she whispered.

We found Sandra and Pinky's Mum was coming down today and will stay at Sandra's for a couple of weeks. Later Anne-Marie carefully hugged her friend, saying she would be down again later but had to get back to Peter and her job.

Thus we left what had been a distressing period, being aware that, despite the care and love of her friends and family, it may take a long time before Pinky truly recovers..

Greg MacBride

CHAPTER FORTY-THREE
Mitcham

It was Cat on the phone. I wasn't too certain about our new found relationship but this was a business call. "Ricci? Hi! We have a new job being lined up. How about you pick me up and we will have a chat about it?"

"Fine." I replied. "Be there in the hour." We seemed to be getting into some sort of a routine. Call from Cat. Pick her up. Go for coffee. Hear the job requirement.

Seated in the café I said, "And what do we have this time." Cat seemed relaxed. "Usual thing. Want us to keep an eye on a couple who are sharing a flat in Mitcham. Seems they are originally from Brixton. Plenty of street cred. Known to have belonged to a street gang with an unpleasant reputation. One is a Brit black guy who has changed his name from Alfred Nobbs to be known as Mohd Maged. His side kick is a white thug born William Surtees who now demands to be called Kalid! Both go around often wearing headgear and professing to be followers of

Mohammed. Started attending a mosque, although they weren't all that welcome and gave it up. Have confused thoughts. Suspects want to become martyrs and join others in Paradise. Not very bright but because of that could become dangerous."

"So why don't they arrest them?"

"They were pulled in by the local cops when they were involved in a gang street fight which included a pistol and knives near Brixton a while back. By the time the police got there two guys were on the ground with stab wounds and another had a bullet in his shoulder. Our guys were suspected of being in the thick of it but typically those who were being held by the cops professed to know nothing. All the police gathered was that our heroes are regarded as nutters, who hate the police and any type of uniforms or discipline. Bunked off school often when younger. Parents have no control over them. Suspected of doing a bit of burglary. The white guy gets disability payments for alleged depression and anxiety problems. Moved to a Mitcham flat when they found they had made too many enemies in their local area. Interest has arisen because the grape vine has thrown up the suggestion they are looking to pick up some shooters. They know there are plenty about if you know the right people. The problem it seems is they are too short of cash at the moment."

Cat leaned back having filled me in on the information available. "I've been given their address. Though we might take a peep and see what we've got."

"This could be interesting," I said as we prepared to move out.

"But not as interesting as Italy!" cat said slyly. I decided to ignore the comment. Just hoping she would soon get it out of her system.

Moving into Mitcham we found their address. One of a number of old two- up- two- down properties off the Church road area. We were pleased to note that the short street of flat fronted properties was a cul-de-sac which meant observation did not necessarily be required within the road itself, offering various viewpoints elsewhere.

We parked away from the road and with a clipboard in our hands wandered into the street of houses, appearing to any inquisitive eyes we were probably from the local council. The general impression, it was rather a down at heel sort of road. The front doors led directly into the living room. Several, obviously purchased from the council by the original occupants had nicely decorated fronts. These stuck out prominently from the majority. The persons in which we had an interest occupied one of the scruffier houses. In front was an old car, in need of a clean. Cat jotted the registration number down. Reaching the end of the cul-de-sac we found the street had been boxed off by the back end of a paint company which accounted for the mixed industrial smells. Satisfied there was no exit at this end we retraced our steps. We studied the photographs of our targets. The details of the black guy showed him to be big boned narrow chested, gangling looking young man with black hair. A close shaved curly design at the side of his head. His friend, white, shorter, heavy chested with a head above a thick neck. Short cropped hairstyle.

"Pair of beauties," I murmured.

"Pair of potential dangerous beauties," corrected Cat.

The following day we chose an inconspicuous parking spot which enabled us to see the front of the house at an angle sufficient to be able to notice any one entering or leaving. We settled in for an observation of several hours. Practical Cat provided coffee and sandwiches. I had an impression that following the talk of Italy and my wrongly held assumption of her sexual preferences, an easier relaxness, a noticeable awareness of each other had become the norm.

Cat was about to make some comment as she sipped her coffee but stopped suddenly.

A slight figure wearing a hoodie fleece had just exited from the house head down, hands in pockets he walked to the end of the street turned left and moved towards the shopping areas at a distant road junction.

"I thought there were only two guys in that house," muttered a surprised Cat.

"Could be just a visitor," I commented.

This seemed to be unlikely. For half an hour or so later we saw the same man returning, a plastic shopping bag hanging from a hand stuffed into a pocket. Cat had a good look at the approaching figure, using the binoculars.

"Asian, maybe Chinese," she studied the man as he turned into the street. "He's got a key to the house," she murmured, as the hooded slight figure entered.

Putting the binoculars by her side, she said, "Now that is interesting. What reason would our guys have in an Asian apparently sharing the rooms. Two bedrooms, a sitting room and a kitchen. In these old houses the bathroom could be on the ground floor through the kitchen." she continued. "One bedroom probably at the front of the house, second bedroom at the rear."

"Can't imagine all three sharing a bedroom, but you never know if we assume the two guys have one bedroom with maybe two beds. The Asian would probably have the other one."

"With the guys we are interested in being the tenants they are maybe charging this guy rent for a room." With their suggested intentions of obtaining guns and knocking off a few uniformed guys I wouldn't have thought they would want strangers around them. Besides, Asians don't mix easily with other nationalities."

"Bit of a puzzle," reflected Cat.

Nothing else of interest happened that day. But the following morning we saw the 'boys from Brixton' as we had dubbed them, leave the house, enter their car, and head into the traffic. Following at a distance we found we were moving through Tooting then Balham and into the direction of Brixton. Near Brixton Market, they parked in a side road and entered a local pub.

Leaving Cat with the car I pushed open the bar door. Half a dozen punters sat at tables, several reading papers over a pint.

I ordered a drink and moved to an empty table, sitting where I could keep our lads in view. They were initially hunched at the bar with a beer. Within a few minutes a tall, square faced middle aged guy strode into the bar nodded to the two men, took a beer and the three of them moved to a table in an alcove.

Looking at my watch, I finished my drink, stood up, and left. Meeting up with Cat I explained, couldn't hear much of the conversation other than the man's name on greeting was 'Ted' and said "If you can take a couple of shots of him I will identify 'Ted' when he leaves the pub. Half an hour later he came out alone into the street. Cat successfully took several shots. I then followed the man until he entered a car of which I took the number.

"We will give our targets a miss for the rest of the day," Cat commented when I returned to her. "Let's get these photos to our people and see if he is known."

Later Cat rang me. She had flashed the photos to somewhere in London. Ted had been identified. Full name was Edward Silven, an ex-armourer in the Armed Forces, with an address in Streatham, age 56, known to have converted various types of weapons including starter pistols into active firing weapons. Had contacts with German, Russian, East European gun dealers. Had served a short sentence sometime in the past. Was regarded by criminal elements as a reliable and canny provider of weapons – at a price.

We sat at a coffee bar. Different places, different qualities of coffee. This one was quite pleasant. We quietly discussed the ex-armourer and our men of interest.

"Seems to me pretty evident they are thinking of purchasing some sort of weaponry," I said. This guy 'Ted' wouldn't be wasting his time with a couple of thugs if he didn't think there was money to be made. Have any idea of the cost of guns these days?"

Cat surprised me. "As a matter of fact I do. We had a police expert on the subject of illegal weapons just before I left the Corps. As I remember he said Glock nine mille automatics are available at around 1500 pounds. Russian eight mille Baikal self-defence pistols converted to fire nine mille ammo requiring a larger barrel which will take a silencer, 1000 pounds to 1500 pounds. He said weapons are flooding in from Afghanistan, Iraq areas. Also from eastern European countries especially Poland and Romania. Kalashnikov rifles are available at a hefty price. German made revolvers in their hundreds which are actually blank firing pistols can be converted with new cylinders fitted which are bought for 60 pounds, add 30 pound for conversion, sold for 700 to 800 pounds. Good profit. Ammo is always kept separate in unusual places. If caught with ammunition as well as a weapon the guilty will get a heavier sentence.

"Most illegal guns are of course used by criminals. Guns are not usually kept at home. Usually kept by an old man with no criminal record several miles away for a small fee."

The continued issue of knowledge never failed to impress me. "So where have the 'boys from Brixton' obtained or are obtaining that kind of money?" I queried.

"If they are thinking of just one hand gun they will at least need 700 pounds to include some ammo. If they are thinking a gun a piece, the cost must be around 1500 pounds. Unless they rob a store which seems to be unlikely. I'm puzzled how they are going to make that amount of money."

We didn't know it but the answer had been in a way staring us in the face. In the next few days we believed we had cracked it.

CHAPTER FORTY-FOUR

Sitting in the car we saw an interesting sight. A large expensive looking motor swung into the street and turning at the end of the cul-de-sac curved around to stop outside the house of interest. Out stepped two Asian males, a third remaining behind the wheel. Cat was busy taking shots of the car and the occupants.

The two men entered the house shortly returning with several large black plastic bags evidently fully loaded. One of the men returned to the house for a few minutes. Returning he entered the car which then drew away.

Later, as we sat there the small Asian figure in his hoody fleece left the house and once again walked in the direction of the shopping centre. A short time later he was returning, a shopping bag by his side. Cat muttered, "Stay here," as she scrambled out of the car. Crossing the road, she walked past the Asian who took no notice of her. Cat walked another fifty yards then turned and came back to the car. Meanwhile the Asian had disappeared inside the house.

"What was that all about?" I asked.

Cat looked at me, a big smile on her face. "I think we've cracked it!"

"How come?"

"I think they have a cannabis farm in the house."

"Cannabis plants?"

"Yes! I caught a whiff as I passed the Asian. I think it makes sense."

I stared at her. "So if they are growing plants they would have to have special gear in there and someone to take care of the heating, strong lighting and watering!"

"The Vietnamese are the main workers in this business and the little guy- maybe an illegal migrant- is the guy who looks after the plants. The guys we saw in the large car are probably enforcers who collect from various 'farms'. They would be paying good money to our suspects for they are providing a perfect front of a normal inhabited house."

* * *

My iPhone rang. It was Catriona. "Ricci, Hi. Look, I have to tell you I'm not feeling all that good today. I was wondering if you would keep up the surveillance without me holding your hand, whilst I rest up at home."

"Holding my hand? That's cheeky! That may be an interesting idea for the future though. So what has caused this sudden illness?"

Cat was quiet for a moment. Then, "Woman's problems. Heavy period. But nothing for you to worry about. It's not catching!"

I was annoyed with my stupidity. "Oh, Cat. I'm sorry. I should mind my own business. Of course I can handle things on my own. Just give me a ring when you are okay. I apologise for being an idiot."

"That's okay. You can't help it! See you in a day or two. Be good! I will phone soon!"

I sat listening to the quiet local news on the radio. Some talk of a freedom of the city march past by an infantry regiment in Kingston. I pondered on whether I should maintain surveillance on the suspects. A thought came to me. I had a better idea.

I moved off in the direction of Streatham. I was about to pay a surprise visit to Mr. Edward Silven, the provider of - weaponry to the underworld. I was aware this was not our normal 'watch and report syndrome'. Catriona would have possibly vetoed my idea. Today maybe my only chance. If I went about my visit the wrong way I would likely be suspended from further operations. Which would mean no sitting alongside Cat and noticing her increasing friendliness. I traced the address and found it to be a small shop type in a narrow lane and off the main business life of Streatham. No sign. It appeared to be closed. A bell with a small note indicated entry. I pressed the bell button and could hear it respond internally. A moment later I heard the door unlock and I recognized Ted standing looking at me enquiringly.

I went into the reason for my visit.

"Mr. Silven. Without naming names at this moment I have been advised you may be able to help me out of a little difficulty I am experiencing. It is in the area of your expertise and I can assure you that a short discussion could be to your financial advantage."

He stood fore square in the doorway. Studying me. "And who are you?" he asked.

"For the purposes of this visit I would like to be known as Martin."

"Are you connected with the police?"

"Good Lord, No. Actually I am a writer. But this will have little bearing other than on a situation I would like to confide in you. Five minutes of your time is all I require. I can assure you I am completely harmless and once I have had the conversation you will not see me again."

"Are you carrying?"

"Carrying? Oh, I grasp what you mean. Good Lord, No. I am quite happy to be searched by you. No weapon, recording aid, or any such items. I just want to speak to you. I think it could be to your financial benefit. Would you mind if I called you 'Ted'? for this would indicate I am aware of your special services."

He looked at me. Nodded. Pulled open the door. "Five minutes," he said. "Thank you," I acknowledged. I entered the room. More of a workshop. A musty smell of oiled metal, the pungent odour of spot welding. He pulled out wooden chairs either side of a battered bench.

"Start talking," he said.

"I understand you are ex-military, having served for a number of years in one of the Anglian Regiments. A former armourer whose expertise is with the repair and otherwise of all types of small arms." Ted looked. Said nothing.

"I will get straight to the point. You recently had an enquiry as to the possibility of obtaining hand guns from a couple of young men, one of black origin and his friend a thick set, white man." My listener continued to look and say nothing. "I am not aware of whether they explained why they were interested in such a purchase. But I imagine they were more interested in what might be available and more importantly at what cost. There is an awareness in some quarters, of your ability to provide weapons of various types to – shall we say persons who deal in criminal activities. I would like you to understand I have no interest in such persons."

I paused, then, "I am aware the military authorities may be considered to have dealt harshly with you. putting that aside, I am sure you had good friends during your time in the armed services"

"Just what is this leading up too?" he broke his silence.

I plunged in. "The two young men seeking to purchase hand guns are wanting them for terrorist purposes. It is unlikely they made you aware of the fact. Probably indicated the possible purchases were for criminal use." I looked at him, he was now showing interest.

"I happen to know it is their intention to kill members of the armed forces. Indeed, I believe I know the precise unit, which is a regiment of infantry not unlike the one to which you belonged. It is very probable they will be making contact with you again in the next few days. For they will have enough money to carry out the purchase of weapons. You will be aware the Terrorist threat is quite real. Whatever the reasons these two men are known to have converted to Islam and are extremely dangerous."

"I will be blunt." I continued, "I can appreciate your possible indifference to providing weapons to the underworld, they tend to use them on each other. But I have met up with you today, for I believe the death or injury to others, particularly those in military uniform, as an ex-army man, would be an entirely different matter." He nodded slightly.

"I have, I believe, a simple solution to this problem, whereby you make a satisfactory sale and you are paid your usual substantial profits and the intention of Terrorist action is thwarted!"

"How come?"

"These young men, apart from everything else are not very bright, have little knowledge of hand guns other than knowing to point and pull the trigger. On the other hand, you know how to activate and de-activate such weapons. For instance, you would know ammunition can be, with care, taken apart and the explosive element removed, making the ammo appear to be active but cannot be fired. Active weapons can have their firing pins filed down avoiding impact on the cartridge. Incorrect ammunition which will fit the breech which would or would not explode in the barrel can be managed. I'm sure you will be aware of many more methods."

I stopped talking. Looked squarely at him. He spoke, "So you are telling me not to sell- if I was about to – weapons to those two who would use them to kill soldiers! Do I have that right?"

I replied, "Not exactly. It would be preferred if as far as these men are concerned the purchase of hand guns was successful and with your advice they accept particular weapons with in their price range – say around 1000 – 1500—pounds with some ammunition. The essential difference is you have ensured the guns cannot fire and they are completely unaware of that fact."

"But wouldn't it be easier if I just refused to sell?"

"No. for refusal would not mean these men would give up on their intentions to cause mayhem. They would seek to obtain weapons from elsewhere or like the deadly attack made on that unsuspecting soldier – sharp bladed weapons. It is the intention of people with an interest in this matter to arrest these men red-handed in the act of terrorism. This will ensure they are off the streets for many years. At the same time, they must be certain the public is not put at risk. This is why your cooperation is so important."

"And I face a jail sentence for supplying!"

"Not so. Your cooperation would be appreciated. These things take place behind closed doors."

"You seem to know an awful lot about this."

I smiled. "Just say I have friends in high places. Terrorism is the scourge of our way of life and I want to be certain actions I've outlined can be carried out."

Ted thought for a moment. Then "Okay. If they call on me I will provide two converted Russian Baitel Hand guns and say couple of dozen rounds. I will ensure the weapons are ineffective and the ammunition cannot be fired."

I relaxed. "Thank you. one final thing just between you and me. It would be appreciated by the unknown soldiers whose lives you may have saved if you would make one phone call to a cell phone number I am about to provide you with, confirming, the purchase. I promise the phone will be immediately subsequently destroyed."

"Okay, will do."

I rose. Shook his hand. Gave him a phone number and said, "this conversation has been conducted between us, and must remain in absolute confidence. Ensure the items sold will not fire. Put the money in your back pocket. One phone call. End of story."

"Rely on me. I may be ex-army and have done a lot of ducking and diving. But this is still my country."

*   *   *

The following day I was in position keeping an eye on our 'Boys from Brixton.' My phone rang. Cat said, "Hi! How are things?"

"All quiet." I replied. "How are you today?"

"Surviving. I will be ready for being picked up if that is okay with you later today. Or I could drive up wherever you are myself."

"Cat, you just relax. Read a book or something. I will keep an eye on our lads for today. Tomorrow, if you are up to it, give me a ring early and pick me up in your car. A change of vehicle will do us no harm and with your hands on the driving wheel I will feel safer."

"Because of my excellent driving?"

"That too."

She snorted. "I've never put a hand on you in my life!"

"Well there is always hope!" her voice changed.

"Are you coming on to me?"

"Now as if I....gotta go. See you tomorrow." I dropped my phone into my pocket, and grinned to myself. The remainder of the day passed without incident. I had my radio on the local newscast. An Army Regiment will take advantage of its Freedom of the City – to make a farewell march in a couple of days' time through the town of Kingston on Thames with pipes and drums prior to its transfer to another location. I wondered if things were moving in a certain direction.

CHAPTER FORTY-FIVE

I was fixing my seat belt in Cat's car the following morning, she said, "To work or have a coffee, first?"

"Coffee and a chat first." We headed for a favourite coffee shop. With drinks before us, I said, "So are you feeling okay, now?"

Cat nodded. "So what have you been up to without my professional advice and guidance?" I thought for a moment. Should I give her details of my actions? I decided she would have to know. "Well I think I know what may be the target of the 'Boys from Brixton'. A Battalion of infantry is to march through the town of Kingston on Thames in two days' time before they move to a different location."

Cat said, "that seems to be a potential target."

"Yeah." I coughed and looked away. Casually, "I'm expecting a phone call sometime soon telling me what weapons they have purchased. If I don't hear today or tomorrow it will be unlikely that this is the potential target."

Cat looked in astonishment. "What do you mean you're waiting for a phone call?"

"From Ted, the ex-armourer."

"The gun dealer?"

"Yes." I swigged coffee, looked at Cats puzzled face, "We had a chat."

"You did what!"

I suddenly felt uneasy. I explained. "It was during a quiet period. I was turning things over in my mind and it came to me if the potential target was a military one, Ted an ex-soldier would not be happy about it. So I decided to pay him a visit."

Cat was for a moment speechless. Then angry. "You made yourself aware to him that we were interested in these two yobs! He is an ex-jailbird about to make a sale to a couple of bad guys. You go and have a chat with him! Are you crazy? All we were supposed to be doing is watching these clowns!"

"Well, firstly I was certain they would have given the impression the guns were for criminal purposes. It is unbelievable they would have indicated otherwise. Ted is an ex-soldier. Despite everything else if he knew the real reason guns were being purchased I was sure he wouldn't sell."

"You don't know that. These sort of underworld guys are only interested in money. Although I understand he may have had second thoughts if he knew the real reason they were after guns."

"He will still get his money. That is why I wanted to have a face to face conversation. Of course he doesn't know who I am other than a writer with interested friends."

"I don't understand what you are on about. How can he make money without selling?"

"We have come to an arrangement. He will sell two hand guns probably of Russian manufacture for around 1000 pounds plus or minus. He will explain they have been converted into killing weapons, and will provide ammunition for them. The 'Boys of Brixton' know little about guns and will go off happy with their purchases. What they don't know is that the guns have been made defective in a way they will not know about until they attempt to fire them. Because they will only have a limited amount of ammunition with more promised later if required they will not test the guns beforehand. If by chance they did, they would be after chasing Ted for an explanation and no harm done at that stage."

Cat searched my face. "What if he tells these guys we are on to them?"

"Ted may be a criminal but he hates terrorists in our midst as much as anyone."

"You are taking a hell of a risk. We had better put a watch on these guys as soon as possible. For the moment we will assume — until we find something different — that the potential target is the Kingston march. Let's just see what they get up to."

I nodded, aware Cat was worried. I hoped the arrangement between Ted and myself would work out. We finished coffee.

With Cat at the wheel we moved off to Mitcham. I thought it better to make no comment on her hands on the steering wheel.

We parked in a convenient place, and watched the house. The old car was out front. We settled in for a long haul. Cat occasionally shooting sly glances in my direction. I tried to make conversation but her replies were short and non-committal.

It was getting later in the day when movement caught our bored interest. The car with the Asian looking guys made another visit to the house. Again, as we watched two guys entered and later returned with loaded black bags. Their car then disappeared towards London. With the three Asians.

Shortly afterwards Mohd and Kalid left the house and drove in the same direction they had done before towards Brixton. We followed.

Near Brixton they parked, used the same pub as before. Ted arrived entered the pub. We noticed he had a folder under his arm. This time the conversation took almost an hour. Ted came out alone and drove away in the gathering darkness. Ten minutes later Mohd and his partner left the pub. Following them we realized they were returning to Mitcham. In the darkness we lost them. But passing the end of their street we saw the old car outside the house and concluded they hadn't stopped on their journey home.

Cat dropped me at my place on her way to Wandsworth having arranged for her to pick me up the following day. The Kingston military show was scheduled to take place the day after tomorrow.

*   *   *

The following day we were back keeping the house under observation. About late afternoon we spotted the car was about to move off with Mohd and Kadir. Mohd was driving. We kept them in view. Firstly, they headed toward Brixton but used a different route, going via Streatham. Off the beaten track they entered a leafy wooded area the single road passing between trees in full bloom. A car was parked off road the driver reading a paper. Noting the car arriving the man put down his paper, flashed his lights and the car with Mohd drew closer to the stationary car. We continued past around the curve, stopped and I hopped out. Cutting through the trees I saw the stationary car driver point towards a large tree under which was stacked a pile of cut logs. Mohd remained in the car as Kadir walked towards the log pile. Here he lifted several logs obviously as previously instructed at some time, and lifted out a black plastic package.

The stationary driver then drove away and disappeared out of sight. Returning to his partner Kadir stuffed the package into the boot, climbed in alongside Mohd who then took off, back the way they had come. We returned to Mitcham and noticed the old car once again before the house.

My phone rang. It was Ted confirming purchase of two Baitel ex Russian long barrelled hand guns had been purchased and collected by the Brixton Boys for 1500 pounds and the guns had been made inactive.

The information now collected was the two suspects were in possession of firearms, a military parade would take place the following day with the strong possibility of being the target. It was time for Cat to pass on the details.

Report by Wandsworth 87 Surveillance Team.
Suspects numbers eight zero and nine zero known as
Mohd Maged and Kadir are in possession of Russian
Long barrelled hand guns. Information is suspects unaware weapons are ineffective and cannot be fired. Target believed to be military parade at Kingston- on-Thames tomorrow. Surveillance to be maintained. Should they travel to Kingston it is likely to be in vehicle 1998 Model Ford, Registration plate number as prev. advised.

The following day Cat picked me up and we commenced an early watch on the suspects. As expected, at an appropriate time they moved off towards Kingston.

Cat informed her contact and also made a report on the suspected cannabis growing situation at the suspects' address, not forgetting to inform them of the existence of the Asian worker within the house. Message received and confirmed, we settled down to what was probably going to be our last surveillance act on

Mohd Maged and Kadir or to remind ourselves of their actual names Alfred Nobbs and the white thug William Surtees. When the suspects entered the car we had noticed they had discarded any Muslim items for normal dress of peaked golf caps and coats above the inevitable jeans.

We were nearly at Kingston-on -Thames and we wondered how they were going to make their move. We were soon to find out. Parking some distance from the main centre they left the car and walked towards the crowded High street where faint sounds of martial music could be heard. A slight bend in the road meant that the marching soldiers would be out of view until they followed the curve just twenty yards or so from where the suspects took positions either side of the road, their weapons out of sight under their jackets. Police stood on the kerbs before the crowds of onlookers at the edge of which stood our heroes. The sounds of pipes and drums grew louder as the parade of musicians followed by marching soldiers came clearly into view. This was the signal for the two men to draw their weapons and aim at the passing soldiers. They aimed, pressed triggers. From each pistol erupted a white flash followed instantaneously by a red flame from the breech as the barrel split apart. Amazement and confusion registered on the faces of the 'Terrorists', as they dropped the shattered useless guns. As Kadir raised his arms he was brought down by armed police.

The black guy reacted. Swinging round he ran diagonally

towards a side street. I leapt out of the car closed on Mohd making a rugby tackle taking his legs from under him. Seconds later he was under a pile of policemen.

I returned to our car to face Cat. She looked at me in silence. Then "So your chat with the gun runner worked."

"We are done here." I replied uncertain of how she was thinking. "Let's leave this now to the police, go home, freshen up, and meet up for a beer." Silently she turned the car towards our own area.

My place was between Kingston and Wandsworth. She slowed the car at Grandma's home. As I prepared to leave the car, I said, "How about I get a taxi later and pick you up and we go for a meal somewhere. We can chat about the day's activities and other things; and we can relax. Now this has been sorted."

Cat hesitated and I noticed. "Please say yes. I know I may have been a bit out of order these last few days and I'm probably not your favourite person, what with Italy, right now, but we may be out of touch with each other until another job turn up."

My appeal seemed to touch a chord. She turned, smiled at me. "Okay. Call for me at eight and I will try and forgive you. You scared me when you hurled yourself at that man. Eight o'clock. See you then."

With that she put the car into gear and roared off.

CHAPTER FORTY-SIX
Catriona

I entered the house, said 'Hi' to both grandmother and Rupinda and kissed the cheek of the older woman who said "You seem to be busy lately for we haven't seen much of you."

"Well I have been helping out Catriona with her work," I said carefully picking words and avoiding having to lie. "In fact I have just left her and after freshening up I am meeting her for a meal later this evening." I changed the subject. "How is that leg of yours progressing?"

"Improving slowly but surely." Gran replied.

"She's making some progress," interjected Rupinda, "As you can see she is back in her favourite chair and we are back to having long conversations and our needlework."

"And how are you, Rupinda? Remember we are indebted to you for being so good with Grandmother Kumari. If there is anything you need or I can help you with, you know I am at your service."

Rupinda's eyes twinkled. "I thank you Ricci, but I'm fine at the moment but I will keep it in mind. Your time seems to be quite taken up. You're so busy these days."

"Oh, the work Cat was doing is now completed. I will have more time to catch up with my writing." Grandmother sat smiling contentedly. Unaware of any hidden messages in our conversation.

* * *

We were seated in a small Italian restaurant. Just finished a fabulous meal of pasta with a bottle of Italian wine to wash it down. Had been discussing the days' events which included confirmation the house had indeed been set up as a cannabis farm and producing centre. The police had found the rear bedroom with hundreds of plants, with the entire floor and built up tier with the usual requirements of plastic sheets, hot bright lights, water supply, and the rest. The Asian had turned out to be, as we had guessed, an illegal migrant of Vietnamese origin. He had been apprehended without any problem.

I sat back and studied Cat. I was uncertain about the immediate future. She hadn't said very much during the meal.

"So we should be rather pleased with the outcome of our surveillance activity," I said trying to encourage conversation.

Cat looked up. "Luckily it worked out well. Our bosses will be happy another couple of dangerous guys are taken care of. And it is mainly down to you and your conversation with the gun dealer."

"Well it is all behind us now. I wonder what the future will bring forth."

Well there are other teams in this part of the world. I have a feeling they may rest us for a while."

"I wouldn't object to that," I commented, "I have a book to finish." I looked at my watch. "Do you fancy making a move to a pub and relaxing over a fresh drink and where I can get a decent pint?"

Cat grinned. "Why not. I'm not averse to a beer myself. Pretty well all we had to drink other than smoothies when I was abroad." I went to pay the bill. Cat said. "It's my shout," and reached for her bag.

"No way!" I said. "You may be a modern woman but in such matters I'm an old fashioned man." And insisted making the payment.

The wine seemed to have made Cat softer towards me. "not only are you a gentleman, allegedly, towards women but an old fashioned one," murmured Cat as she slipped her arm in mine as we left the restaurant. Whether it was a gesture of comradeship or something more I was to remain unsure.

We settled in comfortable seating in a nearby pub. "What are you drinking?" I asked.

"Budweiser."

I returned with a pint and the half pint glass for Cat. Taking a swig from my pint, I looked keenly at my companion.

"It's a funny thing, you know quite a lot about me and yet despite the time we have sat for hours together on watch, I still know so little about you. Is this 'need to know' always going to be a barrier?"

She leaned back. "I hadn't realized it had been a barrier. I thought perhaps with all your other irons in the fire, so to speak, I wasn't of any great interest to you."

I did a double take. "You must know that is not so, I was just being polite and didn't wish to pry. After all, for quite a while I was under the impression you had no interest in -er-the male section of the population."

She laughed at the thought of John Street's warning to me. "I'm like any other female of my age. Hot blooded, like to enjoy myself, but where men are concerned I try to be careful. I've been given heartache before."

I looked at her. She was no longer smiling. "You want to tell me about it or does it come under 'Need to Know' with you?"

Cat sat looking into her glass. Then, "When I was out in Afghanistan I had a regular guy, a boyfriend in my own outfit. We had been going out together for a while and were close. We were both senior NCOS and he was called back to the U.K. to attend a specialist course. Several weeks later he came back to us and naturally I was pleased to see him. We carried on as we had done before. Then one day a Sergeant in the Orderly Room pulled me aside. He said it was none of his business if I carried on as I was, but he was telling me in confidence that my boyfriend had got married whilst in England. I was stunned and said I didn't believe it. Then the Orderly Sergeant told me this guy had registered his marriage and the name of the woman and date as was required to apply for Marriage Allowance. I confronted Alan. I could tell immediately by his face it was true. He tried to make excuses but everything he said, I realized was all lies and he had just been using me. I had really liked him until that day. From then on I hated him. The word had got about the unit. Remember most were males and although the majority reckoned it to be a dirty trick and there was a lot of sympathy for me this really only made me feel worse. I had been considering extending my period of service but this helped decide. Shortly after I handed in my uniform and returned to being a civilian once again."

I sat surprised at the opening up of Cat and the heart breaking situation she had experienced. I wasn't sure what to say. "That was a tough period." I said. "More beer?" Returning with the drink, I said "I'm really sorry to hear of your bad experience."

"It was a while back. I'm well over it, now."

"Have you..." I was about to say.

Cat interrupted. "Now our little jaunt is over I will be able to spend a weekend in Canterbury and relax."

"Canterbury?" I asked, "what's the attraction there?"

She sipped her beer, then looking up said, "Somebody I've been missing, is waiting to put his arms around me."

I grinned at her, "The way you've put it I think it might be your brother!"

"I don't have a brother."

About to make a remark, we were interrupted by the barman picking up our empty bottles and glasses. As he moved away, Cat continued. "So what will you be doing with the remainder of this weekend, meeting up with Rupinda, or is it Lindsey?"

It was obvious the identity of those young ladies was still of interest to a teasing Cat. "I see Rupinda every day at Grandmothers," I pointed out, and don't have a particular reason to see Lindsey at the moment. Mind you I never know what's popping up next – might be my sister, her friend or a tall blonde!"

She laughed. "And I never know what or who is popping up in my hectic life. Maybe a tall, dark, black eyed stranger... Oh!" she said, sweetly, but of course that has already happened."

I didn't have an answer to that. "Yep!" I said. "You want to keep an eye on that guy." I was thinking we were making progress when her IPhone buzzed. She listened. "Okay," she replied. "I'll make a move now. Be there in half an hour."

"What was that about?" I asked with raised eyebrows.

"My cousin ringing me. Had a message from Canterbury. I'm driving down tonight."

CHAPTER FORTY-SEVEN

Days passed. Managed to complete the main draft of my third book and sent off for editing. Grandma Kumari's leg slowly improved and Rupinda's company for her was a blessing.

I find, I was missing the company of Cat. I was tempted to phone her on a number of occasions to suggest meeting up for a coffee or so, but the knowledge she had an interest in a boyfriend in Canterbury, deterred me.

Then my phone rang. It was Cat.

"Hi, Ricci, thought I'd give you a ring to see what you are up to these days."

"Cat! So pleased to hear from you. have we got another job on?"

"A job? Oh, no. Nothing's been mentioned as yet. I-er-just thought I would give you a call- wondered if you would like to meet up for a coffee and have a chat on things in general."

"Be delighted. I'm a free agent at the moment. How about I pop over and pick you up?"

"That's what I like to hear. See you in an hour!"

I pulled up outside her house. Her cousin, a slightly older woman came to a downstairs window on my toot and gave me a wave.

I hadn't seen Cat for a couple weeks. She walked towards the car I realized what a good looker she really was. As she slid into the seat next to me I was tempted to give her a kiss but remembered the boyfriend and just patted her shoulder in greeting.

"So," I said as I drove to one of our favourite cafes. "Have you missed me?"

She laughed. "I've been hoping to hear your lovely voice ringing me up and saying let's have a coffee, but silence." She looked at me. "I did think maybe you had one of your young ladies on a visit abroad, like you do," she teased.

"Well, I considered it. But the young lady I had in mind, would probably have given me two fingers. Anyway she has a boyfriend in Canterbury, so I just carried on with my writing."

She stared at me. "Are you talking about me?"

"The thought passed my mind. To my surprise I found I was missing the company of my co-worker!"

She sat looking directly ahead. "I don't have a boyfriend in Canterbury -or anywhere else for that matter. I went to see my father who happens to be on his own since my mother died a while back."

"Oh!" I didn't know quite what to say. I was sorry about her mother, and yet pleased and surprised on hearing who she had been visiting.

We arrived at the café and sat in an alcove with drinks before us.

"Cat." I said. "I'm really sorry to hear about your mother. I didn't realize you were just visiting your father. No boyfriend, eh?"

"Too busy. Too picky. Once you've been hurt you don't think much about fellows." She looked at me with a mischievous smile. "The good looking ones you have to be particularly careful about. Some have peculiar habits and hobbies."

I flushed. "What I have done is to try to bring happiness to unhappy women."

Cat pondered on my remark. "What if things were reversed. What would you think if I helped a lonely man to find happiness by staying the night sleeping with him?"

The question caught me unawares. I thought about it. Faced the truth. "I have to admit the question you have put to me- in the way that you have put it- would make me sad, unhappy, jealous even." I looked at her, cheekily. "Unless of course that poor, sad, unhappy man was me."

Her eyes widened. "Which leads me to say that I find you interesting, funny, and good to be around. Hell, I like you a lot. You have no idea how often I have wanted to ring you. But I had assumed you had a boyfriend, so I let it be." I grinned. "I also remembered you thought I was a cold fish or suspected I was interested in the same sex as myself."

Cat had her hands around her mug of warm coffee. She said softly. "I have often wondered if you liked me. We've had meals together, been in each other's company for long occasions yet you have never intimated you were at all interested in me."

"Goes, both ways you know. I don't at this moment know how you feel about me. Whether we are friends or something more. On several occasions I have been about to land a kiss on you, but didn't want to get a slap in reply."

Cat smiled. "And to think I have been waiting all this time for some sort of recognition. I think you are a lovely man, there is something that draws me to you and it is not just your good looks."

I glanced around the café. The few customers showed no interest in us. I put my hand over hers and she turned her fingers to press mine.

"If I tried to kiss you would I get a slap?" I spoke quietly.

"There is only one way to find out," she whispered.

The narrow table was no hindrance. I stood up, leaned forward and I touched her lips with mine, lightly. She smiled. "You taste of malted milk," she said.

"You taste delightful," I replied.

CHAPTER FORTY-EIGHT
Kumari

I now found I had a new pleasant interest in life. The barriers down between Cat and myself. The newly discussed closeness between us was evident to others. The theoretical boyfriend/girlfriend we had originally invented had blossomed into a genuine enjoyment of each other. In the past she usually tooted me and I would go out to her car and we would drive away, now she would call and sit with Grandma Kumari and Rupinda, chatting easily. At first I was rather anxious about Rupinda's re-action, but was pleased they got on very well. It was evident Rupinda liked her, although I had the feeling the humorous smile she occasionally gave when I was with her and Grandmother was a recall of our past memories.

*   *   *

It was Rupinda who drew my attention Grandmother was unwell. I was seated at my desk contemplating a new paragraph when there was a soft tap on the door. Surprised I called out to enter and I saw my caller was Rupinda. This was a new event. In fact I couldn't recall Rupinda in my study before. I stood as she entered. Seated in armchairs I listened to her describing the health of Grandmother Kumari.

"I had noticed her cough was getting more frequent and she was reluctant to leave her bed. She was having pain from her hip and I think she is running a temperature. I think despite her protestation you should have a doctor visit and check her condition. She seems to be looking much older lately."

"I hadn't realized she isn't as well as before. If you have a quick chat with her, I will pop in her room and see for myself." Rupinda agreed and five minutes later I was alongside my Grandmother.

"Whenever I asked you, you always said you were fine and not to worry," I said softly, holding her hand. "I have phoned the doctor and he will see how you are."

The doctor called. Following a detailed examination, he reported bad news. Out of Grandmothers hearing he explained her situation to myself and Rupinda. "She has pneumonia. The cause of her heavy coughing. I suspect she has also possible infection of her hip. She is an elderly lady in need of specialist attention. I will arrange for her to be hospitalized."

During the next few days, despite the endeavours of dedicated hospital staff, Grandmother Kumari s condition worsened. An x-ray confirmed pneumonia had taken a strong hold and antibiotics did little to improve her situation. The visiting doctor's own suspicion of infection also proved to be correct. Anne-Marie, Rupinda and myself were continuously supplying a vigil at the private room allocated to Grandmother Kumari. As is often the case with the elderly she seemed to be getting smaller as each day passed. Never a big woman we watched anxiously as this tiny figure between white sheets fought the enveloping poisons in her frail body.

The doctor gave us a descriptive synopsis of her situation, with pessimistic forecast of eventuality. Grandmother Kumari it appeared was allergic to penicillin antibiotic and they were now providing alternatives but with little success, other than halting the disposition of the infection. The main cause of worry was pneumonia particularly as Grandmother Kumari was an elderly patient.

"I regret to say that your grandmother is seriously ill and despite our best endeavours is slowly sinking. I'm afraid you must prepare for the worst. Pneumonia, I'm afraid is difficult to deal with, with little reserves of energy in the elderly.

"So you think there is little hope... When do you think..." I stopped.

The doctor said softly, "Perhaps two or three days, although it is difficult to say. The only consolation I can offer is that with pneumonia the departure is without pain."

The three of us discussed the situation. It was Rupinda who

summarized. "Grandmother Kumari is Hindu. When we have been together she would discuss the necessary actions to be required when her time on this earth came to a close and she was to be prepared to enter the next world. Normally in her passing it would be expected her Hindu family would deal with the requirements of cremation which must take place the day following death, in accordance with traditional rites. Certain arrangements would be necessary when possible immediately prior to her passing. Being in U.K the Hindu service for the departed is held either in a temple or in the home of the deceased. In Grandmother Kumari's service it will be expected of her eldest son who will be dressed appropriately to be the foremost person carrying out a reading and encircle the deceased three times. In this particular circumstance this act will be carried out by her grandson Ricci. A priest will conduct the service. I know of a company which will take care of all arrangements. Following the cremation, the flames of which represent Brahma the Hindu God of Creation, her ashes will be recovered and it is Kumari's desire to have her remains be placed on the holy river of the Ganges to assist her transportation to the next world. There will be twelve days of mourning. On the thirteenth day Saneskara ends with Kriya." This was explained as the final re-incarnation.

It was following this consideration of the near future when Rupinda informed us of her own. "I have been thinking of returning to India. I have a cousin who is a widower and has an interest in me. I have been happy to remain here with Grandmother Kumari. On her passing I have decided I will return to my own land. My final assistance to Grandmother Kumari will be to take her ashes and place them in the holy river of the Ganges thus fulfilling her final wish."

With her Granddaughter, her grandson and Rupinda at her bedside, two days later Grandmother Kumari passed away, peacefully and in no pain.

Knowledgeable and discreet undertakers removed the body to the large room of her home, positioned near the mini grand piano, where it was washed decorated with sandalwood, flowers and garlands. The frail body was wrapped in a white garment her being a widow, two toes tied together with string with her feet facing south.

A priest of the faith gave the Hindu service. Incense perfumed the room. Ricci dressed in white circled the casket three times in accordance with last rites. A large photograph of grandmother Kumari Macdonald took centre place surrounded by flowers and lighted candles.

These formalities concluded the coffin closed and Grandmother Kumari's body was transported to be cremated within the time frame. This requirement was observed by Ricci and Rupinda, Anne-Marie sobbing explaining she could not face this final act. Thus this Indian lady was prepared for Nirvana.

The family in articles of white dress mourned for twelve days following which, on the thirteenth day Saneskara (re-incarnation) ends with the ritual of Kriya when rice balls and milk are placed as an offering to show gratitude for her life fulfilled. A year later food is given to the poor. Rupinda undertook to conduct such actions in India.

CHAPTER FORTY-NINE
Rupinda

Anne-Marie had returned to North London and her boyfriend. I sat with Rupinda discussing the sale of the premises in which we were seated. "I can simplify the disposal arrangements and thus enable you to return to India with a substantial sum of money in your bank account," I was saying. "Should you decide at any time to return to England you will if you so require be able to repurchase this property once again."

We were in the lounge. Rupinda seated on the couch. I was facing her. I had explained how this could come about. The bank that managed my Trust Fund would purchase it on behalf of myself, although the seller would not be aware of my interest in the transaction. It would be purchased at the market price to the satisfaction of Rupinda. The property would be rented out until such time Rupinda confirmed her permanent residence would now be in her country of her birth. The contents would easily be stored for the same period of time in Grandmas house as I still referred to the substantial house in which I was now the only occupier.

"This will certainly be a great help to me," said a thankful Rupinda. She rose and refilled the glass jug of fruit drink returning it to the nearside table. "It's extremely kind of you."

I took her hand. "Rupinda, your kindness to my family, particularly the pleasure you brought to Grandmother Kumari ensures you will always have my deep affection. Wherever you are you will always know I am here for you should you ever require it." I stopped talking then. "On a very personal note, I am forever indebted to you. Whatever type of person I am now you are the cause of it. Your sensitive and gentle manner is only exceeded by your beauty and kindness." I stopped. She was smiling that smile, suggestive, mischievous.

"So you enjoyed the instructional periods?"

"Rupinda, you know the pleasure and laughter it gave me!"

She sat forward. Placed her hand on my knee and gently squeezed. "Would you like to come for a meal this evening? A farewell meal?"

It was my turn to lean forward. I placed my hand on her leg – higher than her knee and squeezed. "What time?" I asked.

*   *   *

I let myself into her house. Immediately aware of pleasant cooking smells. She was just finishing setting out the table when I proffered the bouquet. She stopped what she was doing and came towards me. She was wearing an open necked white shirt and a dark blue skirt.

"Oh! Ricci! What a lovely thought." She took the bouquet from me, roses surrounded by other flowers. "Roses and Sweet Pea!' she laughed. "You remembered!"

She moved towards me and kissed me. "You smell of spices." I said.

"In that case I must shower, later."

"I'll wash your back," I offered.

She laughed. "I'll put these in a vase and thank you again."

Hindu music which I had got used to over time played softly in the background as I settled into a seat. The meal of lamb tikka Masala was delicious, and conversation passed easily between us.

"After spending these years here I suppose you are looking forward to returning to your own country."

"Things change over the years, I was content with my life and enjoyed my time spent with your Grandmother. But with her passing a chapter has closed. For some time I have been receiving requests from a cousin who is interested in me and I believe it is perhaps time for me to return and begin a new life."

"I will miss your presence and friendship," I said sadly.

She smiled, "And I will miss your-er-friendship and particularly your presence." as mischievously as ever.

"To think, this is our last evening together," I replied.

She stood up, about to return used dishes to the kitchen.

"Your life will also take new turns. Let me clear things away. Then I must shower. You say I smell of spices from the cooking."

"Let me help." I said rising.

It was the closeness in the kitchen that decided. As I moved in the confined space Rupinda turned and her shoulder touched mine. We turned toward each other each about to apologize. Our words dried and we looked at each other. Then we found out bodies pressing.

Rupinda pulled away. "I must shower," she whispered.

*   *   *

In her bedroom on a table against the wall was the statue of Lakshmi. Candles circled the Hindu symbol. Dressed in a loose gown, Rupinda, bare footed, caramel skin gleaming entered and hands pressed together bowed before the lotus holding figure. Moving to me she put her hands on my shoulders, kissed me.

*   *   *

"How is it," I said, "That despite long periods of discussion on the merits of interesting, alternatives we always started with the missionary position?"

"Rupinda giggled. "Urgency, comfort, simplicity, and eagerness." She then smiled, softly. "But all that now belongs to the past. Your happiness lies now in the future, seemingly with your beautiful young lady, Catriona. We will always have our memories but you will have your future love." With that she gave me a final kiss as I left her.

CHAPTER FIFTY

Catriona

I returned from the airport. Rupinda had squeezed me and kissed farewell. The carved wooden box containing Grandmother's ashes secured and safely in her luggage. I stood in the centre of the large room feeling lost. In my mind I could see Rupinda sitting next to Grandmother Kumari each busy with their needle and tapestry work, cheerfully chatting happily to each other. Or both sitting smiling quietly as at their insistence I sat, my fingers moving over the grand piano keys playing requests. Now I stood listening to silence and memories.

My IPhone rang. Cat's voice. "Hi Ricci. You okay?"

I came back to the present. "Hi Cat," I replied, "Just taken Rupinda to the airport." I looked at my watch. "She is on her way now to her home country. Standing here feeling a bit lost."

She was silent for a moment. "How about I come over and we head for a pub and a couple of drinks."

"Brilliant idea."

"Be over within the hour," she replied

I heard her car door slam as she parked in the drive and I pulled the door open. She was casually dressed in a white top and blue jeans, a bag hanging from her shoulder her slim figure silhouetted in the evening dusk.

She stepped into the lounge as I was buttoning up a clean shirt after my shower. Dropping her bag on the couch she stood, glance slowly around the room as if being aware of its emptiness. She turned to me, studied my face. "You are sure you are okay?"

I nodded, rather surprised at her obvious concern. "Just seemed a bit strange at first. So used to seeing them huddled together and Grandmother's greeting of 'Hello, darling.' Seeing you had cheered me up." She smiled. That lovely smile. "Nice to know," she said.

"I picked her bag up and handed it to her. Let's go get that drink. There is a decent pub just round the corner. We can walk it."

Cat opted for white wine. I sat with a pint of best. Cat opened the conversation with something of a surprise announcement.

"I've got to start looking for new digs. I'm moving out from Jane, my cousin's place."

I was surprised. "Why? What's brought this on? I thought you and your cousin get on well together."

"Oh, we do. But she's had a boyfriend for quite a while and

well they have decided to be together with him moving in with her. Jane says there is no reason for me to be concerned for there are two bedrooms and I get on quite well with Nick, her boyfriend."

"So what makes you decide to move out?"

"Well, although they are a nice couple, I don't feel like playing gooseberry. Besides, although is a comfortable flat, the walls aren't all that thick and as a single lady I don't want to hear the sounds of love making."

I grinned. "Why? Make you realize what your missing?"

Cat punched my arm. "No! You idiot!" But I noticed pinkness rising from her throat and colour her face.

"Do you believe in coincidences?" I asked.

"Not really, Why?"

"It may not be what you want, but with Rupinda's departure I have undertaken to let her bungalow to a reliable tenant. Of course it is early days and I have yet to make any arrangements to have it advertised. There are a few things to consider, like there is a small garden that needs to be maintained and I imagine you are presently thinking in terms of a flat with no such encumbrances. Also you are probably thinking of accommodation in Wandsworth, whereas this bungalow, which has two bedrooms, one with an en-suite, by the way, is only a few roads from where I live."

"A bungalow?"

"A detached bungalow. Two bedroomed. Bit on the small side. Immaculate condition. Other than a couple of items, ready to be occupied."

"You say it was Rupinda's?"

"It was indeed."

"You know it quite well?"

"I know it is a pleasant location."

"Could I be considered a potential tenant?"

"Cat, presently you are the only potential tenant."

"Could I see it?"

"Of course. Too dark now. How about tomorrow?"

"Terrific, will do!"

I grinned. "Of course there is some alternative accommodation. The rooms are larger and there is no fear of you overhearing other couples-er-enjoying themselves!"

She looked at me, "And where would that be?"

"Where you have parked your car."

She picked up her glass, sipped, holding the glass up to her mouth and said, "And would I get my own room?"

I laughed. "Choice of four. Plus, the bachelor's room is quite comfortable and has a double bed."

"I bet it has," she murmured over her glass.

"You can take a look at the alternative accommodation this evening, if you wish."

"Well I've got to pick my car up. Maybe I'll take a peep at the rooms just-er-to familiarize myself." She had that mischievous look again. She shifted her body, picked up her bag. "Right now I need to powder my nose."

I sat looking at her retreating figure. Things were progressing nicely. Following the light kiss I had placed on her lips in the café we had embraced on our parting with a much longer softer kiss. I was hoping the names of females which seemed to cause awkwardness between us were fading into the past.

Cat returned. I finished my beer and arm in arm we walked back to my place. "Let me show you around," I said. Leading, I theatrically pushed doors open. "I'll start with a guest room. And this is another spare room. And this was my Grandmother's apartment." Pushing against the door. With Cat silently watching I stood in the doorway. The bed had been neatly made up, the wardrobe closed. Everything neat. I felt suddenly a choking sadness. My levity deserted me. No longer did I act like an estate agent. I closed the door quietly and continued offering views of the rooms, my study, finally showing my own bedroom, rather untidier then the others. "And I also have an en-suite." I added.

I turned to face Cat. "It's a lovely house," she said. "You will probably rattle around in it like a pea, being on your own."

I put my hands on her hip. "Stay with me. Stop me rattling. Then we could see the other place tomorrow without you making another trip from Wandsworth."

She sighed. "Do you believe in coincidences?"

I looked at her surprised. "Like you said. Not really, Why?"

She lifted my hands from her hips. "Bad timing. I'm having my period." She held my hands. "I will drive back to my cousin's and come back tomorrow. I'm hoping the bungalow will be suitable for me. Not so much travelling. Be quite near you." she lifted on her toes, put her arms around my neck and pressed her lips to mine. Tongues touched. We stood seeking each other. Then she moved away. "Tomorrow," she said. I stood in the doorway watching her back out. Then with a wave she was gone.

CHAPTER FIFTY-ONE

She loved it. "It's better than a flat! It is ideal, with a backdoor to the garden. Nobody below or above me." Cat turned to me smiling.

"Then it's yours," I said. She wondered who is the owner. "It is owned by an Investment Trust. But you don't have to concern yourself with that. Any problems, speak to me. Later we will get the usual type contract signed and that will be it."

We were standing now in the larger bedroom. "You say this was Rupinda's place and she sold it to this Investment Trust?"

"Yes." She was looking at the neatly covered bed.

"And this is where she taught you-er-certain-positions?"

"Some years ago. Yes, I was technically a teenager."

She turned to gaze at me. "What do you mean, technically a teenager?"

"It was a few weeks before my twentieth birthday."

She turned and pointed to the double bed. "I will replace this bed."

"Sure," I said. "I can take care of that. Would you like a soft mattress or a harder one?"

"Soft."

"Do you want a single or a double or perhaps a king size. I like to stretch out. Would you like me to purchase one or would you prefer we shopped together?"

She laughed, "This is to be my bed. You sound like we are a couple. But I'd like you with me." She said. "When can I move in?"

"Today if you want."

"Really?" she sounded pleased. "How about coming with me to pick up my things from my cousin's place. I have really just clothes and a few items."

"Why not? Then we could have lunch and dinner tonight together. While I think of it, here are the keys to your new home."

*   *   *

Cat drove us to Wandsworth. I met for the first time her cousin Jane, a pleasant women and Cat explained the sudden change of events.

We piled cases, boxes, odd ornaments, books and the rest of the stuff a single woman collects and returned to Earlsfield. Dumping the lot at her new home, we then found a pleasant restaurant and ordered food and drinks.

We are just finishing when Cats phone buzzed. "Hello." I grasped it was a man's voice. Cat listened intently interjecting briefly with where? When? "Well actually I'm in the process of moving house." She listened. I could only hear the deep voice. It seemed she had to make a decision. With it seemed some reluctance, she closed the conversation. "Okay, Ralph, if it will help you out, I'll do it." In reply to a final query she said, "Yes, I will be up in a few hours." She closed her phone.

"What was that about?" I asked.

"That was my old boss, Ralph Watson. The owner of the security and intelligence company I worked for before I decided to go it alone."

I raised my eyebrows. "So?"

"He's got a big job on. Suspected industrial espionage of an important organization. Some of his agents are working abroad and he is desperately short of trained staff. I've agreed to help. It will be for a few days; he will book a hotel room for me. Financially it will be well paid."

"What sort of work will you be required to do?"

Cat was somewhat off handed with her reply. "Oh, a bit of bug hunting, I expect. Making sure the place is clean."

"Seems like 'need to know' has raised its shiny head," I said.

Cat sensed I was disappointed. "I'll only be away a couple of days." She smiled, "You could be doing me a favour whilst I'm away." I raised my eyebrows again. "You could replace that bed with a new one, sort of surprise me!"

"It's not quite what I had in mind this weekend, but I will do that."

She rose and said, "I need to pick up a few things then I must take off."

Back at her new accommodation, having sorted through her clothes and packed a bag, she said "I'll phone you tonight," gave me a hug and a kiss and now the professional business woman, she was off. With nothing else to do I checked out a few bedding stores on the internet, then rode out to take a look at several of them.

CHAPTER FIFTY-TWO
Muriel

I was slowly moving into the supermarket looking for a place to park when I saw Muriel. She was loaded with two heavy shopping bags and heading for the taxi rank. Parking, I saw one of the bags suddenly split and groceries were bouncing and rolling around her. Seeing her plight, I switched off and moved quickly to her side. She was bending trying to recover errant plastic bottles when she realized who it was beside her. "Let me help," I said. "This is an unexpected meeting, I was expecting to see you in an hour or two following John's phone call to come round for a meal."

Thank God you have," she said as we piled groceries together.

"Don't go away," I said to a confused Muriel and dashed into the supermarket and was back in minutes with replacement shopping bags. We refilled the fresh bags, I said, "Where's your car?" Muriel looked up. "No car. I had a taxi bring me and was about to get a taxi back. I only have a provisional driver's license and John who usually comes with me can't drive at the moment."

"No problem, my car is here, Let's put this stuff in the boot. I'll sit you in the passenger seat whilst I dash in and pick up a couple of bottles of wine which is the reason I'm here."

Returning with the wine I secured it in the boot and ensuring Muriel was comfortable and moved off. I didn't notice the sleek black Audi about to park. And I didn't notice the surprised look on the female drivers face on recognizing me as I drove away with a woman by my side. And I didn't notice the black Audi following us.

*   *   *

So why didn't John drive you to get groceries I asked a seated Muriel."

"Tripped on the stairs, fell and has hurt his back. She pondered and grinned at me. "Can't be all that bad. Left him watching the golf on TV. Sports mad!"

I drove up to Muriel's and John's house. I had been once or twice before. Always enjoyed their company. I carried in the groceries following Muriel inside. I could hear the TV commentary on golf as John hailed me from his cushions. I wasn't aware of the black Audi parked across the street.

"He saved me from acute embarrassment." Muriel was explaining my fortunate timed arrival at the supermarket, shouting from the kitchen as she prepared an evening meal. "A good Samaritan!" shouted John in reply. "Remember he gave up a weekend with us to help a friend with car trouble." I smiled but made no comment. I settled down and watched the golf. An hour or so later and our evening meal was ready. I noticed when John moved he had indeed a painful back.

A pleasant meal of roast lamb with mint sauce, roast potatoes plus vegetables, followed by fruit and ice cream, easy going bantering conversation, the golf low on the TV ended. We settled comfortably to watch a film on Netflix. After a while it appeared Johns back was more painful than Muriel had realized and as the film was nearing the end, he said, "Sorry fellers, but I feel I must lie down, my back is killing me!" he stood up in obvious pain. Muriel rose quickly. I'll help you up the stairs. Don't want you tripping up again!"

John waved goodnight to his old rugby pal as Muriel with her arm round him moved toward the stairs. In the bedroom, she switched on the light for darkness had long fallen. They stood silhouetted against the curtained window as he bent and kissed his wife before carefully, with her assistance lowered himself onto their bed.

As Muriel returned to the sitting room I said "Time I was gone – good film." I indicated the TV and she moved to switch it off. Having already said my goodbye to John, I turned to Muriel, kissed her on the cheek and thanked her for a lovely meal and a very pleasant evening.

"We will have to do this again soon," she smiled. Always lovely to have you round." Observing that next time, they must be my guests she turned on the hall light and I returned to my car.

I hadn't noticed the tail lights of a black Audi disappearing into the darkness, the lady driver with tears sliding down her cheeks.

CHAPTER FIFTY-THREE

I was having problems trying to contact Cat. She had said she would phone me when the job with her old firm had finished. I received no phone call and finally I rang her but no pick up. It was now several days since she had left for Central London.

Once again I tried to phone her. This time I was successful. "Been having trouble trying to reach you. Are you okay? Where are you?"

Seemed to be some delay in replying. She then said in a quiet voice. "I am in Canterbury with my father. I will return to the bungalow tomorrow. I've been asked to do another surveillance job. I will speak to you then." The phone call disconnected. I looked at the phone astonished. She had spoken in an unusual level voice. I tried to ring back but no reply. This seemed to be a different Cat. Something seemed wrong.

The following day I decided to walk to the bungalow. It was a clear day and I needed the exercise. It was as I neared the house I saw the front door open. A man was leaving. I was near enough to see he was probably in his late forties, slightly overweight, open necked shirt and carrying a brief case.

Cat stood in the doorway as he departed. She saw me standing on the far side of the street as the man entered the Toyota and drove away. She stood aside as I came to her and together we entered.

"We can sit in the kitchen," she said. No smile of greeting as I said "Hi."

We sat either side of the kitchen table, after Cat had placed two used coffee mug in the sink. "What's happening?" I said abruptly, the atmosphere between us has changed.

"I've been given another surveillance job." she repeated what I already knew.

"So you said over the phone. What I want to know is what is the problem that seems to be between us."

"I was given the job by John Street. I said I will carry out the surveillance but I had no partner. He asked how come and so I said you are not available. The correct team for surveillance is actually three people. But because of the situation they have had to form teams of two. He wouldn't allow me to work alone and said he would provide a locum."

"A locum?"

"In the intelligence world a locum is an experienced operator who is available to stand in for an agent who is ill or unavailable."

"I don't understand. Why would you say I was unavailable?

Was that man I saw leaving a locum?"

"Yes, he is and will be my partner for the immediate future."

"Why?"

Cat hesitated. She looked down. "I don't want to work with you anymore."

I stared at her. I felt I had been punched in the face.

She said, her voice tremulous, "I want you to leave. But before you do I need to know how much you have spent on that replacement bed which I must thank you for and I will repay you. Unfortunately, I signed the contract for this place for a minimum of six months. My father says I should remain for that period but then move away to another area."

"I just don't understand. I thought we were building something between us." I stood up. "I really, really like you. In fact, I feel something else for you. but you want me to go. I am not welcome." I was feeling choked. "Forget the bed. That was a gift. If you don't want it leave it here should or when you go. Just one thing. Why? I think I'm entitled to know why you dislike me."

Cat looked up. I saw her eyes were wet. She sat stiffly. She spoke. Her voice even. "Because I can't trust you. You were honest in telling me of your-er-assistance to women in the past. We discussed it and I thought as we were together that would be the end of it. But I was wrong. Tearfully she said. "I saw you with that woman in the carpark. I saw you put her groceries in your car. I saw you buying bottles of wine. I saw you enter her house. I saw you kissing her in the upstairs room. You were still there when I left at midnight." A tear dropped. "I don't want to be with someone I can't trust- despite how much I liked them."

I stared at her. "You followed me?"

"I had just arrived back from the London job. I thought instead of ringing you I would give you a surprise in my new house. I was in the supermarket to buy groceries when I saw you and that woman. I was surprised my car was still moving when you both left and-well-I was confused- it was unexpected and without really realizing why I followed you and waited till midnight. It was seeing you in the room kissing her that decided you were not a man to be trusted."

I was seeing the light.

"Before I leave can I ask you to do me one final act. I walked here and don't have my car. Would you give me a lift to where I want to go it's not far?" I walked round the table and held her hand. "Please!" I said. She nodded.

"Up here on the left is a florist. If you would just stop there for a moment..." she sat silently in the car whilst I entered and purchased a bouquet of flowers. I came out and placed them in the boot. We moved. I gave directions and we drew up before the house in which I had spent the evening. I left the car, retrieved flowers from the boot and rang the bell. A moment later a surprised Muriel was at the door. "Muriel," I said. "Just passing and thought I'd drop these off in appreciation of a lovely evening."

A delighted Muriel took the flowers and said "What a lovely gesture. You must come in and have coffee. John will be chuffed to see you."

"I have a young lady with me," I said. Muriel craned her neck, saw Cat and said "Bring her with you." She stepped forward and made an invitation to come to the house with beckoning fingers and a large smile. Somewhat reluctantly Cat came to us. "Hi," she said weakly, as Muriel warmly greeted her.

"Cat – Muriel," I briefly introduced them.

"Please come in delighted to meet you. We are just having coffee."

We entered the sitting room. John on seeing a new visitor stood up and introduced himself.

"We are old rugby friends," I said, smiling a bit. "So how is your back this morning?"

"Stiff, but not too painful. So this is Catriona, so pleased to meet you. I understand you have just moved down from Wandsworth to your own place. Ricci was telling us about it."

Cat now realizing the dreadful mistaken assumption she had made had embarrassingly cheered her immensely. Why had she thought the worst of me? Twinges of jealousy, may have been the cause. Warmly she now chatted about her new accommodation as

Muriel brought in the tray of coffee and biscuits.

"So what do you do for a living?" asked John. "Security Consultant," said a smiling Cat, which turned into a discussion of what that actually meant- at least Cat's version of it.

Muriel, coffee cup held in both hands spoke of the unexpected meeting in the supermarket car park. "All the groceries rolling here and there and bouncing because the bag collapsed. I was feeling such a fool and then this Good Samaritan appeared."

"Good Samaritan indeed,' interjected John, cheerfully. "Remember when he helped out that friend whose car had broken down spoiling his weekend with us at our place on the coast." I shifted uncomfortably with Cat's smiling eyes on me. "Just good luck I happened to be on the spot, in both cases, I muttered. "Yes, I've noticed he is always available when needed," smiled Cat, cheekily.

So the conversation flowed until I said, "Well, things to do. Mustn't take up any more of your time, you two." Standing up thanking for the coffee, we moved towards the door. "Don't forget our dinner date in the near future, when your back is okay, John." "I'll hold you to that," he laughed. "A nice foursome."

Driving back Cat was silent. I said nothing just watched the road. Suddenly she said quietly, "Sorry Ricci. I'm so sorry for not trusting you. The things we had discussed. Your helping lonely women, I think I was upset at the thought of you with– I think I was jealous, sad and you are really such a nice man – I thought too good to be true- if you can forgive me."

"Forget it Cat. I'm so desperately pleased you know the truth. I will never ever two time you. You are too precious to me. All I want to do is to sit next to you watching other people misbehaving, loving the smell of your perfume- and you- to hold you, to kiss you, etc., etc.,"

"What is etc., etc.?"

"Drive me to your new home. I'll kiss you, hug you and etc., etc.,"

She laughed. "I still don't know what you mean by etc., etc."

"Oh you will. I promise you. You will!"

We reached her new home. Opening the boot, I removed the two dozen roses I had also purchased. In the sitting room handing a delighted Cat the flowers, I said "There is something you must do. And there is something I must do."

"And what must I do?" enquired Cat.

"Phone John Street. Tell him I have recovered and you will not require the locum for the new surveillance job."

She was already dialling. A quick discussion and she closed her phone. "Sorted," she said.

"You can tell me about the type of job lined up for us, later, but first as I said there is something I must do."

"And what is that?" she asked. I took her hand, and walked towards the bedroom. "We need to test the bed, to see whether it is too soft or too hard." "It is just perfect," she breathed smiling, and, "Is this where I find out what etc., etc., is all about?"

"Better pull the curtains," I said, taking a willing Cat into my arms. "All a question of 'need to know'."

*   *   *

The postman put it through the letter box. The thud of its arrival was heard by Cat. Taking it from its package Cat called out "It's a book!" "What sort of book," said I as she wandered back into the bedroom.

"Hidden Desires." She peered down at the subtitle. "Romantic, Erotic, Humorous. A fascinating love story by Lindsey Ellison!"

She opened two pages. "It's been signed by the author and dedicated to"

Riccardo Macdonald

For bringing me happiness

Greg MacBride

GREG MACBRIDE

'Longing of Lonely Ladies' is the debut book of the author who lives in the Scottish Highlands. Total fiction. Even the author's name is a pseudonym.

Made in the USA
Charleston, SC
20 December 2016